# LONE CALDER STAR

# JANET DAILEY

KENSINGTON BOOKS
http://www.kensingtonbooks.com

KENSINGTON BOOKS are published by

Kensington Publishing Corp.
850 Third Avenue
New York, NY 10022

All Kensington titles, imprints and distributed lines are available at special quantity discounts for bulk purchases for sales promotion, premiums, fund-raising, educational or institutional use.

Special book excerpts or customized printings can also be created to fit specific needs. For details, write or phone the office of the Kensington Special Sales Manager: Kensington Publishing Corp., 850 Third Avenue, New York, NY 10022. Attn. Special Sales Department. Phone: 1-800-221-2647.

Kensington and the K logo Reg. U.S. Pat. & TM Off.

ISBN 0-7582-1300-X

First Trade Printing: June 2005
10  9  8  7  6  5  4  3  2  1

Printed in the United States of America

# LONE CALDER
# STAR

# *Prologue*

Clouds blanketed the Texas landscape southwest of Fort Worth as a stiff wind broomed the countryside, sweeping up anything that wasn't firmly attached. The air was cold with the bite of December's breath, courtesy of the blue norther that had invaded Texas the night before.

A sign swung drunkenly from its gatepost, held by a single chain that creaked and rattled with the effort. The sign itself was pockmarked with bullet holes, making it difficult to read the painted letters that spelled out the name CEE BAR RANCH.

Brake lights flashed red as a fast-traveling patrol car slowed its approach to the ranch entrance. Still the vehicle took the turn a little fast, the rear end fishtailing slightly on the dirt lane. Dust boiled around the patrol car, but not before Officer Ray Hobbs got a look at the dangling sign.

"Looks like somebody's been using that sign for target practice," he remarked to his partner behind the wheel.

"So what else is new, city boy?" Joe Ed Krause, a veteran of some seventeen years on the force, threw a jaundiced look at the young rookie. "Half the signs in the county've been shot up at one time or another. That's just what happens when you put boredom, beer, and back roads together. It don't mean anything."

"Probably not," Ray Hobbs agreed and shifted his attention to the empty landscape, partially obscured by the blowing dust. When the patrol car rolled into the ranch yard, he sat up a little straighter, taking note of the pickup parked in front of an old barn before focusing on the single-story house and the front porch that traversed the length of it. "Looks like somebody's here."

"I wouldn't count on it," Joe Ed muttered and drove straight to the house. Leaving the warm confines of the patrol car, he stepped into the winter-chilled air and clamped a hand on the crown of his hat to prevent the wind from blowing it off.

His partner joined him. Together they crossed to the shelter of the porch. There was an uneven cadence to the heavy thud of their footsteps on the planked floor, the sound partially muffled by the wind.

Without hesitation or caution, Joe Ed opened the screen door and pounded loudly on the wooden door, then waited. As the seconds stretched out, the rookie peered through the dust-coated panes of a side window.

"Don't see any movement," Ray said.

Joe Ed pounded on the door again, rattling the hinges, then reached down and tried the knob. It turned easily in his hand.

"It's not locked?" The rookie gave his partner a startled look.

"Hell, we're in the country," Joe Ed retorted with barely veiled disgust. "Nobody locks their door during the day." He stepped inside and shouted, "Hello? Anybody home?" He paused and called out again, "Evans, are you here?"

But he was met only with silence.

The rookie followed him inside. "I don't think anybody's here."

"No kidding." That observation didn't come as any great surprise to Joe Ed. If he'd been alone, he would have turned around and left right then. But with the green officer at his side, he decided to go through the motions of a search. "We might as well check the other rooms."

The doorway on his right opened into the kitchen. Joe Ed motioned toward it and led the way into the room, floorboards creaking under the weight of his heavy frame. His foray into the room took him to the automatic coffeemaker on the counter next to the sink.

He pulled out the pot and made a face of disgust. "There must be an inch of mold in this pot." More grew on the dirty dishes stacked in the sink. The state of the dishes in the sink didn't bother him, but the coffeepot did. "Every cowhand I ever knew couldn't start his day without coffee. Nobody's made any in this pot for days."

"Do you think we should check out the bedrooms?" the rookie suggested.

Joe Ed shrugged. "Why not?"

A search of the three bedrooms yielded one unmade bed and three empty closets. "This Sam Evans guy that's supposed to be living here has obviously pulled out."

"But how come there's a pickup parked outside?" The rookie, Ray Hobbs, still wasn't satisfied that the situation was as simple as that.

"Yeah. I guess we'd better check it out," Joe Ed agreed with reluctance, regarding it as a waste of time.

The wind howled a greeting as they exited the old ranch house. Heads down, the two officers walked into the teeth of it, taking a straight line to the pickup parked in front of the barn. Like the house, the truck was unlocked. A search of the glove compartment produced a certificate of insurance and registration slip.

"The owner of record is the Calder Cattle Company," Joe Ed announced. "If I'm not mistaken, that's the name of the Montana outfit that owns this place."

# PART ONE

*A lonely star,*
*A Texas sky,*
*A Calder learns*
*That trouble is nigh.*

# Chapter One

~

M other Nature was in an impish mood. While Texas shivered under cloudy skies and a cold north wind, the plains of eastern Montana enjoyed temperatures in the mid-sixties, thanks to a chinook wind that blew its warmth over the high prairie.

In this big and empty land that had once been the domain of the mighty Sioux, today over a million acres of it fell within the boundaries of the Calder Cattle Company, better known throughout the west as the Triple C. Quint Echohawk's roots were sunk deep in its soil. His mother was the daughter of the family patriarch, Chase Benteen Calder, and his late father had been a quarter Sioux.

Quint had inherited his father's smoke-gray eyes, his high, prominent cheekbones and glistening black hair. But there was much of the Calder side in him as well, visible in the granite jaw, the deep set of his eyes, and the muscled width of his shoulders and chest.

As a boy growing up on the Triple C, he'd been dubbed "little man" by the ranch hands. "Little" no longer described his six-two frame, but at twenty-seven, he had made the full transition into manhood.

With the afternoon sun warm on his back, Quint climbed the

steps of the Homestead that had long been the residence of the Calder clan. The towering two-story structure was grand in scale, making it visible for miles like a massive white ship anchored in an ocean of grass.

Thanksgiving had barely passed, but already the big house was decked in holiday dress—a Christmas wreath on the door and a garland twined around its tall pillars. In the bright light of day, its multitude of twinkling lights was invisible, but they were there just the same.

Quint paused at the top of the steps and swung back to survey the ranch yard with its sprawl of buildings. To an outsider, the Triple C headquarters would have resembled a small country town. In many respects it was.

In addition to the usual assortment of barns and sheds associated with the ranching business, there was a commissary stocked with a variety of essential supplies that ran the gamut from foodstuffs and work clothes to hardware and vehicle parts. A few years back an addition had been added to provide space for video rentals and the ranch post office. Other buildings housed a first-aid dispensary, a welding shop, and an elementary school. Besides the old cook shack that served as a restaurant of sorts, there were nearly a dozen houses that provided homes for married ranch hands and their families.

Considering the nearest large town was some two hundred miles distant and the ranch itself covered as much ground as some eastern states, the Triple C had become self-sufficient out of necessity. And the Calder family controlled every inch of it.

That knowledge was at the back of Quint's mind as he idly ran his glance over the large cluster of buildings. If his mother had her way, he would play a major part in the ranching operation, though both knew the reins of the Triple C would eventually pass to her brother's son, Trey. Quint had no problem with that, convinced that it was a role Trey had been born to fill. Still Quint regarded his own future as far from settled. As always, that was something Quint kept to himself.

Hearing the click of the door latch behind him, Quint turned as his mother stepped into view. Cathleen Calder Echohawk— known by all as simply Cat—was a slim, petite woman with green eyes and black hair that showed few strands of gray. Her smile was quick and wide, indicative of a personality that was both vibrant and volatile.

"I thought that was you standing out here," she declared. "You'd better come in. Jessy's looking for you. I got the impression there's a problem of some sort." She continued talking as he crossed to the door. "I hope it's nothing serious, not when we're supposed to leave for England in the morning for Laura's wedding. It would be horrible if the mother of the bride can't be there."

"At least Jessy was present at the first ceremony," Quint reminded her, a glint of teasing humor in his gray eyes.

"Now you sound like your grandfather," Cat chided with affection, stepping aside as he came through the door into the entryway. "He still doesn't see why Laura is having two weddings—one here and one in Britain. But the trip to England would have been much too hard on him at his age, and it simply wasn't practical for Sebastian's family and friends to fly over here."

"I know." Quint nodded. "Where's Jessy? In the den?"

"Yes," she confirmed, then placed a detaining hand on his arm. "I'm glad you decided not to make the trip. The idea of leaving your grandfather here by himself bothers me."

"Don't worry. There'll be plenty of people keeping an eye on him besides me."

"Of course there will." She cast a glance in the direction of the den. "You'd better go see what Jessy wants."

The Homestead's large den was still considered the heart of the Triple C despite the construction of a separate ranch office several years back. It was on one of its walls that the old hand-drawn map of the ranch was hung, outlining its far-flung boundaries and identifying its various landmarks and watercourses on paper that had yellowed over time.

It was in the den as well where the impressive set of horns from a longhorn steer was mounted above the mantel of the massive stone fireplace. The same steer that had led the first cattle drive from Texas to the newly established Triple C Ranch in Montana. It was a room of history and heritage that never failed to make its imprint on Quint. This afternoon was no exception.

The fresh scent of pine emanated from the greenery that adorned the mantel. A cheery fire blazed in the old stone fireplace, casting its glow into the room and adding a welcome warmth for his grandfather's old bones.

As usual, his grandfather, Chase Benteen Calder, sat behind the oversized desk, his once vigorous body now gray-haired and stoop-shouldered, with age lines creasing his rawboned face. The accumulation of years had left the mark on his body, but his mind remained as sharp as ever, and full of a lifetime of ranching knowledge on this northern plain.

Currently, his grandfather's attention was centered on his daughter-in-law, Jessy Calder, who, under Chase's able tutelage, had been running the Triple C for the last twenty-odd years since her husband's death. Jessy sat on a corner of the desk, her boy-slim body angled toward Chase. She swiveled to face the doorway when she heard Quint's footsteps.

"We were just talking about you, Quint." In a single, fluid motion, Jessy straightened up from the desk.

"Mom said you wanted to see me." Quint swept off his hat and walked the rest of the way into the room, dividing his curious glance between the two of them. But there was little that could be read from their expressions. "What's up?"

"That's what we want you to find out," Jessy stated. "How soon can you be packed?"

Quint halted in surprise. "To go where?"

"Texas. We've been leaving messages at the Cee Bar for the last week, but none of our calls were returned. Today I asked the sheriff down there to check it out. I got off the phone with him just a few minutes ago. There was no one at the ranch—and no one had been there for at least a week, as near as his men could tell."

Quint frowned. "I thought you hired somebody from the outside to manage the operation at the Cee Bar."

Jessy released a half-irritated sigh and nodded. "Sam Evans, by name. We hired him about a year and a half ago."

"Have you had any problems with him before now?" Quint asked, following his first thought.

"Not with Sam," Jessy replied without any hesitation. "Although the last few months he has complained that all his hired help kept walking out on him after only a few days' work." Her shoulders moved in a vague shrug of confusion. "I don't know. Maybe he got tired of doing all the work by himself and quit without bothering to notify us."

There was something in the inflection of her voice that told Quint she didn't totally believe that. "You think that would be out of character for him, don't you?" he guessed.

Jessy's innate sense of practicality surfaced. "It doesn't matter what I think. The fact remains he's gone—bag and baggage, according to the sheriff," she added. "We need you to fly down there and take charge of the ranch until we can hire someone else."

"If that's what you want, I can be packed and ready in an hour," Quint stated, then cocked his head at a puzzled and inquiring angle. "But why me? We all know there are any number of men here at the Triple C who have more ranching experience than I do."

The question was directed at Jessy, but it was Chase who answered, "Back in June, Max Rutledge offered to buy the Cee Bar. I turned him down flat. Shortly after that, Evans started having trouble keeping help. It could be just a coincidence. But my gut tells me it isn't."

Max Rutledge. Quint knew the name well. He had met Max's son and heir, Boone Rutledge, during Boone's very brief engagement to Quint's cousin Laura, but he knew Max mostly by reputation. And it was a ruthless one.

The Texan was reportedly worth millions, thanks to his vast petroleum and banking investments. And numbered among his many holdings was the Rutledge family ranch, which just happened to border the Cee Bar.

Quint understood that it was a troubleshooter they wanted more than someone with ranching skills. In that he was uniquely qualified, considering that until a few months ago, he'd been an ATF agent for the Treasury Department. And it was that background in law enforcement they wanted.

"I'll have the twin-engine fueled and waiting for you," Jessy said and reached for the phone.

Winter pressed an early darkness over the Texas landscape. The cold front had passed on through the area, taking the clouds with it and leaving a bright glitter of stars in the evening sky.

The headlight beams on Quint's rental car illuminated the two-lane highway in front of him. At this hour there was little traffic on it, and nearly all of it headed in the opposite direction. As he rounded a bend in the road, Quint noticed a cluster of lights in the near distance that looked to be a mixture of streetlamps and partially lit buildings. According to the directions Jessy had given him, he was to pass through the small town of Loury, Texas, before he reached the Cee Bar.

Within minutes, the city limit sign loomed along the shoulder and Quint reduced the car's speed to match the posted number. The two-lane road cut straight through the center of town. Block buildings, some with brick facades and others with modern awnings, marked the town's business district. Most of the buildings stood empty, a few of them with optimistic FOR LEASE signs displayed in their dusty storefront windows.

In all there weren't more than a half dozen vehicles parked along the street, and a majority of those were in front of a well-lit building on the corner. A large sign above its long windows aptly identified the place as the Corner Café. In big, bold letters painted on the glass, it advertised HOME-COOKED MEALS.

Knowing that it was unlikely there would be anything edible at the ranch, Quint decided to grab something to eat now and save himself a trip back to town. He found an empty parking slot in front of an adjacent building and pulled into it.

There were only five other customers in the restaurant when Quint walked in. Out of habit born of his previous training, he let his glance touch each of them, automatically committing their faces to memory. An elderly couple sat in a side booth, sharing a sandwich, while a rear table was occupied by three men dressed in cowboy hats, pearl-snapped shirts, and faded jeans. Two of them were hunched over their coffee both noting his arrival with idle glances, while the third was busy making short work of a cream pie.

All the stools along the short counter were empty except for the one on the far end. A girl in a waitress' apron was perched on it, an opened textbook on the counter in front of her along with a spiral notebook.

Quint opted for one of the tables closer to the front of the café, pulling out a chair that gave him a view of both the door and his fellow customers. As Quint took his seat, the waitress threw him a distracted glance, reluctantly pushed the book back a notch, and slid sideways off the stool, giving Quint a glimpse of her long hair, fastened together at the nape of her neck with a tortoiseshell clasp. Under the glow of the fluorescent lights, it was the same shiny color of a new penny. He didn't see anything to change his opinion when she approached his table, an attractive girl, on the young side, not over seventeen.

She placed a glass of water on the table and looked him in the eye, studying him with the idle curiosity of a local toward a stranger in town. For the first time Quint noticed the unusual light brown color of her eyes, neither hazel nor golden, but a startling tan.

"Would you like some coffee while you're looking over the menu?" There was an automatic quality to the question that came from frequent usage.

"I'll take coffee and tonight's special."

"You mean the meat loaf?" She gave him a look that clearly questioned his judgment. "Bad choice. You can't pour enough ketchup on Tub's meat loaf to make it taste good." There wasn't a trace of malice or derision in her statement. On the contrary, it came across as a good-natured warning.

Quint couldn't help smiling. "What would you suggest then?"

She responded with a wide-lipped smile of her own. "The safest thing is a hamburger and fries."

"Sold."

"I'll be right back with your coffee," she said, and moved away from the table.

When she returned, Quint used the opportunity to ask some questions and pick up any information he could about the Cee Bar. "Are there any job openings around here?"

"Guy Chalmers is looking for somebody to pump gas on the weekends." Even as she answered, her gaze was making an assessing study of him, exhibiting a maturity that went beyond seventeen. "But I don't imagine you'd be interested in that kind of work."

"Not really. What about the Cee Bar? Somebody mentioned they were hiring."

"You're a cowboy then." Something flickered in her expression that resembled disappointment.

"Is that bad?" Quint countered, amused and curious at her reaction.

"No. You just didn't strike me as one," the girl admitted while a skimming glance took new note of the hat, jeans, and cowboy boots he wore. "After all, half the people in Texas wear boots and hats, but they aren't all cowboys."

Before Quint had a chance to respond, one of the men in back lifted his cup in the air and called, "Hey, Dallas, how about some more coffee?"

"Be right there," she promised, and let her glance ricochet off Quint as she retreated to the counter area.

Coffeepot in hand, she crossed to the table and refilled all three cups. One of them asked her something that produced a shrug before she went to check on the couple in the booth. To Quint's regret she didn't return to his table when she finished. Instead she climbed back on the counter stool and began reading her book again.

Quint wasn't sure why he wanted to talk to this Dallas girl some more. She certainly hadn't given him any useful information. None, in fact. He couldn't tell whether that had been calculated or completely ingenuous on her part. Considering her age, Quint suspected the latter.

Just the same, something about her intrigued him. He couldn't remember the last time a female had aroused more than his sexual interest. It was ironic that it should turn out to be a teenager.

Any other time such a thought would have drawn a smile from him. Tonight, it left Quint feeling dissatisfied and oddly restless.

His glance strayed to a restroom sign with an arrow pointing to a rear hall. The sight of it offered him the ideal excuse to stretch his legs. Quint straightened from his chair and went to wash up before his food arrived.

# Chapter Two

Astocky cowboy at the back table tracked Quint's progress across the café and waited until he had pushed open the door to the men's room, then got up and ambled over to the end of the counter where the waitress sat. He gave his hat a push to the back of his head, revealing a shock of wheat-colored hair, and propped an arm on the counter.

"Just about every time I see you, you got your nose stuck in a book. Your eyes are gonna wear out, Dallas." He waited, but she gave no sign of having heard him. "Heard you and your grand-daddy rented the old, run-down house trailer from Andy Farrell. I figured you'd head to the city."

"You figured wrong, as usual, John Earl," Dallas replied with no visible break in her concentration.

"What did that stranger bend your ear about?"

"Nothing." She scribbled something on a page of the spiral notebook lying next to the book.

"Sure looked like he was asking you a lot of questions. He was coming on to you, wasn't he?" The accusation had a possessive ring to it, enough that Dallas threw him a quelling look.

"No, he wasn't. He was asking about work around here."

"What kind of work?"

"Cowboying."

John Earl Tandy released a short derisive breath. "It's the wrong time of year for any of the outfits around here to be taking on extra hands."

Rankled by his smug, know-it-all certainty, Dallas couldn't resist taking a jab at it. "Is that right?" Her chin came up in challenge. "I wonder where he got the idea the Cee Bar was hiring."

Her response only brought a big grin to the cowboy's face. "He can forget about working there."

"Why?" There was a hard heat in her voice. "Does Rutledge have his eyes on that ranch, too?"

He ducked his head, briefly breaking eye contact with her. "I figured you'd still be sore. But you gotta know there was nothin' I could do about it."

"Just about everybody in town has told us that." Dallas stared at the book's printed page, but her thoughts were on the gray-eyed stranger and the trouble he'd be letting himself in for if he took that job at the Cee Bar. She reminded herself that was his problem, and not hers.

"You've had a rough time of it lately, that's for sure. But things'll get better," John Earl declared with his typical cocksure confidence. "Why don't you let me take you out Saturday night?"

"Is that your idea of things getting better?" Dallas scoffed.

Stung by her caustic retort, John Earl stood up straight, rigid with anger. "I figured you might not think so much of yourself after your granddaddy lost his ranch, but you still act like you're too good for anybody around here."

The accusation was so ridiculous Dallas wanted to hit him, but she attacked with sarcasm instead. "Of course I do. That's why I'm living in an old, run-down house trailer."

John Earl faltered, certain he'd been insulted, but not sure how. "You can't blame me for that. Your granddaddy was a fool to think he could stop Rutledge from getting what he wants. Nobody can go against him and win."

Dallas caught a movement in her side vision and turned as the stranger emerged from the rear hallway and headed back to his table. "You'd better tell the new guy," she suggested.

"No need to," John Earl replied. "He'll find out for himself soon enough."

Dallas was quick to detect a tone that hinted at inside information. "What do you mean?" she demanded and fought to contain the sudden sense of rage that swept through her.

"Nothin' really." But John Earl's smug smile was back. "Just that he won't find anybody there to hire him."

"You mean"—it took her a second to remember the name of the man in charge of the Cee Bar—"Evans left? I hadn't heard that."

"You didn't expect him to put a notice in the paper, did you?" John Earl grinned.

"But why did he leave? No, let me guess. It had to do with his health, didn't it?" Anger seethed just below the surface of her words.

"His health," John Earl repeated in amusement. "Guess you could say that."

Dallas had no doubts that the threats had been subtle, yet very clear. It was almost enough to make her sick. Worse, though, was that feeling of being utterly powerless to do anything about it.

A hamburger platter mounded with fries was shoved onto the serving side of the kitchen's pass-through window and a corpulent hand punched the counter bell, the sharp ding of it signaling to Dallas that her food order was up.

The timing couldn't have been better as far as Dallas was concerned. It gave her a ready excuse to break off the conversation with John Earl. She slipped off the stool and went behind the counter, circling around the cowboy. She collected the hamburger platter from the window shelf, scooped up some ketchup and mustard, and carried all of it to the stranger's table.

"Thanks," he said with an upward glance when Dallas set it before him.

She had trouble meeting his eyes. John Earl was the cause for it—and the things he'd told her about the Cee Bar. She reminded herself that it was the stranger's bad luck and there was absolutely nothing she could do about it.

Instead she glanced at his nearly empty cup. "I'll bring you some more coffee."

When she returned with the pot, the elderly couple were waiting at the cash register to pay. She left Quint's table to take their money, eliminating that chance to strike up another conversation with her.

Quint idly watched as she chatted with the pair. He had the distinct impression that the couple didn't have her whole attention; her thoughts were somewhere else. He decided that was hardly a surprise considering the sizable gap in their ages. By the time she climbed back on her stool, the cowboy had rejoined his friends at the table. Once again the girl immersed herself in the book's printed words.

The trio of cowboys engaged in desultory conversation, the low, lazy drawl of their voices providing a backdrop to Quint's meal. Occasionally the easy quiet of the café was broken by the clink and clatter of glasses and pans coming from the kitchen.

As Quint chewed the last bite of his hamburger, the cowboys pushed their chairs back from the table in ragged order. One dug some coins out of the side pocket of his jeans and tossed them on the table for a tip. Together they ambled toward the cash register counter near the door, their glances sliding curiously to Quint.

One of them abruptly came to a decision and swung toward his table. Quint was quick to recognize him as the same cowboy who had been talking to the waitress earlier.

"Dallas told me you were looking for work," the man said without preamble. "She said you'd heard the Cee Bar was wanting a hired hand."

Quint leaned back in his chair, giving the appearance of one fully at ease. But there was an instant sharpening of all his senses. "That's right."

"Now, it's no skin off my nose what you do, but if you're open to some friendly advice, you'll forget about that job."

Quint cocked his head at a curious angle. "Why's that?"

The cowboy paused over his answer. "Let's just say you wouldn't like working there, and leave it at that." He concluded the statement with a curt bob of his head and moved off to rejoin his buddies.

There was no change in Quint's expression as he digested this tidbit of information, aware that his conversation with the waitress had netted results after all. He thoughtfully sipped his coffee, aware there were two possibilities—that the former ranch manager Evans had been something of a tyrant or someone was deliberately creating problems—just as his grandfather had suspected.

Even in these modern times, there were few ranches of any size that could survive without some hired help. And it was an absolute necessity for one with absentee ownership.

Quint waited until the cowboys had gone and the young waitress had cleaned their table, then made his own way to the cash register. His gaze traveled over her face when she joined him, noting its clean, smooth lines.

"Was everything all right?" Her glance briefly made contact with his, but not long enough to renew his fascination with the tan shade of her eyes.

"Fine," Quint replied, conscious of a male interest stirring despite her youth and his better judgment. "The hamburger was a good choice."

"Better than the meat loaf." A smile edged the corners of her mouth.

"I'll take your word for that." He laid a twenty-dollar bill on the counter. "Your cowboy friend advised against taking that job at the Cee Bar. He said I wouldn't like working there. Do you know why?"

Quint sensed her sudden withdrawal; it was almost a physical thing.

Yet the shrugging lift of her shoulders seemed to be a natural gesture of ignorance. "John Earl usually knows what he's talking about. It would be smart to listen to him." She placed his change on the counter and turned away, adding a perfunctory "Y'all have a good night."

Quint studied the straight, almost stiff, line of her back and considered pursuing the subject. He knew, better than most, that the young were rarely skilled at withholding information for long. The cook emerged from the kitchen, using the hem of his stained apron to mop up the sweat rolling down his multiple chins.

The corpulent man threw an indifferent look at Quint and waved a fat hand at the waitress. "Might as well lock up after he leaves and call it a night." He grabbed a glass of ice from the rack and pushed it under the Coke dispenser.

The announcement effectively made it difficult, if not impossible, for Quint to linger and question the young waitress further. He decided it might be for the best. If Rutledge was behind this, then it was better not to involve the girl—even indirectly.

There were fewer vehicles parked along the street and no traffic moving when Quint left the café. But he scanned the street in both directions, mainly out of habit, as he made his way to the rental car.

Dallas watched him through the café's plate-glass window while she gathered up the dirty dishes from his table. She was surprised and a little puzzled when she saw him slide behind the wheel of a late-model sedan. Every self-respecting cowboy she knew drove a pickup—except for the occasional married ones.

Dallas tried to remember whether he'd been wearing a wedding band, but she had no recollection of one. Not that it mattered. It wasn't likely she would see him again anyway.

With her side work finished, Dallas filled out her time card, stuffed her textbooks and papers into a canvas tote bag, called a good night to Tubby Harris, and left by the back door. She wrenched open the driver's side door of an old white pickup, shoved her tote bag onto the passenger seat, and climbed in after it.

It was a five-minute drive from the café to the old Farrell place on the outskirts of town. Dallas parked the pickup next to the single-wide trailer that had been home for the last eight months. The outside light was on, the yellow fixture throwing an amber glow over the wooden steps to the trailer's front door.

A bluish light flickered across the living room window, a distinctive pattern that said the television was on. Dallas smiled knowing that she would likely find her grandfather snoozing in his recliner.

The smile didn't last, though. Losing the ranch had been hard on her grandfather, but not as hard as finding himself with all this time on his hands and nothing to do with it. Jobs were scarce in Loury, and there were fewer still for a seventy-eight-year-old man.

Suppressing a sigh, Dallas slung the tote bag strap over her shoulder and climbed the steps to the front door. The hinge screeched in protest when she pushed the door open.

Instantly the recliner snapped upright and the footrest thudded into place. "Who's there?" her grandfather barked.

"It's just me." Dallas walked on in and halted at the sight of the shotgun gripped in his gnarled hands. "I thought you promised me you'd lock that in the gun cabinet, Empty."

Born Mordecai Thomas Garner, the rancher had been known by his initials M.T. since his cradle days. No one recalled who had first mistakenly spelled his name as Empty, but it had stuck. Everyone in the area knew the big-chested, bandy-legged old man as Empty Garner.

Empty had the grace to shift uncomfortably under her disapproving look. "I had to clean it first," he grumbled in his own defense and motioned to the gun-cleaning kit on the table next to his chair.

She skimmed the tabletop and noted the absence of any shells. "That's loaded, isn't it?"

"What good is it to have a gun around if it isn't loaded?" he argued, then attempted to change the subject. "What in tarnation are you doing home so early anyway?"

"It's Wednesday. Tubby seldom has many customers on a weeknight." Dallas let her tote bag slide to the floor and crossed to his chair, extending her hand in a demanding fashion. "Give me the shotgun, and I'll lock it up."

His eyes narrowed in sharp temper. "Don't you be giving me orders, little girl. I'm not the youngster around here."

But it wasn't in Dallas to back down when she knew she was right. She pointed a rigid finger at the tall gun cabinet on the wall next to the television. "Then you go lock it up before you accidentally shoot somebody."

He glared at her. "How can I when you're standing in my way?"

"I could throttle you sometimes," she declared and stalked over to scoop up her tote bag.

Empty Garner levered himself out of the recliner and crossed to the gun cabinet, moving with the side-to-side rocking gait of a man who had spent most of his life in a saddle. "Someday you're going to be sorry you insisted on this," he said to her back as Dallas carried her bag of books to the table in the adjoining kitchen. "Especially if Rutledge sends one of his boys prowling around here."

"You don't have to worry about Rutledge." Dallas plunked herself on one of the kitchen chairs, feeling as cranky and out of sorts as her grandfather. Deep down she knew it had nothing to do with the shotgun. "He's after the Cee Bar now."

"How do you know that?" Keys rattled on the metal ring as Empty flipped through them, searching for the one for the gun cabinet.

"John Earl was in the café tonight."

Her news caught Empty off guard. His brow furrowed in thought as he stowed the shotgun in the cabinet and locked the door. He shoved the key ring in his pocket and ambled into the kitchen, still mulling over her statement.

"I know John Earl's belt doesn't go through all the loops, but I didn't think he was dumb enough to volunteer something like that."

"He didn't exactly volunteer it," Dallas admitted and pulled her English Lit book out of the tote bag.

"How did it come up then?"

Dallas sighed in exasperation, regretting that she had mentioned anything about it. But once said, she couldn't take it back. And knowing her grandfather, he wouldn't give her a moment's peace until he knew the whole story. She should have remembered that any mention of Rutledge was like a red cape to a Spanish bull.

As concisely as possible, Dallas told him about the stranger looking for work and asking about the job opening at the Cee Bar, followed by John Earl's questioning her conversation with the stranger and his cocky response about the unlikelihood of the stranger getting hired.

"He didn't say it in so many words," Dallas said in conclusion, "but it was obvious that Evans had been run off."

Her grandfather nodded in agreement. "More'n likely he got the fear of Rutledge put into him. It'd be easy to buy him off after that. By God, I'd give anything to be around when Rutledge gets his comeuppance." Acrimony riddled his voice. "He's played it high and wide too long."

"Nobody's stopped him all these years," Dallas reminded him, stifling her own bitter resentment of the man. "It isn't logical to think any one will."

"You're probably right," he grumbled and watched as she flipped through the pages of the textbook. "I suppose you'll be up half the night studying."

"I have to. Finals start next week."

"Just remember you need your sleep, too. Studying won't do you any good if your brain's too tired to take it in." With that bit of wisdom delivered, he started to turn away, then swung back, pinning his gaze on her. "Who's tending the stock out at the Cee Bar?"

"Nobody, I guess," Dallas replied absently, already turning her attention to the subject before her.

"It wouldn't bother Rutledge if they went hungry," Empty muttered, unaware that Dallas had already tuned him out. "He'd probably like it if they starved. Then he could report it to the authorities and cause more trouble for the owners."

Dallas made an agreeing sound, without having heard a word he'd said.

"What time you got to be at the feed store in the morning?" he demanded suddenly. "Eight o'clock, isn't it?"

"Eight?" She gave him a blank look, then his question belatedly registered, and Dallas nodded. "Yes, eight o'clock."

"I'm gonna need to use the truck tomorrow, so I'll take you to work in the morning."

"Fine," she said and went back to her studies.

All was dark, shadows lying thick around the buildings, when Quint pulled into the Cee Bar ranch yard. The single-story house stood off by itself, half hidden under the enveloping shade of a live oak. Quint parked the sedan in front of it, retrieved his duffel bag from the trunk, and crossed to the covered porch that ran along the front.

The door was unlocked, making the spare key in his pocket needless. Quint stepped inside and felt along the wall for the light switch. Finding it, he flipped it on. Light spilled from an overhead fixture, illuminating the center area of the living room while leaving its corners in shadow.

His gaze traveled to the old stone fireplace along the wall. Soot from countless fires stained the front of it, revealing its age. Quint wandered over to it, ignoring the creak and groan of the uneven floorboards when they took his weight.

Idly he ran a hand over the wooden mantelpiece and smiled, recalling the winter holidays he'd spent here when he was eleven, and the many stories his grandfather had told him about the ranch. Quint felt the swirl of history around him.

And it was Calder history. The origins of this ranch and its house dated back to the Civil War era when it had been the home of Seth Calder and his son, Benteen—the same Benteen Calder who had eventually driven a herd of longhorns north to Montana and established the Triple C Ranch.

Well over a hundred years had passed since a Calder had lived on the Cee Bar. That seemed wrong somehow.

Pushing that thought aside, Quint turned from the fireplace and the past, focusing once again on the job he had come to do.

# Chapter Three

Wakened by a rooster's crow shortly after dawn, Quint rolled out of the strange bed and padded into the hallway. The floorboards creaked companionably under his bare feet as he made his way to the closet-sized bathroom off the hall. He wasted little time relieving himself and washing the sleep from his eyes. Back in the bedroom, he pulled a clean set of clothes out of his duffel bag and put them on.

Leaving the rear bedroom, he headed for the kitchen where he'd left the coffeepot and dirty dishes soaking in a sink full of sudsy bleach water the night before. There was just enough coffee in the canister to make a pot. He spooned some into the basket filter and made a mental note to add coffee to his grocery list as he thoroughly rinsed out the now mold-free glass pot.

After plugging in the coffeemaker, he filled its tank with water and listened to it gurgle to life. Just as he poured his first cup, the telephone rang. Quint crossed to the wall-mounted phone and lifted the receiver.

"Cee Bar Ranch."

His mother's familiar voice responded, "I was hoping I wouldn't waken you."

"You didn't," he assured her. "As a matter of fact, I'm drinking coffee and making a grocery list. The cupboards here are bare."

"What are you going to do for breakfast?" she asked with instant concern.

"I'm looking out the window at a bunch of chickens scratching in the yard. There's bound to be some eggs somewhere out there waiting to be gathered."

There was an element of relief in her soft laughter. "Sometimes I forget how resourceful you've always been."

"Now you've been reminded." Affection gentled his voice. "I thought you would have left for Laura's wedding by now."

"We're about to walk out the door, but I wanted to call you first and tell you good-bye."

"Let Laura and Sebastian know I'll be thinking about them."

"I will. And you take care of yourself down there."

It was his own suspicion of trouble coming that made him admonish, "Don't start worrying about me, Mom."

"I'm not," she said with ease. "I don't think you realize how proud I am that Jessy wanted you to put things back in order at the Cee Bar. It shows that she recognizes you can shoulder that kind of responsibility. I hope you can see that so we won't have to argue anymore about how much of an asset you can be to the Triple C."

"We would just argue about something else," Quint teased.

That drew the expected protest from her. They talked a few minutes more before exchanging final good-byes. Quint hung up and finished his coffee, then unhooked his denim jacket from the chair back and headed out the door.

The instant the screen door banged shut behind him, the rusty red chickens in the yard ran to meet him, clucking noisily. Their clamor was echoed by the eager whickering of the horses in the small fenced pasture next to the barn.

"We all have empty stomachs this morning, don't we?" Quint remarked as the chickens crowded around him, clucking and flapping their wings.

They trailed after him, running to keep up with his long strides as he struck out for the barn. The grain barrel was empty of all but the bottom leavings. He dumped that out for the chickens and looked through the rest of the barn. He found a half dozen eggs, but only one square hay bale.

He used an empty grain bucket for an egg basket and set it outside the barn door. The four horses in the corral broke into eager whickers at the sight of Quint with the bucket. A big bay gelding whinnied a shrill protest when he disappeared back inside the barn.

A few seconds later Quint emerged from its shadows, carrying the bale by its twine. Short of the fence, he broke the bale apart and, one by one, tossed its squares into the corral. The landing of the first brought a flurry of flying hooves and bared teeth, but the squabbling soon ended as each horse tore eagerly into its own mound of hay. He watched in grim silence, aware there was too little hay to satisfy their empty bellies and that the few patches of grass in the large corral had already been chewed to the roots.

It was one more thing Quint held against the former ranch manager. Walking off the job without telling anyone was bad enough, but leaving without turning the horses loose was something that Quint couldn't easily forgive.

After dragging a hose from the barn and filling the corral's water tank, Quint carried the egg pail to the house and scrambled some eggs. Breakfast finished and washed down with a second cup of coffee, he added his own dirty dishes to the ones still soaking in the sink, stuck the grocery list in his shirt pocket, and plucked the ignition key to the ranch pickup from its hook by the back door.

He wasted thirty minutes trying to get the truck to start before he gave up and climbed behind the wheel of the rental car.

Located well off the more heavily traveled routes, the town of Loury attracted mainly local traffic. Downtown had a deserted feel to it when Quint drove through that morning. The breakfast crowd at the Corner Café had already come and gone, and it was too early for the town's old-timers to gather there for coffee and their morning bull session.

The grocery store had seven cars in its lot. Quint bypassed it for the time being and drove straight to the feed store on the east end of town. He pulled into the graveled lot and parked next to two pickups that stood in front of the metal building. When he climbed out of the sedan, his glance flicked to the passenger door panel of the truck beside him, and the sign painted on it that read SYKES FEED & GRAIN. The words were an echo of the board sign above the door.

A chalky white dust coated the front windowpanes, obscuring Quint's view of the interior. But an ingrained caution had him scanning the dim interior for any sign of movement. Upon entering the feed store, he automatically stepped to one side, well clear of the glass door.

Dust motes danced in the few shafts of sunlight that penetrated the windows, and the air had that familiar, musty smell of grain. A grumbling murmur of male voices came from the open doorway that connected the store with its warehouse area.

Quint glanced in their direction just as a female voice called out a somewhat absent "Be right with you."

Quint was quick to locate the woman. She was seated at a desk well to the rear of the front counter, facing a computer screen, her back to the door. At almost the same instant, he caught the faint, tinny tap of fingers moving rapidly over a keyboard.

He crossed to the counter and idly leaned a hip against it to wait until she was through. After another thirty seconds, she swung her chair around and stood up. She was dressed in jeans and a sweatshirt that stopped at midhip. A cap, emblazoned with the name Sykes Feed & Grain, covered her head, its bill casting a shadow on her face.

As she approached the counter, something about the way she walked nagged at Quint. Not until his curious glance encountered her pale brown eyes did recognition strike. It was Dallas, the waitress from the Corner Café. Pleasure kicked through him, warm and unexpected. He smiled when she faltered in midstride, revealing her own surprise at seeing him again.

"I thought you would have been long gone." Her mouth curved in a small smile that seemed to say that she was glad he wasn't.

"And I thought you'd be in school."

"School!" There was a note of incredulity in her short, amused laugh. Then understanding dawned in her expression. "You must have seen me studying. I go to college three nights a week. Second year." Despite her attempt to sound matter-of-fact, a faint note of pride crept into her voice.

"You're in college?" His initial assessment of her underwent a rapid revision as he added a few more years to her age.

"That's right," Dallas replied, then hesitated, a flicker of regret shadowing her eyes. "If you're here about a job, I can tell you now—they aren't hiring."

"No problem. I'm here to get some grain."

She shot him a quick, curious look, then masked it with an air of easy efficiency. "You came to the right place. What do you need?"

"One hundred and fifty pounds each of corn and oats, and a hundred pounds of top dress—whatever you carry in the way of a vitamin and mineral pack," Quint replied, as two men filed into the store from the warehouse.

The taller of the two had a round beer belly and sharp eyes that sized Quint up as a stranger. He threw him a curt nod and mumbled, "Mornin'."

Quint nodded back.

"Cash or charge?" Dallas asked him.

"Put it on the Cee Bar account," Quint told her.

Her head snapped up, her look one of disbelief. Before she could say a word, the big man snapped gruffly, "The Cee Bar doesn't have an account here."

"Since when?" Quint asked in cool challenge.

The big man hitched his pants higher around his fat belly and swaggered over to the counter, his bulk forcing Dallas to the side. "Since it got closed," the man replied, matching Quint's tone.

Quint didn't hesitate. "In that case, I'll pay cash." He pulled a wallet from of his hip pocket. "You do take cash, don't you?"

Clearly annoyed, the man shifted his glare to Dallas. "What's he wanting?"

She seemed to deliberately avoid any eye contact with Quint as she read off his request.

When she finished the man grunted and turned his narrowed eyes on Quint. "There's nobody here to load it for you. Come back in an hour or so, and we'll see if we can't get you fixed up."

"No problem. I'll load it myself." Retaining an outward calm, Quint flipped open his wallet and said to Dallas, "How much do I owe you?"

For a long tick of seconds, his question was met with a heavy silence. Never once did Quint acknowledge the hard stare the man directed at him. Instead he kept his attention centered on the sheaf of bills in his wallet.

Finally the man swung a cold look at Dallas and snapped, "Take his money an' show him where it's at." Off he stalked to the desk area.

Her face was an expressionless mask as she punched the sale into the computerized register, took his money, and handed him back the correct change and a printed receipt. Not once during the entire transaction did she meet his steady gaze.

"This way." Dallas seemed to push the two words through clenched teeth as she pivoted sharply toward the warehouse door.

She crossed the intervening space with quick, stiff strides. Quint followed at a seemingly leisurely pace, conscious of the anger that emanated from her in waves.

"Corn there. Oats here." She pointed to two separate rows of fifty-pound bags stacked on wooden pallets.

"Thanks." He continued past her, dragged the first sack partway off the stack, and hoisted it onto one shoulder. As he turned to carry it out to the car, he saw Dallas manhandling a fifty-pound sack of vitamin and mineral pack onto her shoulder. "I can get that," he said.

"So can I," she retorted.

Quint smiled crookedly. "You sound like my aunt," he said, knowing it was exactly the sort of thing Jessy would say.

"I hope she's brighter than you are," Dallas stated, without so much as a glance in his direction as she headed for the wide door that led outside.

But only a deaf person would have missed the caustic sarcasm in her voice. And Quint was far from deaf. He stiffened with a sudden surge of anger and followed her out of the warehouse all the way to his car. He held his tongue long enough to pop the trunk open and dump the sack of corn into it.

"Would you care to repeat that?" he challenged cooly as he hauled the bag off her shoulder and tossed it on top of the other.

She squared around to face him, her glance raking him with a look of disgust mixed with contempt. "You are an utter fool," she declared. "John Earl warned you about going to work at the Cee Bar, but you were too stupid to listen. Obviously you don't have the brains God gave a goose."

A fury, hotter than anything Quint had ever known, swept through him. Before he had a chance to unleash any of it, she spun away and struck out for the warehouse, shoulders straight and head high. Quint was slow to follow as he struggled to rein in his temper, unable to recall a time when he had come this close to losing it—simply because some woman with light brown eyes thought he was a fool.

Mouth firmly shut, he went back inside the warehouse and met her on her way out, toting another bag of the vitamin and mineral pack. "I'll take that." Giving Dallas no chance to object, he relieved her of the sack and shifted it onto his shoulder.

Strong fingers gripped his arm, checking his swing away from her. She threw a quick, wary look in the direction of the feed store, then said in a low voice that wouldn't carry, "Get smart. Dump this grain off at the ranch, then climb back in your car and get the hell out of there."

"Not a chance."

She stepped back, something resembling sadness in the look she gave him. "Like I said, you're a fool."

"Everybody's entitled to an opinion," Quint stated and walked out of the warehouse.

Dallas lingered a moment, half irritated that she had wasted her breath on him. He had already been warned once. She wasn't sure why she had bothered to do it a second time. He was nothing to her, just a good-looking cowboy new to the area—who had obviously landed on his head a few too many times. But that always seemed to be true of the good-looking ones, she thought wryly.

But no amount of reasoning could rid her of that heavy feeling she had when she went back into the feed store. When she started toward the computer and the rest of the grain shipment waiting to be added to the inventory, her glance skipped to the dusty windows, catching a glimpse of the cowboy on his way back into the warehouse.

Her boss Holly Sykes was at his desk, his chair tilted at a precarious angle and the phone pressed to his ear. As loud as the bell in the warehouse was set, Dallas knew she would have heard the ring of any incoming call. Which could only mean Sykes had instigated the phone call. Dallas didn't think she needed three guesses to figure out who that was. It was bound to be either Max Rutledge or his son Boone.

That old feeling of resentment left a bitter taste in her mouth when she sat down at the computer and reopened the inventory file. Only half of her attention was on the work before her; the rest was tuned to the one-sided phone conversation.

"He never blinked an eye when I told him the account was closed," Holly Sykes declared. "He just pulled out his wallet and said he'd pay cash for it." There was a lengthy pause while he listened. "No, he didn't give his name, and I had no call to ask for it with him paying cash." Another pause followed. "He looked like your ordinary cowboy—tall, dark-haired, on the young side. Didn't talk like he was from around here." The third pause was much shorter. "No problem. I figured you'd want to know about this guy."

The desk chair screeched noisily as Sykes rocked his considerable bulk forward and hung up the phone. The front door opened and Sykes demanded, "Is there something else you need?"

Quint paused inside the door. "Do you know of anybody with hay for sale?"

"Not off the top of my head, but you're welcome to post a notice on the board over there." Sykes waved a hand at the bulletin board on the wall by the door. Its surface was already cluttered with a mix of posters advertising the stud services of local stallions and scraps of paper offering to sell anything from vehicles and trailers to dogs and vegetables.

Quint walked over to the counter. "Do you have some paper I can use?"

"Get him some, Dallas," Sykes ordered.

Feeling oddly reluctant to face the stranger again, Dallas tore a page off the notepad on her desk, walked back to the counter, and handed it to him.

"Thanks."

But there was a coolness in his look that stung. Dallas supposed she deserved it after the things she'd said to him. Yet she found herself missing the easy warmth that had been in his gray eyes all the previous times. She waited at the counter while he jotted his message on the paper, telling herself that the sooner he found out there was nobody around here he could trust, the better off he would be.

Finished, he walked over to the bulletin board, posted his notice on it, and headed out the door. In big, block letters, he had written: HAY WANTED. Directly below it, he'd put the name of the ranch and its phone number.

Beyond the windows, dust swirled as the sedan reversed away from the store and swung toward the highway. The minute it turned onto the road, Holly Sykes pushed out of his squeaky chair and walked over to the bulletin board, removed the notice, and retreated again to his desk. He dropped the handwritten message on the desktop and picked up the phone, punched a series of numbers from memory, and lifted the receiver to his ear.

"Yeah, it's Holly Sykes down at the feed store. I need to talk to Mr. Rutledge again." After receiving an obviously negative response, he said, "That's all right. Just give him a message for me. Tell him the cowboy came back in, wanting to know where he could buy some hay."

The receiver rattled back onto its cradle as Dallas turned from the counter. Holly Sykes wadded the notice into a ball and tossed it into the wastepaper basket next to his desk. With a self-satisfied smile, he lowered himself into his chair and clasped his hands behind his head.

"It'll be a cold day in hell when he finds any hay for sale around here. And I'd bet money on that," he declared and rocked his chair back.

A little nudge was all it would take to overbalance the chair and send him flying ass over teakettle. Dallas had to remind herself how much she needed this paycheck. She suddenly had the uncomfortable feeling she wasn't any different from anyone else in this town. The discovery didn't set well.

Paper sacks stuffed with groceries in the rear seat sat atop the bags of grain that Quint hadn't been able to fit in the sedan's trunk. More sacks occupied the front passenger seat.

When he slowed the car to make the turn onto the lane, his glance skipped to the ranch sign, hanging perpendicular to the ground. But it was one of many signs of neglect that he'd noticed about the place. He couldn't help wondering how much more he would find when he finally ventured farther than the ranch yard and lane.

Idly, Quint scanned the gentle slope of hills on either side of the winding lane on the off chance he might spot some of the cattle, but there were none to be seen. Considering there was little in the way of graze, other than scrub grass, Quint wasn't surprised. Years of abuse from overstocking and overgrazing had taken their toll. The land was certainly nothing like the rich grassland of the Calder ranch in Montana with its thick mat of buffalo grass and stands of blue joint. It would require some aggressive land management to turn the Cee Bar into productive rangeland again.

He rounded a curve in the driveway and the ranch yard opened before him. Automatically Quint pointed the car toward the house, intending to unload the groceries first. But there was something amiss; he sensed it at once and slowed the car.

The horses weren't in the corral.

With a quick whip of the steering wheel, Quint swung the car toward the barn. He braked to a stop in front of it, threw the gearshift into park, and climbed out of the car.

The instant he took his first stride in the direction of the corral, a male voice barked, "Hold it right there, mister."

The voice seemed to be coming from the barn area. Quint made a half turn, and the voice barked again with new harshness, "Damn it, I said hold it right there!"

In his side vision, Quint could see the double barrels of a shotgun protruding from the opened barn door. But the man holding it was little more than a hatted figure cloaked in the barn's interior shadows. For the first time in months Quint missed the weight of the Glock he had once carried in a shoulder holster.

But even if he had been carrying the Glock, he was in no position to argue with a shotgun and Quint knew it.

"Who are you?" he demanded instead, careful to hold himself motionless.

"I'm the one holding this shotgun on you, and that's all you need to know," the man countered in a cold, hard voice. "Now you just climb back in that car and go tell Rutledge that whatever mischief he was wanting you to do here will have to wait for another time."

The man thought he was one of Rutledge's men. Quick to seize on that slim opening, Quint said, "You've made a mistake. "I'm—"

"No, you've made a mistake," the man broke in, a heat in his voice that warned against further argument. "Now you get back in that car and haul your ass out of here. I'm not going to tell you again."

The ominous click of a cocking hammer lent its own emphasis to underscore his words.

"All right. I'm going," Quint conceded.

With deliberate, unhurried movements, Quint retreated to the car and slid behind the wheel. The shotgun barrel followed him every inch of the way, but Quint still couldn't get a good look at the man holding it.

Taking his time, Quint reversed the car away from the barn and made a wide, lazy swing toward the lane. All the while his gaze scoured every inch of the yard. Logic told him the man had definitely not arrived at the ranch on foot. His vehicle was parked somewhere. Since the area behind the barn was blocked from his view, it seemed reasonable to assume that was the site.

Quint followed the lane's curving route until he was certain he was well out of sight of the ranch yard. Leaving the car parked on the shoulder, he slipped between two sagging fence wires and set out across the pasture, intent on circling around to approach the ranch yard from the rear.

The terrain offered little in the way of cover, forcing Quint to keep to the hillsides. With the barn's roof peak serving as his guide, he worked his way around to the back. He crept forward for a look. There, parked in the full glare of the morning sun, was an old white pickup, its finish dulled with a coating of road dust and its edges eaten with rust.

A scan of the area failed to turn up any sign of its driver. With a good forty yards of bare ground to cross, Quint could only hope the man was still in the barn and still watching the lane.

Alert for any sign of movement, Quint rose in a crouch and took aim on the pickup, the closest cover. With silence more important than speed, he moved as quickly as he dared over the hard-packed ground. He didn't draw an easy breath until he reached the cab of the pickup.

He hugged close to its side for a moment, listening. But there was little to be heard beyond the clucking of a chicken and the faraway bellow of a cow. Quint waited a few beats, then left the protection of the pickup for the barn. Pressing close to its rough siding, he listened for any sounds coming from within.

He caught a faint rustle, but it was impossible to tell if it was made by a human or a chicken. With the rear barn door closed and no windows on this end, Quint had no choice but to edge around to the side. He stopped short of the window frame and removed his hat before stealing a look inside. He glanced first at the open barn door without really expecting the man to still be standing by it.

For an instant Quint could hardly believe his eyes when he saw the shotgun propped against the door. A hen squawked and scurried into view, disturbed by something or someone on the opposite wall of the barn. Quint ducked down and shifted to the other side of the window. When he peered through its dusty pane, he immediately spotted a hatted figure poking around in the manger of one of the horse stalls, his back to the window. That was all he needed to see.

Moving away from the window, Quint glided swiftly around the barn door and paused inches from its opening. More faint rustling came from the vicinity of the stalls. Hearing it, Quint stepped inside the barn and almost simultaneously scooped up the shotgun.

With no hesitation at all, he broke it open, removed its two shells, and snapped it together, no longer caring that the sound betrayed his presence. The rustling noise stopped instantly.

"You might as well come out of that stall," Quint called. "I know you're there."

A narrow-hipped man, wearing a lined jacket that gave extra bulk to his torso, stepped out from behind a partitioned stall. The brim of his dark cowboy hat shaded his eyes, but it didn't conceal the lower half of his age-weathered face or the tufts of gray hair that poked from beneath the sides of his hat. He didn't say a word, just stood there glaring at Quint.

"All right," Quint said, "let's try this again. Who are you?"

"Empty."

Quint thought he was referring to the shotgun, currently cradled against the crook of his arm. "I know it's empty. I unloaded it."

"No," the man grumbled irritably. "That's my name—Mordecai Thomas Garner. M.T. for short."

"What are you doing here?"

The old man spunkily cocked his head to one side. "I don't know that it's any of your damned business."

"I can promise you it is." Quint smiled and began a leisurely approach to the man. "If you had given me a chance to explain earlier, I would have told you that I don't work for Rutledge." He halted a few feet from him and gave the shotgun a toss into the old man's arms. "I work for the Triple C."

Empty Garner clutched the shotgun and stared at Quint for an uncertain instant. "The Triple C—that's the Montana outfit that owns this place, isn't it?"

"That's right," Quint confirmed.

The old man eyed him leerily. "How do I know you're who you say you are? That car you're driving has Texas plates."

"That's because I rented it after I flew down here."

"That's what you say," Empty scoffed, still skeptical.

"I did give you back your shotgun," Quint reminded him.

"You kept the shells, though."

Quint smiled. "I'm not stupid."

"Neither am I," the old man retorted and patted the bulging side pocket of his jacket. "I got a bunch more shells right here. If I thought you were lying, I could have this loaded in two seconds."

"In that case, you have a decision to make. Because one of us is trespassing and it isn't me."

Empty thought about that a moment, then ducked his head. "I guess that'd be me then." When he looked up, there was fire in his eyes again. "But if you're that Evans fella, you've done one helluva poor job of running this place."

"I don't know where Evans is," Quint admitted. "My name's Echohawk. Quint Echohawk."

"That's an Indian name."

"That's right. Now would you care to tell me what you're doing here?" Quint asked in light challenge.

"I guess you've got a right to know," Empty Garner admitted. "My granddaughter mentioned last night that Rutledge had run off this Evans guy. It got me to thinking about the livestock. I knew Rutledge wouldn't care one whit if they starved to death. And I was right, too. When I got here, I found the horses in the pen, nosing in the dirt to find the last few scraps of hay, and nothing but nubbins for grass. So I turned them out."

"And I have a half dozen bags of grain in my car." Quint smiled at the irony of it. "Now I have the fun of catching them again."

"You won't have any trouble," the old rancher declared. "Just rattle some corn in a feed bucket and they'll come running."

"Probably," Quint agreed, turning away.

"Where'd you leave your car?"

He swung back. "Halfway down the lane."

Empty Garner responded with a slow nod of comprehension. "When you left, I figured you'd head to the Slash R for reinforcements. Never occurred to me you might sneak back here. That was my mistake." He paused, his sharp-eyed glance giving Quint the once-over. "My truck's out back. Why don't I give you a lift to your car and save you hiking all the way back to it?"

"That's a deal."

Leaving the gloom and musty odors of the barn, they exited through the rear door and made their way to the white pickup. Empty Garner stowed the shotgun in the gun rack mounted across the cab's back window and hauled himself behind the steering wheel. Quint climbed into the seat beside him and pulled the creaking door shut.

At a turn of the ignition key, the engine sputtered, then rumbled to life. The way the old pickup bounced across the rough ground, circling to the front of the barn, Quint suspected its shocks had given out long ago. The going was a little smoother when they reached the ranch yard.

Empty nodded in the direction of the pickup parked in front of the barn. "How come you didn't haul the grain in that truck?"

"It wouldn't start."

"You'll probably find that somebody dumped sugar in the gas tank." There was no humor in the smile that twisted Empty Garner's mouth. "Don't bother hiring anybody around here to fix it. They'll just drag their feet about getting it done, knowing that's what Rutledge would want them to do. Spend the extra money and get a tow truck to haul it to a garage in the city. While they're at it, you might as well have them install a lock on the gas tank, or it'll just happen all over again."

"Thanks for the warning."

"I'd tell you to get a mean dog, but it wouldn't do any good. They'd just wait until you were away from the place and either poison it or shoot it."

Quint eyed him with growing interest. "I get the feeling you're talking from experience."

There was a tinge of bitterness in the grim set of the old man's features. "I used to own the Robles Ranch south of here until Rutledge squeezed me out." He sliced a hard look at Quint. "Mind you, I can't prove that. Rutledge is too clever to leave any trail that'll lead back to him. But it was his doing—and him who ended up with my place."

"How'd he go about it?" In Quint's experience, people rarely changed their modus operandi.

The pickup jolted over a pothole, but Empty Garner didn't seem to notice as his thoughts turned back. "I guess the trouble started when Fred Barlow quit after being with me nearly ten years. He said he got a job in a big feedlot north of Dallas that would pay him more money, plus give him health benefits and paid housing. I didn't see Rutledge's hand in it at the time, but looking back, I know it was there now. After that, everybody I hired kept quitting on me. Some lasted a month or two, but most walked after a few days. Pretty soon I couldn't get anybody to work for me. Now I grant you, my ranch wasn't a big spread, but there was more work than I could handle by myself. If it hadn't been for my granddaughter pitching in like she did, I'd have had to hang it up sooner than I did."

"What tipped the scale?"

"Hay," Empty replied. "My cattle kept mysteriously getting into my hayfield. First time a gate was open; then a fence kept going down. One time it looked like a rotten fence post, and another rusted-out wire—the sort of things that could lead you to think you were having a streak of bad luck. Anyway, you add the drought in and I didn't get enough hay out of the field to feed my cattle through the winter. When I started looking to buy some, there wasn't any to be found within fifty miles. Seems the Slash R had bought it all up, claiming they needed it to winter-feed their cattle. The cost of importing hay from up north was more than I could afford. Which meant I had to sell off part of my herd. A lot of other ranchers were doing the same, driving the price down. There I sat without enough money to pay the note payment, and the bank refusing to give me an extension, when up walks Rutledge's son Boone, offering to buy the place. That's when I started seeing his hand in all that had gone on before."

Quint couldn't help observing, "That's not much to hang your hat on."

Empty released a contemptuous snort. "I told you Rutledge was cagey."

"Just the same, that's a stretch."

"Think so, do you?" He threw Quint a look of disgust. "I guess I didn't mention that I told him to take his offer and stick it where the sun don't shine. That's when the meanness started—the dog crawling off to die from a bullet wound, the sugar in the gas tank, places where I'd had credit for years suddenly demanding cash on the barrelhead, banks turning me down all over the place when I tried to refinance, wells getting poisoned, cattle rustled. I managed to hold out for another year—" His voice tightened up on him. He paused, dragging in a deep breath, and continued. "Rutledge bought it out of foreclosure. The Homestead law let me keep the house. It galled me to wake up every morning and see Slash R cattle out the window grazing on my grass. When I found out Rutledge wanted the house for one of his hired hands to live in, the strangest thing happened." A dark light danced in his eyes. "The house caught on fire. Musta happened shortly after I left for town."

"What did the insurance company say?"

"They wouldn't pay up," Empty admitted. "Called it suspicious. Naturally everybody figured Rutledge was to blame. Now folks around here are even more afraid to cross him."

The pickup rattled to a halt alongside Quint's rental car. The old man draped his left arm across the top of the steering wheel and angled around to face Quint.

"Understand, now, Rutledge isn't what you'd call a greedy man," Empty said. "He only wants land that butts up to his. And it looks like he's after the Cee Bar. So you might want to let your boss in Montana know what he's going to be coming up against. Right now all the squeezing is the subtle kind, aimed at making the operation too costly to keep going. Rutledge probably figures your boss won't want to hang on to a ranch that's a losing proposition, 'specially one located so far from the home spread."

"I'll pass the word." Quint reached for the door handle and smiled crookedly. "Between you and me, though, if you push a Calder into a corner, he comes out swinging every time."

The old man's chin came up a notch, his gaze sharpening as he considered Quint's words. "You know," he began thoughtfully, "there isn't anywhere I need to be for a while. If you want, I can give you a hand unloading that grain. Seeing how I'm the one who turned your horses out, I could catch them up for you, too."

Quint accepted. "I'd appreciate the help."

# Chapter Four

A few minutes before five o'clock, Empty Garner swung the pickup into the feed store's parking lot and pulled up in front of the door. The chalky white dust had barely settled to the ground when Dallas walked out of the metal building and climbed into the pickup. She flung herself against the backrest and pulled off the feed store cap that trapped her hair atop her head. She dropped the cap on the seat and dug her fingers into her scalp.

"I itch all over from that grain dust," she muttered. "I can hardly wait to get in the shower."

"Guess I don't need to ask how your day was," Empty surmised and pointed the truck at the highway.

"It wasn't all that bad, I guess," she replied.

But the minute Dallas let her thoughts drift over the day's happenings, only one incident stood out from any others. The weariness that comes at the end of the day kept Dallas from considering the wisdom of relating it to her grandfather.

"Remember that cowboy I told you about," she said, "the one that came into the café last night? Well, John Earl had to have been wrong. Evans must still be working at the Cee Bar, because that cowboy came into the feed store today. He's working at the Cee Bar."

"I know." Gravel churned under the truck's wheels as the pickup accelerated onto the highway.

It was a full second before his response penetrated her fatigue. When it did, Dallas sat up. "What do you mean? How do you know?"

"I swung out by the Cee Bar this morning to make sure the stock had plenty of food and water. That's when I met him." Empty was careful to omit any mention of the business with the shotgun. "And Evans is gone. This new guy is from the Montana outfit that owns the place. His name is Echohawk. Part Indian, I guess."

"I wonder how long he'll last," Dallas murmured absently, privately regarding the ultimate outcome as a foregone conclusion.

"This one's not gonna be easy to scare off."

Dallas slid her grandfather a dryly skeptical look. "You wish."

"The cowboy's got sand," Empty stated, unswayed by her cynicism. "Must be why the Calders sent him down here. You know the Triple C has a huge spread up in Montana, covering over a million acres," he added thoughtfully. "Could be Rutledge is trying to take a bite out of an outfit that's too big for him."

"But it's up there. Down here, Rutledge calls the shots—or have you forgotten?" The instant the acerbic comment left her mouth, Dallas regretted opening old wounds. Still, the truth was the truth. "And how much is a big outfit like that going to care about a measly little spread a thousand miles away? Every rancher with any business sense at all knows that sometimes you have to cut your losses and sell."

Empty chose to ignore her latter remark. "The Cee Bar isn't as measly as it once was. It takes in close to five thousand acres now. And it's got this big creek that curls right through it. It's never been known to run dry either. It's the water; I'll bet that's what Rutledge is coveting."

"You're full of information, aren't you?" Dallas turned a suspicious look on him. "And you got all this from one brief meeting with this Echohawk?"

"It wasn't all that brief." He deliberately avoided her eyes. "I pitched in and helped him unload the grain and catch up his horses. I knew nobody else would be making any neighborly gestures. Lord knows I didn't have any other demands on my day except to sit in that trailer and go stir-crazy."

But Dallas refused to be diverted by his attempt to change the subject. "Just how long were you there, Empty?"

"How should I know? I didn't keep track of the time." He puffed up, all stern-looking and indignant. Not for anything would he admit that he had left the Cee Bar barely twenty minutes ago. "I don't see what difference it makes anyhow. All I did was lend him a hand with a few things. From the way the place looks, Evans let a lot of things go slack these last few months. Course, that ranch is too big for one man to handle by himself. That Quint Echohawk will need a hired hand. There's no two ways about it."

"We both know he hasn't got a snowball's chance in hell of finding one," she stated flatly, yet inwardly struggled with the heavy feeling of regret that washed over her.

"Watch your language, there, little gal. Why, your grandma would be rolling over in her grave if she heard you cussing like that." There was sharp reproach in the look he slanted in her direction. "You were raised better."

"I know."

Empty caught the note of defiance in her voice. "You've gotten hard, Dallas." It hurt him to see that in her. "It comes from carrying too much on those young shoulders of yours. Guess that's my fault."

"Don't be ridiculous," she said in annoyance. "It's nobody's fault. It's just life."

"Maybe so," he conceded. "But that doesn't make it any easier to watch you working two, sometimes three jobs and going to school nights to better yourself, while I sit around, twiddling my thumbs, waiting for my Social Security check to arrive. Lord knows why, 'cause it's hardly enough to pay the rent on that run-down old trailer."

Dallas knew it was his pride talking. "Anyone who has worked as hard and as long as you have is entitled to a life of leisure," she reasoned. "And I'm not working any harder than you did at my age."

"I suppose you think I'm like an old horse who's supposed to be happy about getting turned out to pasture. Well, for your information, little gal, I'm not on my last legs yet."

Dallas sensed some hidden message in his statement that instantly made her wary. "What do you mean?" A frisson of alarm shot through her. "Wait a minute, Empty. You aren't thinking of taking that job at the Cee Bar?" She checked the impulse to tell him he was too old. "You can't do it," she protested instead. "We don't need any more trouble."

"Rutledge has you buffaloed, doesn't he? I thought I raised you to have more backbone than that."

Stung by his words, Dallas reacted with heat. "I only know that we have to live here while your Mr. Echohawk can go back to Montana any time he chooses."

"In the first place, he isn't my Mr. Echohawk," Empty retorted. "And in the second, Rutledge has already got my ranch. There isn't a whole lot more he can do to hurt me."

But there was, and Dallas knew it. Several months ago, while filing some papers, she had stumbled upon a sale document transferring ownership of the feed store to Max Rutledge. Sykes continued to front for him, but Rutledge owned it. She had never mentioned anything about it to her grandfather, fully aware he'd be furious if he knew she was working—even indirectly—for Max Rutledge.

One word from Rutledge and she would be out of work. The chances of finding another full-time job in the area were virtually nil. And her chances of convincing her grandfather to move to the city were just about the same.

All those thoughts ran through her mind, but Dallas didn't voice any of them, saying instead, "Personally, I don't want to find out what kind of trouble he might cause us. I just want to forget he exists. And I want you to forget about that job at the Cee Bar."

Empty made the swing into the driveway a little too fast. Gravel flew when he slammed on the brakes. The pickup screeched to a stop short of the steps.

"I never said a word about taking the job. You're the one who got the idea in your head. And you haven't quit harping about it ever since." He climbed out of the pickup and slammed the door shut behind him.

"Fine," Dallas snapped, slamming her own door. "Then let's both stop thinking about it."

"Suits me." He grabbed hold of the handrail and pulled himself up the steps ahead of her. "You got school tonight?"

"Yes." Her thoughts made the lightning leap to more mundane matters. "I thought I'd add some rice to that leftover chili and fix that for supper tonight. Is that all right with you?" she asked, thinking that she should have enough time to hop in the shower while the chili was heating.

"Bowl of that'll be good enough for me. Don't have much of an appetite anyway." He walked through the door straight over to the recliner and plopped himself in it.

Both were careful to avoid any further reference to the Cee Bar Ranch. But the thought of it was never out of Empty's mind. He did experience a twinge of guilt when Dallas stopped by his chair on her way out the door and brushed his cheek with a kiss.

"I'm sorry for arguing with you earlier." Her lips curved in a rueful smile even as her eyes teased him. "But you're such an old war-horse that I could easily imagine you letting yourself get talked into something."

"Nobody can talk me into anything," he insisted gruffly. "I make up my own mind about things."

"Always," Dallas agreed and crossed to the door, her book bag in hand. She swung back, smiling at him. "I don't know what I was so worried about anyway. It isn't likely your Quint Echohawk would even consider hiring you."

His head came up. "Why not?"

"Because men his age never think that someone as old as you are would still be capable of doing that kind of hard work." It was a matter-of-fact statement, with no undertone of anything else. She opened the door. "I'll be late coming home—as usual. I've got my key, so be sure to lock the door before you go to bed."

He waved a hand in answer. After the door closed behind her, Empty gathered up their supper dishes and carried them to the sink.

The pickup's headlight beams arced across the window behind it. He peered out to make certain she had pulled onto the road. The instant he caught the red flash of taillights, he crossed to the end of the counter and dug around until he located the telephone book among the clutter. He flipped through the pages and kept his finger on the number for the Cee Bar while he dialed it.

"Echohawk? It's Empty Garner," he said the minute the phone was answered. "I've been thinking about all the work needing to be done out there. It's no secret you're going to have a tough time finding a hired hand. Since I'm not doing anything but sitting around, I thought I'd offer to help till you do."

He paused and heard the silence that followed. Sensing the hesitation on the other end of the line, Empty rushed in.

"I know I'm an old man," he said. "But I'm not so weak I can't mend a fence or doctor a sick cow. And it's for sure there isn't a whole lot about ranching that I don't know. In fact, it's the only thing I do know."

"You're qualified, all right." There was a smile in Echohawk's voice, but no sound of commitment.

"You can say that again." Empty worked to sound bluff and hearty and keep the sense of desperation out of his voice.

Until now, he hadn't realized how much he wanted the job. He wanted to feel like a man again, useful and productive, instead of a washed-up old codger who couldn't fasten his own pants. As a result, Empty wasn't above using a little emotional blackmail.

"With the holidays coming on, that extra money I'd get from working for you would give me a chance to buy my granddaughter something nice for Christmas. It's a little hard to make my Social Security check stretch to include presents. So . . . you want me to start tomorrow?" Tension held him motionless, not breathing.

"No, I won't be here most of tomorrow. A tow truck will be here first thing in the morning to haul the pickup in for repairs. I need to return the rental car and pick up the loaner. By the time all the paperwork is finished, it will probably be late in the afternoon before I get back to the ranch. Let's make it the day after."

"Sounds good," Empty said, and hesitated. "I just got one problem. Would it be too much trouble if you picked me up? We've only got one vehicle, and my granddaughter needs it to get back and forth to her job. I can be ready by eight."

After a long pause, the reply came. "I'll pick you up at eight then."

The setting sun made an inglorious departure from the sky, leaving behind only a pale golden arc on the horizon to mark its passage. The west-facing windows of the Slash R's sprawling ranch house briefly reflected the amber glow of its dying light. Built low to the ground with wide overhangs to block the penetration of the summer sun's hot rays, the house made a giant footprint on the hilltop, its square footage massive enough that no visitor could doubt the wealth of its occupant.

And Max Rutledge was a full-fledged Texas billionaire. The Slash R ranch was only a minuscule part of his vast holdings, but it was his showplace and personal retreat.

Max Rutledge wasn't a man that anyone would ever mistake for an ordinary Texas rancher. Crippled in a car accident that had taken the life of his young wife and forever robbed him of the use of his legs, he was confined to a wheelchair, albeit the most advanced wheelchair money could buy.

The sight of the wheelchair and the atrophied legs might evoke an initial reaction of pity, but one look at his thickly muscled torso, the harsh gauntness of his face, and the hooded glare of his dark eyes, and any sense of pity instantly vanished. No one walked away from a meeting with Max Rutledge still harboring any doubt that his reputation for being utterly ruthless was not well earned.

Manipulating the hand controls with practiced ease, Rutledge sent the wheelchair gliding across the living room's stone floor, its motor emitting little more than a soft hum. The double doors to the den stood open, revealing the bright blaze of flames burning in the fireplace, the room's focal point. With a flick of the controls, he swung the wheelchair toward the open doors.

It was a decidedly masculine room, paneled in lustrous wood with exposed beams providing a rustic touch. The decor had the requisite Texas touches. The overstuffed armchair by the fireplace was upholstered in leather and cowhide. A Russell bronze stood on the fireplace mantel while a Navajo blanket lay artfully draped over the leather sofa.

None of it caught Max Rutledge's eye when he wheeled into the room. His hard gaze continued its scan until it landed on the tall man standing at the window, staring out at the twilight's gray landscape, a drink in his hand. His hair was dark and thick, with an unruly tendency to curl. There was a muscled trimness to his physique that exuded strength and power. But it was the rough and raw virility that stamped his features that always claimed attention.

This prime specimen of manhood was his son, Boone Rutledge. But Max's heart didn't lift with pride at the sight of him. If anything, it turned stone-hard.

"I should have known I'd find you in here." His voice had a contemptuous edge to it. "Instead of standing there doing nothing, make yourself useful and fix me a drink."

Boone turned, a banked anger in his dark eyes. "Bourbon and branch?"

"That'll do." Max engaged the controls and glided over to the fireplace, positioning his chair to face the warming flames.

He stared silently into them and listened to the firm tread of his son's footsteps as Boone crossed to the bar. The sound was followed by the thud of a glass on the leather-topped counter, the clink of ice cubes, and the splash of liquid over them. Then footsteps approached his chair. Max took the proffered drink without glancing up.

"Sykes called this morning," Boone said. "He thought we'd want to know that a cowboy came into the feed store this morning and tried to charge some grain to the Cee Bar. When Sykes told him the account was closed, the guy paid cash for it." He swirled the cubes in his drink. "So it looks like the Triple C has managed to hire somebody."

"What are you doing about it?" The question was more in the way of a challenge than a demand for an answer.

"I thought I'd send Clyde Rivers over there tomorrow and see what he can find out about this new man."

Max released a derisive snort and shook his head in disgust. Boone reacted with an angry glare.

"What's wrong with that? That's exactly what we've done every time a new man came on board."

Max lifted his grizzled head and viewed him with contempt. "You don't have the slightest clue why this time should be different, do you?" He observed the flicker of confusion and turned away. "Why did I get stuck with a son with more muscles than brains?" he muttered.

His jaw ridged in anger, Boone pivoted sharply and stalked back to the bar. "Maybe you'd care to let me know what you think the next move should be," he taunted and snatched the whiskey bottle off the shelf, then sloshed more liquor into his nearly empty glass.

"You're the one who's going over there, not Rivers," Max snapped.

"Me?" Shock held Boone motionless for an instant. Confusion reigned in his expression when he recovered. "Why would you want me to go? You've always insisted we have to keep our distance from all of this."

"Since you're obviously not smart enough to figure it out on your own, I'll tell you. Now that Cee Bar is without a ranch manager, what's the most logical thing for the Calders to do to fill that void—temporarily, if nothing else?"

Boone's frown deepened. "Hire somebody. What else can they do?"

"Send one of their own down here, that's what," Max retorted with impatience. "They won't want to take some stranger's word for what's going on down here. They'll want to check it out for themselves."

"That still doesn't explain why you want me to go over there," Boone protested, recrossing the room.

"Then you might try remembering how much time you spent at the Triple C this past summer trying to convince that Calder girl to marry you. Unsuccessfully, I might add," Max tacked on spitefully.

"It isn't my fault that she was stupid enough to marry that fortune-hunting Englishman instead of me." Boone stood facing the fireplace, a rigid set to his shoulders.

Max ran an assessing eye over his son and muttered, half under his breath, "Unfortunately, her choice wasn't all that stupid. But that's whiskey in the river." He sighed a dismissal of the subject. "You must have met quite a few of the ranch hands while you were at the Triple C, certainly ones in positions of responsibility. That's why I want you to pay a 'neighborly' call on the new man. With any luck, you'll recognize him."

Understanding at last dawned in Boone's expression. "That makes sense."

"At least you can see that. Of course I had to spell it out for you first."

Boone whirled around, a black rage glittering in his eyes. "Damn it, will you lay off me?"

Max almost wished Boone would summon up the guts to hit him, but he knew that would never happen. "Save that show of toughness for a time when you'll need it. We've got our work cut out for us now. I've heard those Triple C riders are a close-knit bunch, supposedly loyal to the core. But first we have to find out who it is they sent. Then we'll decide our next move."

The cold front had retreated to the north again, leaving behind a startling blue sky, swept clean of all clouds. The high, rolling Texas hills lay beneath it, basking in the warmth of the midmorning sun. But the air remained invigoratingly brisk.

A lone tan-and-white pickup traveled along the paved state road, its doors emblazoned with the name SLASH R RANCH. Boone Rutledge occupied the driver's seat, his hands gloved in the finest calfskin leather. He dipped his head to peer ahead and locate the entrance to the Cee Bar Ranch. Spotting it, he slowed the truck to make the turn.

The board sign above the gate sported a shiny new chain on one end, but the wood itself still carried the scars of old bullet holes. The pickup rolled beneath it and headed up the winding tract, bouncing over its many ruts and potholes. If this was Slash R land, Boone knew he would have long ago called in a grader to blade the drive and smooth out its roughness.

Chickens squawked and flapped their wings in panic as they scurried out of his path when he pulled into the ranch yard. But they were the only sign of life he saw. There were no vehicles around, no horses in the corral. Nothing.

Boone wasn't fool enough to think that it meant that there was no one about.

He pulled up to the old ranch house, stepped onto the truck's running board, and reached back inside to give the horn a couple of long blasts. He listened, his gaze scanning the pastures beyond the yard. A horse whinnied in the distance and a chicken clucked in annoyance, but there was no other response. Boone swung to the ground and gave the door a push. Its closing sounded loud in the stillness.

In no hurry, Boone idly gave his gloves a tightening tug and surveyed the ranch yard and its few structures. All of them had a dingy, timeworn look that not even a fresh coat of paint could cure. It definitely wasn't a place a man could point to with pride.

For the life of him, Boone couldn't guess why the Calders hung on to the ranch. Supposedly it had once been owned by a long-ago ancestor. Yet it had been years since any of the Calders had set foot on it.

Considering that a ranch this size could never show much of a profit, the Cee Bar couldn't be anything more than a headache to the Calders. Boone smiled, thinking how much worse that headache was going to get. Sooner or later they'd wash their hands of it and sell; it always worked that way.

After another look around, he headed for the house. He paused at the door and rapped loudly on it. As he expected, there was no stirring of movement inside.

With curiosity getting the better of him, Boone cast a quick glance behind him and tried the knob. It turned easily under his hand. He pushed it open and stepped inside.

Still cautious, he called out, "Hello? Anybody home?"

There was nothing but the echo of his own voice.

Satisfied that he was alone, Boone wandered through the old ranch house, snooping to see what he might find. The place was remarkably tidy and clean. All the beds were made, and dishes sat in the drying rack next to the sink counter. Boone found virtually nothing of interest lying about.

Even a search of an old desk in the living room failed to unearth anything of importance. The kitchen table yielded the only noteworthy items: two local newspapers folded open to the want-ad section. Circles had been drawn around ads offering hay for sale.

Boone smiled when he saw them. He'd given his foreman orders yesterday to buy up all the hay in the surrounding counties.

He knew there was no longer any to be had in the area. Calder would have to truck in his hay, and that wouldn't be cheap.

He lingered in the house a while longer. When no one showed up, he let himself out, climbed back in his pickup, and drove away.

It was after three in the afternoon when Quint arrived back at the Cee Bar. He had managed to switch his rental car for a black pickup that came equipped with a gas tank lock and security system. Both of which he'd left instructions to be installed in the ranch pickup once its repairs were complete.

He collected the part for the broken windmill from the pickup's rear bed and started for the house. Sundown came early at this time of year and there might not be enough daylight left to get the parts switched and the windmill up and running before dark. He decided to give Empty the task tomorrow while he did a little fence-riding and checked on the cattle and pasture conditions.

Quint pulled the screen door open, caught it with his shoulder, and reached for the thin black cord he had shut in the door when he left. But it was lying on the threshold.

There had been a visitor at the Cee Bar while he was gone.

# Chapter Five

It took Empty Garner most of the morning to get the windmill back in operation. After lunch, he gave Quint a hand replacing a long stretch of fence, using steel posts in place of old tree limbs and stringing new wire. By then, it was after four o'clock; time to call it a day.

Empty hauled his muscle-weary body onto the black pickup's passenger seat and settled back for the ride into town. His thoughts drifted back over the day's work. It had been months since he had felt this tired. But it was a good feeling, a kind of honest, achy soreness.

He cast a considering glance at the man behind the wheel, recalling how Quint had sweated and strained right alongside him, sometimes even shouldering more than his share. It wasn't a trait he'd necessarily seen in young cowboys anymore—especially ones that had gotten a taste for giving orders. Those usually did more telling than doing.

It never occurred to Empty to comment on his observations. He was of the opinion you didn't praise a man for doing what he should. When he did speak, it was as a former rancher. "I don't know how many cattle you're supposed to be running, but I've got the feeling if you do a count, you're going to come up short."

"That's what I thought, too," Quint acknowledged.

"Most people think the days of cattle rustlers are long gone. Hell, it's probably easier now than it was back in the eighteen hundreds. Back then, you stood a chance of tracking them. Today they load cattle into trucks, and those wheels don't leave any tracks on concrete roads."

"How true."

Empty gazed at the road ahead of them, a thoughtful furrow creasing his brow. "I wish I could give you an idea of what Rutledge's next move might be."

"He might have already made it," Quint replied.

Empty sat up, his weariness temporarily forgotten. "What do you mean? What'd he do?"

"Somebody came by the ranch yesterday while I was gone."

"How would you know that if you weren't there?" His frown deepened.

"There are ways. Some papers in the desk were out of order, plus some other things that weren't in the exact place that I left them."

Empty shook his head. "I swear those Rutledges are as bold as the most brazen hussy that ever walked the streets. Next thing you know they'll come sneaking around at night." He pinned a piercing look on Quint. "You've got yourself a shotgun, don't you?"

"I didn't bring any firearms with me. I thought there would be a rifle of some kind at the ranch. But if there was, it's gone now." Nearing the outskirts of town, Quint slowed the truck and made the turn onto the back road that would take him to Empty's trailer house.

"I've got a whole gun cabinet full of weapons—shotguns, rifles, handguns, you name it and I've got it. Why don't you come in with me and pick out what you want?"

"I can't tonight." Quint swung into the driveway and parked near the steps. "Maybe when I come to get you in the morning."

"It's your funeral," Empty said with a shrug and climbed out of the cab despite the protest of stiffening joints.

"I almost forgot." Quint leaned sideways across the seat. "I need directions to the Slash R."

"The Slash R!" Incredulity claimed the old man's lined face. "Why in billy blue blazes do you need that?"

A slow smile spread across Quint's mouth. "I decided I should return the favor and pay them a call—one neighbor to another."

"You're kidding." But Empty could see that he wasn't. "Just what do you think that's going to accomplish?"

"You never know." His smile turned into a full-fledged grin. "Since it seems the Slash R has bought every available bale of hay around here, maybe I can talk them into selling me some."

"You've got as much chance of that as a fly getting loose from a spider's web." But Empty relented just the same and gave him directions.

"Thanks. See you in the morning."

"Sure thing." Empty gave the door a push and stepped away from the truck.

As it reversed away from the trailer, Empty headed for the steps. He caught a flash of white out of the corner of his eye and turned. There was Dallas coming down the road in their old truck. And he knew she couldn't help but see the black pickup pulling out of the drive. It didn't matter that they wouldn't be passing each other. A strange pickup in their driveway was bound to spark his granddaughter's curiosity.

Empty realized he would have to step quickly around this. Which wouldn't be easy. Dallas was about as sharp as his wife had been at spotting a lie.

He resumed his path to the steps and managed to get halfway up them before Dallas drove in. She hopped out of the truck, her gaze locked on the departing pickup halfway up the road.

"Who was just here?" She wore a puzzled look when she came around the white pickup to join him.

"The guy from the Cee Bar, Quint Echohawk." Empty knew he had to keep to the truth—as much as possible.

"What did he want?" The question had all the earmarks of simple curiosity, which suited Empty just fine.

"You wouldn't believe me if I told you." He climbed the rest of the steps to the trailer door.

"Wait a minute." Dallas caught up with him before he could step inside, her gaze sharp with suspicion. "He didn't ask you to go to work there, did he?"

"Nothing of the sort," he declared as if the possibility were completely out of the question. "He wanted directions to the Slash R."

"But he could have gotten them from anyone. Why did he come here? For that matter, how did he know where we live?"

"Somebody must have told him."

"But that same somebody could also have told him how to get to the Slash R."

"True. But it's likely they would have got on the phone the minute he left and reported it to Rutledge. And I got the impression Echohawk wanted to arrive unannounced. I expect Echohawk knew I'd sooner jump off a cliff than give Rutledge the time of day."

His explanation appeared to satisfy her, but Empty could see she was still chewing on what he'd told her. "I can't imagine why he would want to see Rutledge." The wheels continued to turn in her mind as she tried to figure it out.

"He said he was going to try to buy some hay off him."

"Hay?" An abrupt laugh slipped from her. Then she shook her head in dismissal. "The man is clearly a fool."

Empty wasn't sure, but he thought Dallas sounded a little bit sorry.

"You can't miss it," Empty had insisted after he'd given Quint directions to the Rutledge ranch. The minute Quint encountered the pristine white fencing that ran for nearly a mile, he knew the old man was right.

The entrance itself was recessed from the road and flanked by high white wings. Arching across to connect them, tall enough to allow a semitrailer rig to pass beneath it, was a span of wrought iron. Scrolled in its center and gilded in gold was the Slash R brand.

The gleaming black iron gates stood open. Quint wouldn't have been surprised to find them shut. He turned onto the paved driveway, bordered by more white fence. Sun-seared grass covered the pastures on either side of the manicured lane, with no scrub brush or mesquite thicket to be seen.

A good half mile back from the road, the arrow-straight driveway opened into the ranch yard with its assorted sheds, stables, and barns all painted a pure white. The white paint accented the ranch's immaculate look, all scrubbed and ready for inspection. Quint found it hard to believe the Slash R was a working ranch. It was more like something Hollywood would come up with.

Off to his left, he noticed a paved road that branched away from the ranch and curved into some trees. He followed it. Within seconds he spotted the sprawling ranch house on the hilltop, hidden from the ranch yard by a screening of trees.

Rock columns supported a low, wide portico that marked the home's front entrance. Quint parked beneath it and climbed out of the truck. On impulse he hit the remote, locking the pickup's doors and activating its alarm system, then slipped the keys in his jacket pocket.

A burly man with a crew cut answered the door when he knocked. Blue eyes made a swift, assessing sweep of Quint.

"If it's work you're wanting, you'll need to go to the ranch office and fill out an application," the man said.

"No, I'm here to see Mr. Rutledge if he's available. Mr. Max Rutledge," Quint added in clarification.

The man's impassive expression never changed. "Is Mr. Rutledge expecting you?"

"No. But he'll see me," Quint stated, one corner of his mouth lifting in the smallest suggestion of a smile.

"Your name?" the man requested, unfazed by Quint's claim.

"Quint Echohawk with the Cee Bar Ranch."

After a small hesitation, the man stepped back to allow admittance. "Wait here, I will inform Mr. Rutledge that you're here. But I can't say whether he will see you."

"I understand." Privately, Quint had no doubts at all that Max Rutledge would agree to see him.

He stepped through the doorway and moved to one side, allowing the man to close the door behind him.

"Wait here," the man repeated the instruction and withdrew.

Out of habit, Quint removed his hat and made a visual inspection of his surroundings. The spacious entrance hall provided glimpses of its adjoining rooms, but not enough to encourage exploration. Like all the rest of the ranch, the house seemed designed to impress the visitor, both with its scale and its artful appointments.

The whisper-soft tread of the man's footsteps faded into another part of the house. With typical patience, Quint waited as the seconds ticked by.

The snicking click of a latch drew Quint's glance to the front door an instant before it swung open and Boone Rutledge walked in. He flicked a disinterested look at Quint, then came to a dead stop when recognition set in. He stared at him in bald-faced shock.

"Hello, Boone." Quint nodded, aware that he was likely the very last person Boone expected to see.

As expected, Boone didn't bother to extend a hand in greeting, honest not to pretend a civility he didn't feel. A dark displeasure was in the narrowed look he aimed at Quint.

"What are you doing here?" But there was a ring of falseness in the question that revealed Boone had already guessed the answer.

Before Quint could reply, the servant reappeared in the entry hall. "Mr. Rutledge will see you now."

Boone made a quick dismissal of the man. "I'll show him to the den, Harold." With a slight nod, the man moved away. "Follow me." Boone struck out, taking the lead, then cast a questioning look at Quint. "I guess I should have asked if this was an official visit."

"No." Quint smiled, knowing it was the first question he should have asked, but Boone didn't appear to be very adept at thinking on his feet. "In fact, I quit the ATF shortly after my father's funeral."

"I didn't know."

"There's no reason why you should."

Crossing to a set of double doors, Boone pushed them wide as he walked through the opening into the spacious den. A wheelchair-bound Max Rutledge glided silently from behind a gleaming wood desk and rolled forward to meet Quint when he entered.

Boone rushed quickly to make the introductions. "I don't believe you've met Quint Echohawk, Max. He's the grandson of Chase Calder."

"I've heard of you, of course. Welcome to the Slash R, Quint." After a slight pause, he added, "Although I can't help wondering what brings you here."

The unabashed curiosity in Max Rutledge's expression seemed utterly genuine. Quint took it as a warning of the man's canny shrewdness.

"He didn't come on official business." Boone crossed to the bar. "Quint's already told me he quit the ATF."

"I didn't think for one moment he was here in any official capacity," Max said easily.

"I suppose you could call it official," Quint said with a smile and added the qualification, "at least in the sense that Jessy asked me to come down and take charge of the Cee Bar."

"Really?" Max said with a startled widening of his eyes. "I guess I assumed you would be looking after your mother's ranch. Although I seem to recall it adjoins the Triple C. I suppose it would be a simple matter for the Calders to assume management of it."

"That's right." From the bar area came the clatter of ice dropped in a glass.

"Do you have time to join us for a drink?" Max asked.

Quint's hesitation was only slight, but deliberately calculated. "Sure," he agreed. "Whiskey Seven."

"Pour Quint a whiskey Seven, Boone," Max ordered. "And I'll have my usual bourbon and branch." He swung his wheelchair toward a conversational grouping of chairs and swept out his hand in an inviting gesture. "Have a seat."

"Thanks." Quint crossed to a cowhide-upholstered chair and laid his hat on its wide armrest as he folded his tall frame onto the seat.

"How's Chase these days?" Max positioned his wheelchair in the open space within the grouping.

"Doing remarkably well, considering his age."

"Your grandfather is a remarkable man in many ways."

"I agree," Quint said and smiled. "Although naturally I am prejudiced."

"As you should be." A smile grooved deep lines in Max's gaunt cheeks. Then a small line furrowed his brow in a faint show of puzzlement. "You said earlier something about taking over the Cee Bar. What happened to the ranch manager you had running it? What was his name?" He turned a frowning look to Boone for the answer when he arrived with their drinks.

"Evans, I think it was."

"He's gone now." Quint took his drink from Boone's out-stretched hand.

"Help is always a problem, isn't it?" Max remarked in a commiserating fashion. "The good ones are too often lured away by better offers. And the bad ones—well, you don't want to keep them anyway."

"Very true." Quint raised his glass in a toast. "To finding good help and keeping them."

Boone and Max acknowledged the toast with a slight lift of glasses. The gesture was followed by the muted clink of ice against the glass sides as each took a sip. Boone drifted off to the side and hooked a long leg over the high armrest of a leather sofa, but

Quint was conscious of the heavy bore of his gaze. If, as he believed, the Rutledges were orchestrating the current spate of trouble at the Cee Bar, the son was likely the muscle behind it, and the father, the brains. And it was on the latter Quint centered his attention.

"It just occurred to me," Max began, "did your mother come with you?"

"No," Quint replied with a slight, negative movement of his head.

"I thought she might have welcomed a change of scenery, not to mention the warmth of a southern winter. And with Tara in Fort Worth, it seemed likely. I know they are former sisters-in-law, but it's always been my understanding that the bond between them has remained a close one."

"I know Tara is of that opinion." Quint's impression was that his mother had retained a healthy suspicion of Tara. Although in recent years Tara had been more of a pain in the neck to the Calders than the troublemaker she once had been. "Actually my mother has moved back to the Homestead to look after Chase. Right now, though . . ." He paused, idly swirling the liquor in his glass. "Most of the family is in England to attend Laura's wedding."

The remark was designed to get a rise out of Boone. Quint observed Boone's reaction to the comment in his side vision—the faint jerk of his head and the white-knuckle tensing of the hand holding the drink glass.

"Yes," Max interposed smoothly. "I recall reading something in the society page about Tara flying over to attend the nuptials."

"I thought she'd already married him." Boone's jaws barely moved as he pushed the words out.

"There was a ceremony in Montana," Quint confirmed. "But it was a small one. And you know Laura—she likes things on a grand scale."

"That's Laura, all right." There was something wistful about the smile that briefly touched Max Rutledge's mouth. But when he looked at his son, there was something hard and unforgiving in his eyes. "It was a sad day for this family when Boone let her slip through his fingers."

Boone straightened from his perch on the armrest with the swiftness of a scalded man. "The mistake was hers, not mine." He growled the words, his voice low and hot.

"Unfortunately"—Max's lip curled ever so slightly in derision—"the mistake was mine for ever believing she would marry the likes of you. Now go freshen your drink and shut up." Making it clear that he regarded that particular discussion to be closed, Max smoothly swung his attention back to Quint. "I'm surprised you didn't go to England with the rest of your family."

"We couldn't all go." Quint smiled, conscious of the cold fury that emanated from Boone in waves, holding him motionless.

"I suppose not," Max agreed, completely ignoring the looming figure of his son. There was no doubt in Quint's mind whose will was stronger. He wasn't surprised when Boone abruptly turned and carried his drink to the bar. "So when did you arrive in Texas?"

"The first part of the week," Quint replied, certain that Max already knew that. "It took me a couple of days to familiarize myself with the place and get a handle on things or I would have stopped by sooner."

"I understand," Max assured him. "I imagine you had your hands full when you arrived. After you're here awhile, I think you'll find that things in Texas are different from the way you're used to them back in Montana."

"There isn't much doubt about that." Quint knew Max was referring to more than just ranching methods.

"You know"—Max clasped his hands together in a thoughtful pose, his elbows resting on the arms of his wheelchair—"it's been a good many years since a Calder set foot on the Cee Bar. It's almost like the ranch has been the Triple C's forgotten stepchild."

Quint was forced to agree with that assessment. "I suspect it has."

"It's never been a secret that I would like to make the Cee Bar a part of the Slash R," Max declared, his hands separating to grip the ends of the armrests, rather like a king on his throne. "I offered to buy it from your grandfather, but he wasn't inclined to sell. Businesswise it makes no sense to hang on to it. The Cee Bar's too small to show much of a profit, especially when you have to pay someone to run it."

Quint was slow with his answer. "I have a feeling that he bought the Cee Bar for the same reason that makes him determined to keep it. And that reason had nothing to do with its viability as a working ranch."

"Whatever his reason, let him know my offer stands if he should change his mind."

"I'll tell him."

"Good. And I hope we have you as a neighbor for a while." Another possibility seemed to occur to him. "Or will you be staying only long enough to find a replacement for Evans?"

"It's hard to say how long I'll be here," Quint admitted. "It depends on many other things."

"If you're still here when the holidays roll around, I hope you'll join us for Christmas dinner. My ward called a few minutes ago to say that she was planning to come. She is the daughter of a late business partner of mine, Hamilton Davis."

"I'll keep the invitation in mind," Quint promised and took a small sip of his drink.

"I hope you do," Max said. "In the meantime, if there is anything you need, just give us a call. We'll be happy to help if we can."

"I'm glad you said that." Quint seized the opening. "There is something I need."

"I hope it isn't a hired man," Max cautioned. "We're too short-handed to spare any of ours."

"My biggest need right now is hay. I have a load coming in next week, but I could use some square bales to tide me over until it arrives. I thought I might talk you into selling me some."

"Only a few bales? We can spare that," Max replied without hesitation.

"Consider them sold," Quint stated. "If it isn't too much trouble, I'll throw them in the back of my pickup when I leave."

"No trouble at all," Max assured him. "Boone, ride down to the barn with Quint and give him a hand loading the hay."

Boone responded to the order with a resentful glare, but offered no objection. "I'll take you down whenever you're ready to leave," he said to Quint.

"Let's make it now." Quint set his half-finished drink aside. "I don't want to overstay my welcome."

"You come anytime," Max insisted.

But the minute Quint left the room, his smile turned into a thin angry line, lips tightly compressed. Hunching his shoulders in thought, Max went back over their conversation in his mind, studying each word Quint had said and considering the ones he hadn't. None of it was to his liking.

In fact there was nothing about his meeting with Quint Echohawk that Max did like.

He was still in the same spot, deep in thought, when Boone returned to the den twenty minutes later. Max reared his big head and flipped the control stick to pivot his chair around.

"Echohawk left, did he?"

"He was halfway down the lane when I came in." Boone flicked a cold look in his direction and walked straight to the bar. He took a fresh glass from the shelf and proceeded to pour himself another drink. "I thought the plan was to make sure he didn't get his hands on any hay." He threw an accusing look at Max.

Max returned the look with one of contempt. "You would have been stupid enough to openly declare war over a half dozen bales, wouldn't you? It's a measly amount. Why do you think he asked for it? He knew if we refused, we'd be tipping our hand. Aren't you smart enough to figure anything out?" He whipped his wheelchair around and sent it speeding toward the desk, then stopped and swung it back. "It's that semi load of hay he's got coming in next week that you have to make sure he never gets to use."

"And just how the hell am I supposed to do that?" Boone shot back as he roughly shoved the bottle of bourbon back in its rack. "Hijack the truck?"

"Leave it to you to come up with a harebrained idea like that." Max shook his head in disgust.

"I suppose you have a better one." The attempt at a jeer fell short of its mark, mostly because Boone knew he wasn't as clever as his father. And it was this feeling of inferiority that he hated more than almost anything—except the way his father constantly reminded him of it.

"I can easily come up with a half dozen, but the hay isn't something we have to be concerned about until next week. Right now we have other things to worry about."

"Such as?" Boone resorted to sarcasm and quickly bolted down a swallow of liquor to cover his own ignorance of the answer.

But Max was already aware of it. "Such as why Echohawk is here."

Boone frowned, regarding the answer as obvious. "Just like he said—to take over the Cee Bar."

"But why him? Why not one of their veteran hands with years more ranching experience?"

"I don't know," Boone muttered, irritated at how out of his depth he felt. "They were tied up and he was available."

"It's a possibility," Max conceded. "But I'm convinced it's a remote one. Somehow the Calders sensed the Cee Bar wasn't having ordinary problems. That's why they chose Echohawk. He was raised on the Triple C so he's bound to know enough about cattle to handle that end of things. But it was the training and experience he had working for the government. They know he won't accept things at face value. He'll probe to find out why and how—and who."

Understanding registered in Boone's expression. "Then coming here to the Slash R could mean he suspects we're behind it."

Max raised an eyebrow in mock approval. "Well, well, you can add two and two after all."

"That's why you sold him the hay," Boone realized. "To try to throw him off."

"And four and four makes eight. Amazing. And?" Max questioned in a prompting fashion.

But Boone could only frown. "And what?"

Max sighed. "And that's why I insisted you help him load the hay—so he wouldn't have a chance to question any of our ranch hands and maybe get his hands on information that he shouldn't."

"They don't know anything," Boone declared with arrogant unconcern.

"They know enough. Don't kid yourself," Max muttered. "And there's another thing that bothers me—he never said anything about needing a hired man. Twice I gave him a chance to bring up the subject, and he ducked it both times. Why?"

"You already told him we were shorthanded, so he already knew you wouldn't be sending anybody his way if they came here looking for work."

"Maybe." Max had considered that. "Or maybe he's already hired someone."

Boone released a scoffing laugh. "Not a chance. People around here know better than to go to work for the Cee Bar."

Max didn't dispute that. "Unless the man isn't from around here."

"Where else would he—" Boone cut off the question. "You think he might have brought one of the Triple C ranch hands with him?"

"You've added two and two again. Maybe there's hope for you yet," Max said dryly.

"But if he does, what then?"

"First let's make sure that's the case. Then we'll decide what to do about it." He wheeled his chair toward the desk.

# Chapter Six

There is something about Saturday night that has always drawn a cowboy to the lights of town, and Quint was no exception. While drinking and carousing had never been part of his nature, a cold beer, a good meal, and a change of surroundings held a definite appeal for him.

Fort Worth with its array of nightspots sat northeast of the Cee Bar with other towns of varying sizes lying in between. Quint left the ranch with no particular destination in mind, but he turned in the direction of Loury. The Corner Café hadn't crossed his mind until he saw the fluorescent glare of its lighted windows. The sight summoned up an immediate image of Dallas with her pale copper hair and unusual light brown eyes.

Quint found himself wondering whether she was working tonight. At almost the same moment, he remembered all the times in the past when he had been a stranger in a strange town and experienced the loneliness that could be found in a crowd. A familiar face suddenly had more appeal than a beer and a good meal. In the blink of an eye, the decision was made and he swung the pickup into an empty parking slot in front of the café.

Dallas saw him when he walked through the door. One glimpse

of his high cheekbones, the slight bronze cast of his skin, and the black gleam of his hair when he slipped off his hat, and she identified him instantly. Oddly, her spirits lifted. The night suddenly didn't seem to be as dull and ordinary to her as it had before he arrived.

The touch of his gaze was almost a tangible thing when he saw her crossing to a booth, a heavily laden serving tray balanced on one arm.

She nodded to the table he had occupied on his previous visit. "You can sit at your old table if you like," she told him.

"Thanks." His eyes smiled at her.

There was a warmth in their gray depths that Dallas didn't recall noticing before. Considering some of the things her grandfather had told her about him, she had a feeling she might have been too quick to dismiss him as an ordinary cowboy.

After she finished distributing the food orders on her tray, Dallas collected a glass of ice water and a cup of hot coffee from the counter and carried them to his table.

"I didn't expect to see you in here tonight." She set the water and coffee before him.

His eyes gleamed with amusement. "You didn't really think I'd leave town just because you told me I should."

"It was good advice." Dallas still believed that. "Or have you found that out? I heard you went to the Slash R."

"News travels fast," he replied, neither confirming nor denying.

Dallas realized that he had seldom given her a direct answer. "It's a small town. And anything to do with the Rutledges spreads like crazy. And the news that you bought hay from them went through this town like a category-four tornado."

"They were just doing the neighborly thing." He reached for the menu and flipped it open.

Dallas liked the way he played down the purchase. "Maybe, but the Slash R has never been known for making neighborly gestures."

"Maybe no one's given them a chance," he suggested, tongue-in-cheek.

Dallas reacted with a crooked smile that grooved a dimple in one cheek. "Yeah, right."

His smile widened into something dazzling and warm that snatched at her breath. "For a minute there I thought you were going to accuse me of being a fool again."

The remark was an instant reminder of the futility of one man attempting to stand against the Rutledges. It sobered her. "I don't think you realize how big the odds are against you."

An amused dryness entered his expression. "I imagine the odds were long that I'd get any hay, too." Without giving her a chance to reply, he asked, "Is it safe to order a steak?"

"Yes. It's just the meat loaf you need to avoid," she told him.

"In that case, I'll have a T-bone, medium rare, and a baked potato with all the trimmings."

"What kind of dressing on your salad?" Dallas pulled the order tablet from her apron pocket and flipped to a new sheet.

"Blue cheese, if you have it."

"Coming right up," she promised and moved away.

When she left, that lonely feeling closed around Quint again. Looking at the empty chairs pushed up to his table, he realized that it was her company and conversation he wanted.

There was a glimmer of rare annoyance in the glance he flicked at the scattering of other customers. Their presence forced Quint to put aside any hope he might have entertained of persuading Dallas to join him at the table. The knowledge left him with an edgy, irritated feeling, something that was new to him.

The sensation didn't fade until she returned to his table a few minutes later and placed a salad liberally drizzled with blue cheese dressing before him.

"I thought it would be busier than this on a Saturday night," Quint said to prevent her from walking away.

Her easy smile gave him the impression that she didn't mind being drawn into conversation, perhaps even welcomed it. "The supper crowd always comes early. By now the homebodies are back in front of their televisions and the rest are bending their elbows at Tillie's."

"Tillie's. That must be the local bar," Quint guessed. "Is it here in town? I don't remember driving by one."

"It's a block off the main drag, so it isn't a place that you would happen by," she explained. "Tubby's sister owns it. I keep telling him they should merge the two businesses. He'd have more customers if he sold beer and she'd have more if she sold food. But he just turns a deaf ear to the idea."

"Sounds like a good one to me. We have a place like that back in Montana," he said, thinking of the former roadhouse called Harry's in Blue Moon that had always sold both food and liquor. "Come Saturday night, it's packed to the rafters."

She tipped her head to one side, curiosity entering her expression. "Is that where you're from—Montana?"

"Born and raised there," Quint confirmed with a nod. "How about you? Are you a native Texan?"

"Of course." There was an impish light in her eyes. "Care to guess where I was born?"

Quint laughed softly in response. "Something tells me it might be Dallas."

"It's a little obvious, isn't it?" she agreed.

"I'd say you were lucky the hospital wasn't in Fort Worth."

"True. Although my mother told me that if she had gone to Fort Worth to deliver, she would have named me Gentry. But when I was born in Dallas, she thought it would be more original to name me after the city of my birth. Of course, you have to understand, she had an absolute aversion to commonplace names. Her own was Mary Alice, and she hated it."

Made sensitive by the recent loss of his father, Quint was quick to note her use of the past tense in referring to her mother. "How long has she been gone?"

"It was seven years ago this past spring."

"It's hard losing a parent," he said, speaking as much for himself as for her.

"Yes." But she seemed a little surprised that he understood that. After an instant's hesitation, Dallas glanced down at his untouched salad. "You'd better dig in," she told him. "Your steak will be up soon."

Left alone again, Quint picked up his fork and started on the salad with a renewed appetite, only distantly aware that his conversation with her, brief as it had been, had stimulated a male kind of hunger as well.

During the course of his meal, he had more occasions to talk to her, some exchanges longer than others. On a subconscious level, Quint knew it was all part of an age-old dance between a man and a woman. He had long ago become familiar with the steps to it, the advance and retreat, and the waiting and watching for that signal from the woman indicating her interest, or lack thereof.

With the only other remaining customer at the cash register, Quint let his attention focus on Dallas, recalling the small, personal things he had learned about her tonight and the thousands more he still wanted to know—things like whether her hair felt as smooth as it looked, and the look of her light brown eyes when passion glazed them.

There was a natural grace to the relaxed, yet erect, posture of her body, long and slim and unmistakably feminine in its well-proportioned curves.

His bill paid, the man at the register headed out the door, and Dallas emerged from behind the counter and looked directly at Quint, her eyes bright and alive to him.

"Ready for more coffee?" Her warm smile was an encouragement to agree.

But Quint wasn't really interested in another cup of coffee. "What time do you close?"

"Usually whenever the last customer leaves," she admitted easily. "But don't let that stop you from having another cup if you want it."

"I think I'm coffee-ed out."

"Are you sure?"

Quint detected a kind of regret in her look, giving him hope that the evening wouldn't be coming to a quick end. "I'm sure." Rising, he collected his hat and the check for his meal, then followed Dallas when she retraced her steps to the cash register counter. He slid the check and the cash to pay it across the counter to her. "Do you have a way home after work?"

She nodded, explaining, "I'm parked out back."

"Since I can't offer you a ride home, maybe I could buy you a drink over at Tillie's when you're through." Her hesitation was immediate and obvious. He could only think of one reason why that would be. "Sorry," he said. "Maybe I should have asked if you're married."

"I'm not." The denial came in a rush, but it didn't change the mix of uncertainty and regret in her expression. "It's just that—"

"It's just what?" He didn't understand why the answer wasn't a simple yes or no. Yet it clearly wasn't for Dallas. "It isn't this thing with Rutledge, is it?" That thought was followed instantly by another. "Are you worried that Rutledge will cause trouble if you're seen with me?" The possibility aroused all his protective instincts in a surge of anger.

"Heaven knows he's capable of it." Looking at Quint, Dallas couldn't help remembering the way friends and neighbors—people she had known for years—had shied away from any contact with her and her grandfather during their battle with the Rutledges. A public shunning couldn't have been much worse. "But that has nothing to do with my problem. I have finals next week. Tonight and tomorrow is the only free time I have to study."

"I understand." There was a polite curve to his mouth that seemed to match the expressionless set of his features.

She couldn't let the night end like this. Dallas couldn't even say why she felt that so strongly, but she did. "Of course," she began, "an hour one way or the other shouldn't make that much difference. Maybe I could join you for just one drink before I head home and hit the books."

"I promise I won't try to talk you into two." His gray eyes sparkled with a warmly intimate look.

"You wouldn't succeed if you tried," Dallas countered even as her pulse quickened and she felt that little curl of excitement in the pit of her stomach. Both were purely a physical response to a man's attention. It had been so long since she had allowed herself to feel such things that it was almost like the first time.

"How do I find Tillie's?" he asked, taking his change from her.

"Turn right at the first block north of here. You'll see a parking lot on the corner, probably jammed with vehicles. Next to it will be a one-story building with a neon sign in the window advertising Lone Star beer. That's Tillie's."

Armed with directions from Dallas, Quint drove straight to the bar. He pulled into the corner lot as another pickup drove out, leaving an empty slot in the row that faced the building. Quint parked his pickup in it and made his way to the entrance located in the center of the building's limestone front.

A muffled mix of music and voices reached him even before he opened the door. The volume grew decidedly louder when he walked into the dimly lit bar. His glance made a quick scan of the bar's long and narrow layout.

A scattering of tables, all occupied, took up the front section with booths lining one short wall. A long, wooden bar, darkened with age, dominated the middle part, complete with a row of tall stools in front of it. A jukebox stood on the opposite wall, its speakers blasting out a rowdy drinking song by Toby Keith.

In between the two were more tables and chairs with a small space left empty in front of the jukebox, creating a dance area of sorts, but there were no couples making use of it. At the bar's rear area, players were clustered around two pool tables, the green of their surfaces illuminated by the hooded fixtures suspended above them. Every now and then the crack of one ball striking another made itself heard above the blare of music and the din of voices.

Spotting an empty stool at the end of the long bar, Quint made his way to it, aware of the curious glances strangers always attract. He slid onto the stool and swiveled it slightly so he could keep an eye on the door.

There was a short, squat woman tending bar, a voluminous white apron tied high on her front, almost completely hiding the pink dress she wore. She had small dark eyes and a mop of tight red curls, a bright color that obviously came from a bottle. Quint surmised that she had to be Tillie.

After an initial, sharp glance in his direction, she pulled a pair of long necks out of a cooler, popped their tops, and set them out for the waitress to collect, then wiped up a water ring before she ventured to his end of the bar.

"What'll you have?" Her dark eyes made a close and thorough study of him.

"A beer," he replied. "Whatever you have on tap is fine."

Without an acknowledging word, she moved off, grabbed a clean mug off the shelf, filled it with beer from the tap, and carried it back to him. She stopped short of setting it on the counter before him, her eyes narrowing into dark points.

"Are you that new guy that took over the Cee Bar?" she demanded.

"Yes."

"I figured you probably were." She plopped the mug on the counter. "That'll be two dollars, cash." She stood there, making it plain that she wasn't about to leave until he paid for his drink.

Quint took a couple one-dollar bills from his pocket and pushed them across the counter to her. She scooped up the money and stuck it in her apron pocket, then reversed direction and headed to the opposite end of the bar.

Within minutes, Quint sensed a change. There were no more curious glances directed his way. Any that he happened to encounter were quickly averted. One by one the stools closest to him were vacated until only those at the opposite end of the bar were occupied.

For the first time, he questioned the wisdom of asking Dallas to meet him here for a drink, aware that his reasons were completely selfish. He had just decided to leave before she could arrive when she walked through the door.

He was held motionless by the sight of her. Her hair was down, falling loose and soft about her face. All the previous times it had been confined by a clasp or tucked under a cap; the change was stunning.

But it was more than her hair that was different. Gone was the plain white blouse that she'd worn at the restaurant. In its place was a snug-fitting T-shirt that molded itself to the rounded contours of her breasts and stopped a centimeter short of her waist. It was a soft green color that highlighted the coppery sheen of her hair and the tan shade of her eyes. The result was all woman, breezily confident and subtly sexy.

Quint tried to be sorry that he hadn't left before she came, but he couldn't. Those twinges of conscience weren't nearly as strong as the raw desire he felt.

"Hi." She climbed onto the stool next to him, her lips glistening with a fresh coat of coral gloss that seemed to invite him to test their slickness. "I got through sooner than I thought."

"Sooner than I expected." He was glad about that.

"Hello, Tillie." She smiled at the woman with easy unconcern. "I'll have a beer, same as him," she said, pointing sideways at Quint.

Quint had the money out and on the counter when she returned with Dallas's beer. Tillie glanced at the bills, then shot a pointed look at Dallas.

"Are you going to let him pay for it?" The question bordered on a warning that forcibly reminded Quint of his previous misgivings.

"That's the general idea," Dallas replied.

The woman shook her head in mild disapproval, swept up the money, and stuffed the bills in her apron pocket with the rest.

Quint waited until she moved out of earshot.

"Maybe it was a bad idea for you to meet me here," he said, still keeping an eye on the bartender.

Dallas glanced sideways at him, a smile showing. "I knew what I was doing when I came. But it's nice that you're a little concerned."

"If Rutledge retaliates over this," Quint began, anger fisting inside him, "I want to know."

Dallas smiled at his noble words, wise enough to know there was absolutely nothing Quint Echohawk could do about it if Rutledge chose to make an example of her.

"A warning is likely all I'll get," she replied, knowing that the threat would come only if she repeated the offense.

"He has that much leverage that a warning would be enough?" Quint lifted the beer mug and took a sip from it.

"This is a small town," Dallas reminded him. "If he isn't the landlord or employer, then he's the biggest customer. He has the leverage. As the old saying goes—it's his way or the highway."

"What keeps you here?" There was something more personal than idle curiosity in the warm probe of his gaze.

"Right now it's practical. The rent's cheap, my job at the feed store pays above average, and it's an easy commute for my night courses at college." Dallas omitted any mention of her grandfather and his reluctance to leave the area. "And if everything goes according to plan, in a couple more years I'll have my degree. It's hard to say where that might take me. Somewhere else though, I'm sure."

"Have you decided on your major?"

"Business administration," she answered without hesitation. "Although I still haven't decided if I want to focus on the financial side or management."

"Either way you'll be carrying a bunch of accounting courses."

Dallas was surprised that he would know that. There was only one logical conclusion to be drawn from that. Still she hesitated.

"Did you go to college?"

"I have a feeling you've never met a cowboy who knew his way around a university campus before." His look was lightly teasing. "You might be surprised to learn that it isn't uncommon these days for a Triple C ranch hand to have a degree in his pocket."

Dallas realized that her initial impression of him as an ordinary cowboy had colored much of her thinking. But a common ranch hand wouldn't have been sent here to take over the Cee Bar.

"I think I remember hearing somewhere that the Triple C is a big ranch. Is it?" she wondered.

"Bigger than most."

"Is it bigger than the Slash R?"

"Yes."

Dallas had only to consider the immense power and wealth Max Rutledge could wield to know that Triple C's size was irrelevant when it was well over a thousand miles away.

"Have you worked at the Triple C long?" she asked instead.

"No, not long. Why?"

"Just curious," Dallas admitted, aware that her motive was nothing more than a simple desire to know more about him. Although he hadn't been exactly forthcoming in his answer. It made her wonder why he was so guarded. She laughed out loud when a possible reason popped into her mind. "If you're worried that Rutledge is using me to get all the information I can about you, you can forget it. I promise you, I'm not his pawn."

"I'm glad to hear that." There was a smoky intensity to his steady gaze that sent her pulse skittering all over the place.

"You're smart to be cautious, though."

His smile widened. "That sounds like a compliment."

"It is."

"Now that your opinion of me has improved a little, maybe you might accept if I asked you to dance."

The suggestion, coming as it did from out of nowhere, caught

Dallas by surprise. Up until that moment she had blocked out the honky-tonk music coming from the jukebox. Now she heard the ballad being played. And the woman in her wanted to know what it would be like to feel his arms around her.

"Are you asking?" she said, unconsciously holding her breath.

"Are you accepting?" he countered.

She had expected him to smile an answer, but his expression, while warm, was on the serious side.

Letting her actions speak for itself, Dallas slid off the bar stool and turned toward the dance floor. An instant later she felt the light pressure of his guiding hand on the curve of her waist. The contact produced a delicious little tingle.

When they reached the cleared space in front of the jukebox, two other couples were already making use of the slow music. Dallas turned into his arms, surprised at how very natural it seemed to slide her hand onto his shoulder.

Hands linked, Quint made no attempt to draw her close as he guided her into the opening steps. But with each turn around the dance floor, the space between them lessened until their legs were brushing and he felt the occasional rub of her breasts against his chest.

The top of her head came just to his nose. Every now and then he felt the evocative stir of her warm breath against his jaw and caught the faint fragrance of the strawberry-scented shampoo she used on her hair.

A silence swirled between them, charged with the stimulating effect of physical contact. With each step, each rocking sway of motion, they came a little bit closer together, their bodies automatically adjusting to the contours of each other.

Quint was conscious of a thousand things about her—the long sweep of her brown eyelashes, the supple grace of her body, and the heat that emanated from her.

In spite of the rightness he felt holding Dallas in his arms, he was gripped by a growing frustration that came from knowing he didn't dare see her again—not for a while, not until this business with Rutledge was concluded. And not just for her sake, but also for his own.

If Max Rutledge suspected that Quint cared even a little about Dallas, it wouldn't trouble his conscience to use her as a means to get to him. Quint couldn't afford to let Rutledge have any kind of hold over him.

After tonight, he needed to stay well away from Dallas. He had no other choice.

John Earl Tandy stood to one side of the pool table, his hands wrapped in a stranglehold around the cue stick while he stared holes in the back of the stranger circling the dance floor with Dallas. It sickened him the way the stranger was coming on to her, sickened and infuriated him.

"Hey, John Earl." Somebody poked him in the shoulder. "Have you gone deaf or something? It's your turn."

John Earl turned a scowl on his fellow ranch hand, Deke Saunders. Before he had a chance to reply, one of his other buddies spoke up. "Hell, haven't you noticed? John Earl always turns deaf, dumb, and blind whenever he's in the same room with Dallas."

"That's her dancing with that new guy from the Cee Bar, isn't it?" Deke Saunders observed. "Sure looks like she's getting mighty friendly with him."

John Earl leaned onto the pool table and took aim at the white cue ball. "If you'd been watching, you'd know, he's the one getting friendly with her. I have half a notion to go over there and cut in on him."

"Why don't you?" his other buddy, Chuck Reno, taunted.

"Maybe I will." John Earl was quick to take up the challenge, straightening from the table when the cue ball took a nosedive into the corner pocket.

"Too late," Deke informed him. "The song's over."

John Earl turned to look, his eyes narrowing at the sight of that tanned hand riding so familiarly on Dallas's hip when the stranger guided her back to the bar.

"Somebody needs to let that guy know he isn't welcome here," he declared stiffly. "And maybe do a little rearranging of his face at the same time."

"Now you're talking, John Earl. Go get him," Deke urged.

"Don't think I wouldn't like to, but I talked to him before. He's liable to remember me." He eyed the trio around him with sudden speculation. "He's never seen any of you, though."

L.B. Brody, always the quiet one, drew back in uncertainty. "Wait a minute, John Earl. Rutledge might not like the idea of us roughing him up."

"Hell, he's liable to pay you a bonus for it," he retorted. "And if he does, you damned well better share it with me."

"Why should you get anything when we're the ones taking the risk?" Deke wanted to know.

"There won't be any risk, not the way I got it figured," John Earl stated and motioned them closer to explain his plan.

At the bar, Quint waited until Dallas had climbed onto her bar stool before he slid onto his tall seat. There was distance between them again, but it didn't eliminate the new awareness that sizzled between them. Quint knew he had to do something about that.

He signaled to the woman behind the bar. "Two more beers, Tillie."

Dallas spoke up quickly. "Don't order any for me. I still have half of mine."

"But that's warm by now," he countered smoothly.

"It's not that warm," she insisted, sliding him a glance that was slightly confused and uncertain. She forced a smile. "Besides, I told you my limit was one drink. Then I have to go hit the books."

Quint shrugged. "You can't blame a guy for trying," he said and flashed her a smile.

"I suppose not," she agreed and studied him with a new carefulness as Tillie walked up and shoved two more beers onto the counter in front of them. "You should have listened, though. Now you have two beers to drink."

Quint made no reply to that and fished more money out of his pocket, then slid it over to the bartender. "Bring me some change for the jukebox, will you?" He eyed Dallas with a knowing look. "There's bound to be a few more slow songs on it. You can help me pick them out."

"Maybe another time," Dallas replied, oddly saddened that he would resort to such a ruse to get her to stay longer. She reminded herself that men were like that, and wondered why she had thought Quint was different from any other male on the prowl. She took a long drink of her nearly warm beer, determined to bring this meeting to a quick end.

"I thought you liked dancing," he remarked with subtle persistence.

"I like it well enough," she said, refusing to lie about it. "But I have some heavy-duty studying to do, and that has to come first."

"The night's young. You have plenty of time to study later," Quint reasoned.

"Hey, Dallas," Tillie shouted from halfway down the bar. "You got a phone call. You can take it in the back room." She jerked a thumb toward the rear of the building and immediately resumed filling the next drink order.

"Excuse me." Dallas darted a short glance in Quint's direction and slipped off the stool, striking out toward the dimly lit hall just beyond the twin pool tables.

Quint was quick to notice the shine was gone from her eyes when she looked at him. It was proof, if he needed any, that he had succeeded in his role of a cowboy on the make. But he felt no satisfaction in it, just a resenting anger that it had to be this way.

He wrapped a hand around the icy cool sides of the fresh beer mug and carried it to his mouth, drinking down several long swallows. But the cold beer failed to rid him of the sour taste.

Engrossed in his own dark thoughts, Quint paid little attention to the stocky cowboy sauntering toward him until he stopped by his stool. He skimmed the man's face in a glance, identifying him as the cowboy who had warned him about working at the Cee Bar his first night in Loury, the one Dallas had called John Earl.

"You're from the Cee Bar, aren't you?" After making his opening gambit, the cowboy waited for Quint's reply.

"I am." Quint tensed ever so slightly, not sure what was coming, but ready for it.

"Some guy outside wants to talk to you. Said it was important."

Aware that it was one of the oldest ambush tricks ever used, Quint shrugged. "If he wants to talk, tell him to come in here."

John Earl scoffed at the suggestion. "Tell him yourself. It's Saturday night and I'm too far behind on my drinking to be carrying messages," he declared and walked down to the middle of the bar where he slapped a hand on the counter. "Give me a beer, Tillie. Tall and cold as they come."

Quint sat on the stool a minute longer. The message reeked of a trap. Yet there was a slim possibility that Empty Garner was out there. At the same time, Quint knew that if Max Rutledge was dealing this hand, he had to play it. He threw a glance at the dimly lit hall, but there was no sign of Dallas.

Leaving his change on the counter, Quint stepped down from the bar stool. When he reached the door, he pulled it open and paused within its frame, scanning the area immediately outside. Seeing nothing suspicious, he exited the bar with a sideways step that put his back against the building, letting the door swing shut on its own.

He stood there for a long moment, tuning in to the night sounds and sifting out the man-made ones, every sense alert. Logic said the parking lot was the obvious location for a trap. He concentrated most of his attention on it.

His caution paid off when he caught the faint scuff of a boot on gravel, the kind of sound that might be made when a person shifted his weight from one foot to the other.

"If someone wants to talk to me," Quint said in a low voice, "he'd better show himself or I'm going back inside."

A sudden stillness gripped the night. It was soon broken by the faint rustle of clothing and the soft tread of footsteps, both coming from the parking lot area, just as Quint expected. A second later, he spotted a movement in the shadows at the building's corner. A hatted figure in a bulky, insulated jacket exposed a shoulder, briefly lifting a hand.

"Over here," he said in a voice as low as Quint's had been.

Although he could see nothing of the man's face, Quint knew at once the man wasn't Empty Garner. His caution tripled.

"Step out where I can see you," Quint ordered.

"Like hell I will," the man retorted in a voice that was lower still. "I can't risk being seen talking to you. You either come over here or forget you ever saw me."

The response had just enough ring of truth in it to draw Quint forward, but he took a course that kept him wide of the corner. When he was level with the tailgate of the pickup parked closest to the sidewalk, he turned into the lot, crossing behind the truck, and stopping in the dark space between it and the next vehicle.

The man still stood by the corner, cloaked in deep shadow now. After a moment's hesitation, he shifted past the pickup to stand directly opposite Quint. Just enough light from the street reached him to enable Quint to see the turned-up collar of his jacket and the downward angle of his hat brim, both intended to conceal.

"What did you have to tell me?" Quint prompted, alert for any movement to the side of him.

"You're a cautious one," the man muttered. "Guess you can't blame me for being cautious, too."

Hesitating again, the man threw a glance at the street, giving Quint a glimpse of a thick dark mustache. Then he was in shadow. He seemed to come to a decision and moved briskly forward.

"This is gonna be short and quick," he said and started feeling around in the pocket of his jacket. "It ain't what I got to say. It's what I got to give you."

The man's swift approach forced Quint to center his attention on him while maintaining a healthy amount of disbelief that his intention was as innocent as his words.

Almost too late, he detected the roll of gravel to the side of him, the sound masked by the heavy crunch of the man's footsteps. Someone lunged at him out of the darkness. Ducking sideways, Quint eluded the brunt of it and instinctively grabbed the arm that tried to wrap itself around his neck, lowered a shoulder, and flipped him over his back into the path of the first man.

Before Quint could straighten, a third man slammed into him, knocking him against the parked truck. He came away from it swinging and had the satisfaction of hearing a startled grunt when he buried a fist in the man's coat-padded midsection.

He never had a chance to deliver a follow-up blow as the second man scrambled to his feet and grabbed Quint's arm. He twisted free of his grip in time to block a swing from the third. By then the second man had recovered and managed to land a glancing blow along Quint's jaw.

A fist clipped the side of his head and sent his hat flying. The action was coming too swiftly. Quint no longer bothered to discern which one was pressing the attack. He had his back up against the pickup's side bed, using the protection it offered to prevent any assault from the rear.

As long as they kept coming at him one at a time, Quint was able to hold his own even though he was outnumbered. But they were bound to wise up any second and coordinate their efforts.

A head snapped back, rocked by a hard jab from Quint. Out of the corner of his eye, he caught a glimpse of the cocked arm that was taking aim on his middle. It was pure reflex that turned him sideways, letting the fist ram itself into the side of the pickup. The man yowled and grabbed at the hand he jerked away from the truck. Quint had a split second to hope he'd broken a bone or two in it.

Someone jumped him from behind and wrapped his arms around Quint's shoulders. "Come on. I got him," he called in quick excitement, his breath sawing near Quint's ear. "I got him!"

But Quint's hand-to-hand training stood him in good stead. Without a conscious thought, he seized the man by one wrist, ducked under his arm, and twisted the wrist behind the man's back. A quick chopping blow delivered between the man's shoulders sent him sprawling face forward at the feet of his cohorts. Both reached down to help him up.

In the brief interval of inaction, Quint was conscious of the heavy pounding of his heart and the heaving of his chest to draw air into his lungs. There was a roar in his ears. Blows had landed, but adrenaline blocked any of the pain from them for the time being.

The street remained empty of traffic and no one had ventured out of the bar. Quint was dimly aware of the muffled noise from inside the building, but his focus was on the curses and muttered oaths of three men as they regathered themselves.

Quint tried a bluff. "Pack it up and get out while you can still walk."

"Like hell," one muttered.

The response seemed to galvanize the other two. As one they hurled themselves at Quint. As good as he was, three was more than he could handle at one time.

Fists flew. Knuckles smashed against bone, and the air had the tinny smell of blood in it. Grunts, gasps, and curses all mixed together in a seamless sound of confusion.

In the bar's makeshift storage room and office, Dallas dug through the jumble of papers that littered the solitary desk and uncovered the black telephone hidden beneath them. She picked up the receiver and punched the button with the blinking light.

"Hello, this is Dallas."

"Dallas?" a woman's voice repeated on an incredulous note. "What are you doing there?"

The voice was a familiar one, but Dallas couldn't place it. "Who is this?"

"It's Kelly Rae. Kelly Rae Thomas," she added in clarification.

"Kelly Rae," Dallas said, recalling the brunette who had been one year behind her in high school. "What did you want to talk to me about?"

"Tillie said I wanted to talk to you?" Again she sounded surprised.

"She just said I had a phone call."

"I can't believe this," Kelly Rae declared in disgust. "I told her I wanted to speak to *Alice*. Alice Mitchell. That old fool needs a hearing aid. If I wasn't so furious right now, this would be funny."

Dallas remembered the two girls had been almost inseparable during high school. "Let me see if Alice is here."

"No! Wait," Kelly Rae rushed. "Maybe you can help me. I'm trying to find out if Bubba Franks is there. Have you seen him?"

"I don't remember seeing him here, but I wasn't really looking for him either."

"What about the Poindexter brothers? Bubba usually hangs out with them."

"I definitely don't remember seeing them," Dallas answered with confidence. Both men, former defensive line standouts in football, topped six feet and three hundred pounds.

In frustration Kelly Rae launched into her tale of woe about a family get-together Bubba was supposed to attend, complete with a threat to return his engagement ring if he didn't walk through the door in the next ten minutes. A promise from Dallas that she would send Bubba on his way if she saw him finally satisfied the girl, and Dallas hung up.

The loud music and raucous voices hit her the minute Dallas exited the relative quiet of the back room. She hesitated, briefly toying with the idea of slipping out the rear door, avoiding any further attempts by Quint to persuade her to stay. But it smacked too much of cowardice.

Squaring her shoulders, she set out for the far end of the bar. As she passed the pool tables, John Earl intercepted her.

"Hey, Dallas." His avid gaze devoured the close fit of her cotton top. "Don't you look sweet tonight?"

"Thanks." But he was easily the last man she wanted to notice that. Dallas continued past him with hardly a break in stride.

He quickly caught up with her. "Not so fast. I was just going to buy you a drink."

"Sorry, but I'm with someone." Even as she made her claim, her glance skipped ahead. Her steps faltered when she failed to see Quint sitting at the far end of the bar.

"If you're talking about that stranger, he left."

Dallas wanted to take issue with that, but the evidence seemed to be all on John Earl's side. Quint was nowhere to be seen. She hadn't expected him to walk out without waiting for her to come back. She told herself that it was just as well he had. It saved her from having to deal with any attempts by him to get her to stay longer.

"Good," she said. "I have to be leaving anyway."

"You can't go yet," John Earl protested, catching hold of her arm before she could walk away. "I want to buy you a drink."

"No, thanks. I have to go home and study."

"And I said you're going to stay," he insisted with an angry scowl. "Forget about those damned books for a while."

"Why?" Dallas was suddenly suspicious. He seemed more anxious than eager for her to stay.

"Because I want to buy you a drink. Why do you think?" He turned a big smile on her, but there was an edge of desperation in his voice that was impossible to ignore.

"What's going on, John Earl?" she demanded.

"Nothing." The denial came a little too quickly. And the pause was a little too long before he remembered to say, "I just want to buy you a drink."

"Where exactly did Quint go?"

"I told you he left." John Earl tried to appear cocky and indifferent, but only succeeded in looking nervous and uneasy.

"And rather suddenly, too. Did you have anything to do with that?"

"Me? Whatever put a crazy thing like that in your head? I don't even know the guy. Forget about him, and have a drink with me." He tucked a hand under her elbow and tried to turn her toward the bar.

Dallas pulled her arm free and bolted for the door.

"Hey! Where are you going?" a dumbfounded John Earl called after her. "Damn it, come back here."

Dallas knew without looking that he was coming after her. She broke into a run the last few feet. But the flat of his hand pushed the door shut a second after Dallas had pulled it open.

"You can't leave yet." There was anger and something else in his eyes.

"Watch me," she replied and simultaneously gave the door a hard jerk before he had a chance to set his weight against it.

The suddenness of her action enabled Dallas to open the door wide enough that she could slip out before John Earl could recover. By the time he came charging out the door after her, she was halfway to the parking lot.

"Come back here, you damned, spooky broad!"

She threw a glance over her shoulder and saw that he had stopped to glare at her, jaw ridged in a tight, angry line. In that same second, he pivoted away and bulled his way back inside the building.

In the next breath, Dallas heard the hasty thud of running footsteps, more than one set, the sound mixed in with the hiss of whispers. She reached the parking lot's graveled lot in time to see the dark shapes of two hatted figures ducking behind the building.

"Quint?" she called in a low, hesitant voice.

There was a scrape of a foot on gravel somewhere close by, off to her left. She turned toward the sound. There, in the shadowy gap between the two parked vehicles, she saw him half standing and half leaning against the side of a pickup. A light from the street revealed the black gleam of his hair and the glisten of a dark wet streak running from temple to jaw.

"My God, Quint. You're hurt," she murmured and rushed to his side.

"I'm all right." He brushed aside the hand she stretched out to him, and shifted to make his legs take more of his weight, but Dallas could see the effort it took.

"You are far from all right," she informed him.

Blood continued to seep from a nasty gash along one eyebrow. There was a swollen area along the opposite cheekbone that was already showing the discoloration of a bruise. One side of his mouth was puffy, with more blood trickling from the corner.

"It's nothing," he insisted and pressed two fingers to his mouth, winced, and stared at the coagulating blood on them with a kind of groggy recognition.

"Just the same, I think we'd better be safe and get you to a doctor." Dallas didn't like the vaguely dazed look he had.

He dragged in a deep, long breath, then slowly released it. "Nothing's broken, only bruised. I know the difference."

Unable to argue with that, she swung away. "I'm calling the police then."

"Don't bother," he said in a weary voice. "I didn't get a good enough look at their faces to recognize any of them again—unless you did?" His gaze sharpened on her when Dallas turned back to him.

"No," she admitted.

"Then it would be a waste of time and paperwork." He frowned and lifted a hand to his bare head before making a scan of the ground near his feet. "Where's my hat?"

Dallas found it lying half under the pickup and retrieved it for him. He took it and eased it carefully onto his head. Then he seemed to focus on her for the first time.

"You'd better get out of here and go home," he told her.

Dallas hesitated. "What are you going to do?"

"The smart thing—go home and nurse my wounds." He brushed past her and angled across the lot while fishing a set of keys from his pocket. Dallas watched, half expecting his gait to be a staggering one, but he walked a slow but straight line to the rear of a black pickup, then took aim on the driver's side. She saw the interior light come on when he opened the door.

There was a slight pause between the time he opened the door and pulled himself into the cab. Then the light went off, and the engine rumbled to life, tail- and headlights coming on.

When the black truck reversed out of the parking slot, Dallas started toward her own vehicle. Despite all his assurances, she wasn't totally convinced that Quint was okay. Rather than be nagged by her conscience, she followed him at a discreet distance all the way to the entrance of the Cee Bar.

She slowed as she approached the gate, and caught a glimpse of his taillights disappearing around a bend in the drive. Satisfied that he would make it safely the rest of the way, she turned around and headed home.

# PART TWO

*An evening star,*
*A Texas moon,*
*A Calder trusts,*
*But is it too soon?*

# Chapter Seven

Morning light streamed through the windows as Boone entered the Slash R's formal dining room. He winced at the bright light that flooded from the huge chandelier above the table. The harsh glare of it sharpened the pounding in his head, the lingering result of one too many whiskeys last night.

To avoid the light's direct assault, Boone tipped his chin down and crossed to his usual chair, situated midway on one long side of the table, grateful for the plush area rug that muffled the heavy tread of boots. As usual, the hangover made his hearing much too acute, magnifying the smallest sound.

As he took his seat, he slid a glance at his father, already ensconced at the head of the table, then reached for his napkin, shook out its folds, and dragged it across his lap. A connecting door to the kitchen swung open and a servant glided into the dining room, carrying a steaming bowl of oatmeal on a serving tray. Boone's stomach rolled a little at the sight of it.

"None for me, Vargas," Boone stated, intercepting the servant's quick look at him.

"I suspect Boone needs one of the cook's tomato juice concoctions before he tackles any food," Max informed the servant. The servant nodded, placed the bowl in front of Max, and left the dining room. The stirring scrape of a spoon across the bottom traveled up Boone's back like the screech of chalk on a blackboard, setting his teeth on edge.

"I understand it was after three o'clock when you finally staggered home." The comment had an offhand quality to it, but Boone heard the underlying tone of disgust.

"That's probably about right," he agreed and took considerable pleasure in adding, "I know it was right around two o'clock when I got back to the ranch."

"Two?" The single word carried a demand for an explanation for the hour's difference in time.

"Two," Boone confirmed as the servant swept back into the room and placed a tall glass of the cook's personal hangover antidote, the ingredients of which he refused to divulge, before Boone. Boone downed a healthy dose of it and felt the spicy bite of it on his tongue and throat, its fiery flavor burning away much of the dullness in his head.

"If you were back by two, why did it take you an hour to get to the house?" Max eyed him with sharp suspicion.

"When I pulled into the ranch yard, I happened to see Tandy struggling to get one of his buddies out of his pickup. I figured the guy had probably passed out, so I stopped to give John Earl a hand." He paused deliberately, savoring that rare feeling of knowing something his father didn't.

"That couldn't have taken you an hour," Max stated with certainty. "What did you do—tip a few glasses with the boys?"

"You always told me that whiskey is a sure way to loosen a man's tongue." Boone was well aware that whiskey hadn't been necessary. Tandy, Saunders, and the other two had been only too eager to tell their story. "And it was an interesting tale they had to tell about how they got the cuts and bruises, black eyes, and cracked ribs they sported."

Max laid his spoon aside, his gaze growing hard with impatience and intolerance. "The only thing that could be of any possible interest would be who they had the fight with."

"Exactly." Smugness marked the curve of Boone's mouth. "It seems they cornered Echohawk in the parking lot at Tillie's and roughed him up a bit."

Elbows resting on the arms of his wheelchair, Max clasped his hands together and coolly regarded him. "Did you put that idea in their heads?"

The icy contempt in his father's voice suddenly made Boone uneasy and defensive. He lifted one shoulder in a nervous shrug.

"They came up with it themselves. The opportunity was there and they took it. What's wrong with that?" He frowned, confused and not liking the feeling. "They didn't do anything different from what you've wanted done in the past."

"But in the past," Max began, speaking slowly, drawing out each word and coating it with sarcasm, "the target was always some hired man. It was never a Calder!" He issued the last with explosive heat.

The hangover left Boone with a short temper of his own. "I don't see what difference that makes," he fired back. "Echohawk's never laid eyes on any of them before. He can't connect them to us."

"Do you really think he's as stupid as you are?" Max jeered, then waved aside the question in disgust. "Don't bother to answer that."

"What the hell difference does it make what he might suspect?" Boone demanded, his voice raising. "He can't prove a damned thing. He never even called the police. Tandy hung around Tillie's to make sure of that."

"The police are the least of the problem," Max said, dismissing that as a concern. "I can pull enough strings to handle a scuffle outside a bar."

"Then what the hell's your problem?"

Max ignored the question. "You said the boys roughed him up. How bad was he hurt? Or did you even bother to ask?"

"I didn't know I was supposed to care," Boone replied with sarcasm. "But he couldn't have been hurt all that bad. Tandy saw him behind the wheel of his pickup, driving out of the lot. Odds are, he got home under his own power."

With that concern eliminated, Max's thoughts went down another road. "I wonder why Echohawk went to Tillie's in the first place," he mused aloud. "Was he hoping to invite the kind of trouble he got? I wonder."

"Now you're giving him credit for being smarter than he is." Boone smiled without humor and downed some more of his hangover cure.

"Am I?" Max countered in open doubt. "Then maybe you can tell me what he was doing there? And don't give me any nonsense about just stopping in for a beer. Echohawk didn't strike me as the type who goes carousing just because it's Saturday night—like somebody else I won't bother to name."

Boone reacted to the none-too-subtle dig with more sarcasm. "He had a drink there, all right, with Dallas."

"Dallas," Max repeated and frowned. "You mean Empty Garner's granddaughter?"

"There's no one else around here named Dallas that I know of," he retorted and drained the tall glass, ice clinking against its sides.

"I wonder how he met her," Max murmured thoughtfully.

"Could have been the café, or the feed store—or both." As far as Boone was concerned, it didn't really matter.

"She works both places, doesn't she?" Max said in idle recollection. "It's our bad luck that he hooked up with the Garners so soon after he hit town. But it could explain why Echohawk was so quick to look our direction for the source of the Cee Bar's problems. It's odd though," he added on further thought.

"What is?"

"Let me put it this way—Empty will likely go to his grave still nursing a grudge against us, but I thought the girl had let go of the past."

"She met with Echohawk, didn't she?" Boone reminded him.

"But why at Tillie's? Why at a place where she had to know we would be told about her meeting?"

Boone shrugged. "Maybe she doesn't care if we know."

"If she doesn't, she will," Max stated with a finality that suggested that matter was settled in his mind. He picked up his spoon and dipped it into the oatmeal. "As for the three men who jumped Echohawk, right after dinner you can go tell them to pack their bags and head for the feedlot outside Plano. I don't want them showing their faces around here until all their bruises have disappeared."

"If you say so." But Boone regarded it as a needless precaution. "You should know, though, that they're hoping for a bonus."

"I'd say they've already gotten one. They aren't fired. Maybe they'll get the message to do what they're told—and nothing more than that." Max scooped more oatmeal into his spoon. "What have you learned about Echohawk's hired man? Is he from the Triple C?"

"I don't know yet."

"Then find out," Max ordered with thinning patience. "I want to know who he is, what he drives, and where he's staying. And I want to know it yesterday!"

"I wish you'd make up your damned mind," Boone muttered, pushing the words through tightly clenched teeth. "First you're telling me to do something about that semi load of hay he's got coming. Now it's the hired man."

Max threw him a scornful look. "What's the matter? Can't you do two things at once?"

The words were a verbal slap. "Of course I can!" Boone asserted in a voice that vibrated with pent-up fury.

"Then do it," Max snapped in return.


Saddle leather creaked, a companion sound to the muffled thud of hooves on hard-packed ground. Overhead, the afternoon sun sat at a high angle, its yellow glare shining in a milk-blue sky. An idle breeze wandered over and down the Texas hills, its breath carrying the warmth and faint tang of the gulf shore.

Quint sat easy in the saddle, his hand light on the reins. The bruise along his cheekbone was a colorful swirl of purple and green, but the swelling had gone down. A simple bandage covered the cut above his eyebrow. Other than a lingering puffiness around one corner of his mouth, he looked none the worse for his run-in with the trio in Tillie's parking lot.

A quick drumming of hoofbeats came from his right. Quint glanced that way as Empty Garner flushed two cows out of a draw and sent them trotting after the rest of the herd. Twenty feet beyond him was the fence line, every inch of it without cover and empty of cattle.

His job finished, Empty reined his horse away from the cows and took aim on Quint, lifting his mount into a lope to rejoin him. Quint pulled up to wait for him and dug the notepad and pencil out of his pocket to add the last two animals to his tally.

With a short tug on the reins, Empty checked his horse's gait and swung alongside Quint. "Like it or not, that's the last of them in this pasture." He eyed the marks on the notepaper in Quint's hand. "Is the tally the same as the first?"

"Exactly the same." Quint wasn't surprised by that, but he wasn't pleased either as he returned the tally book and pencil to his pocket.

"I didn't figure we'd missed any, but there was always a chance we might have." Empty rested both hands on the saddle horn, one on top of the other, and slanted a knowing look at Quint. "I told you to expect it."

"To be honest, Empty," Quint said, allowing a slight smile to curve his mouth, careful not to let it be too wide and open the cut inside the corner of his mouth, "I would have been shocked if you were wrong."

Empty grunted an acknowledgment and declared, "Rutledge don't miss a trick and that's a fact." He ran a sidelong glance over the multicolored bruise high on Quint's cheek. "Though, I've got to admit I never figured he'd sic his boys on you so quick."

"It was my mistake for stopping in there for a beer." But it was Dallas that Quint was thinking about, just as he had countless times in the last two days.

By now she would have heard from Rutledge, either directly or indirectly. Quint could only hope that a warning was all she received. As much as he wanted to make certain she was all right, he knew he had to keep his distance from her.

"Best do your drinking here at the Cee Bar from now on—and damned little of it," Empty advised.

"I've never been much of a drinking man." Quint collected the reins and swung his horse toward the ranch yard.

Empty followed suit, riding parallel with him while automatically running a rancher's assessing eye over the pasture condition. "Good thing you got hay coming. The graze is getting pretty thin."

"I noticed."

"It could be worse, though," Empty continued. "Old Ellis Baxter used to own this section. He was one of those progressive kind, always hot to do what some government expert claimed was right." Empty punctuated the statement with a derisive snort. "It wouldn't have surprised me if Baxter had seeded his whole place with that damned government Love Grass. It's the most worthless stuff ever put on earth. Cattle won't eat it. But that damned Love Grass chokes out all the native grasses. As far as I'm concerned, it's nothing but a fire hazard."

As always, Quint listened when the retired rancher opined on a subject. The old man reminded him of the veteran hands at the Triple C, whose storehouse of knowledge and experience they had always been ready to share with him, from the time he was knee-high. They had taught him a healthy respect for the old ways, which often turned out to be the best ways.

"Thought I'd tackle that mesquite in the south pasture tomorrow," Empty remarked. "You turn your back on that stuff and before you know it, it's taken over the whole pasture. Then you gotta play brush-popper to get the cattle out of it, and I'm too old to be tearing pell-mell through a bunch of scrub. You only need to drive to the coastal plains or over in west Texas to see what a plague mesquite's become. An old-timer once told me that whole area used to be a sea of grass. Now it's damned near a forest of mesquite."

"I heard." In his mind, Quint summoned up an image of the grass ocean that covered the Triple C Ranch in Montana. The image quickly dissipated, scattered by the muted jingle of the cell phone in his jacket pocket. Retrieving it, he flipped it open. "Cee Bar."

His aunt's familiar voice responded with sharp clarity, "Hello, Quint. It's Jessy."

"Back home, are you?" he guessed. "How was the wedding?"

"Huge and beautiful—everything Laura wanted it to be. I'm just glad it's over and I'm back home where I belong," she stated with conviction. "How are things down there? Laredo mentioned that you'd run across some problems."

Quint brought her up to date on the current status. "I talked to the mechanic this morning. It was sugar in the gas tank. But all the repairs on the pickup should be finished next week sometime. As for finding another feed store to supply us with grain, there's no need to do that until I start running low. We just finished the tally on the cattle and came up twenty-seven head short."

"Stolen, no doubt."

"That's my guess. Since I don't know how many were in any given pasture, I can't even pinpoint where the loss occurred."

"Or when," Jessy added.

Quint hesitated only briefly. "You might as well know that I was jumped by three men Saturday night," he said and gave her a thumbnail sketch of the events, omitting any mention of Dallas. "I came out of it with nothing more than a little cut and some bruises, but I'd appreciate it if you wouldn't mention anything about it to my mother."

"I won't say anything for now," she agreed. "But I don't like the sound of this, Quint."

"Don't blow it out of proportion like my mom would. We're talking about three cowboys trying to pound home a message. If professionals had delivered it, I'd probably be talking to you from a hospital bed."

"Just the same," Jessy began with an obvious note of concern for his well-being.

"Nothing's changed, Jessy," Quint stated calmly. "There's no one at the Triple C better qualified for this than I am."

"That's true," she said. There was a smile in her voice when she recalled, "When you were a boy, you always finished any job you started. You haven't changed in that. I would feel easier, though, if you had someone there with you. Laredo mentioned that you'd found a hired man to work at the Cee Bar? Is he someone you can trust?"

"Without question."

"That's good then. What about the hay you ordered? Has it arrived?"

"It's supposed to be here Wednesday morning," he told her.

"Good." After a few more questions, Jessy drew their conversation to a close. "Keep me posted on what's happening, especially if you have any further trouble. I won't tell you to be careful. I know you always are."

"Always." Quint smiled. "Tell Mom I'll talk to her tonight."

"I'll tell her," Jessy promised.

Lines of thought creased her forehead as Jessy hung up the phone. The sound of the receiver rocking into its cradle roused the aged Chase Calder from his idle daydreams. More and more these days his mind had a tendency to wander, finding little to hold its attention for any length of time.

Yanked unexpectedly back into the present, Chase struggled to ascertain what that was. Flames leaped and crackled over the logs stacked in the den's massive stone fireplace. Chase was vaguely conscious of the warmth radiating from it and of the weight of the blanket robe that covered his legs.

Almost belatedly he focused on the tall, slender woman behind the desk, but he was quick to detect the slightly troubled look in her expression. He had an instant recall that she had picked up the phone to call Quint in Texas.

"What's wrong?" Chase couldn't remember hearing Jessy talking to anyone. "Wasn't Quint there?"

"I talked to him," Jessy confirmed, the small lines vanishing from her forehead, her expression again showing the calm, steady composure that served her so well. "He has everything under control there."

Chase leaned forward in the wing-backed chair. "You told him about the hay, didn't you?"

Jessy gave him a bewildered look. "The hay? He said it wasn't scheduled to arrive until Wednesday. Was I supposed to tell him something about that?"

Chase sank back in his chair, not at all certain that he had told Jessy of his suspicions. "I can't see Rutledge letting him have it. He'll try something. He'll have to. Quint needs to know that."

"He said he was going to call Cat tonight. I'll let her know that I need to talk to him—and mention it then."

Yet Chase's concern only reminded Jessy of the assault on Quint by three men. When she had sent Quint to Texas, she had strongly suspected, like Chase, that the Cee Bar's problems were caused by an outside source. But Jessy had never really believed she was putting Quint in any physical danger. Now she couldn't ignore the possibility.

"Chase, is it really important that we keep the Cee Bar?" Ultimately such a decision was Jessy's to make, but the habit of seeking her father-in-law's counsel was too deeply ingrained for her not to ask the question of him. "It's always been more of a financial liability than an asset to the Triple C."

She expected him to come back with his usual answer—that Calder land was never for sale. This time Chase didn't speak off the top of his head, but gave her question considerably more thought before offering a reply.

"The day may come when selling it is the right move. But it will never be right if someone is trying to force that sale. You'd be showing weakness. Others will see it." His gaze was hard with warning. "When they do, you could find yourself in a fight for the Triple C."

Jessy recalled the number of times something similar had happened during Chase's life. She wanted to believe those days were gone, but she realized that the old-time range wars weren't all that different from the hostile takeovers of modern day. Only the tactics had changed.

After wrapping up a report on the current trend in the grain market, the radio announcer moved on to opening livestock prices. Dallas listened with only half an ear and smothered another yawn, fighting the fatigue that came from burning the midnight oil too long the night before. She reached for her coffee cup only to find it nearly empty.

With a frustrated sigh, she rolled her chair back from the desk and carried her cup over to the coffeepot that sat atop the table along a side wall, accessible to any customers of the feed store. She refilled her cup with the strong brew and glanced idly at her boss.

Holly Sykes stood in front of the big window facing the highway. He'd been standing there when she arrived for work at eight o'clock, and had hardly budged from the spot since. Dallas had the impression he was watching for something or someone, but she was too tired to summon up any curiosity as to who or what that might be.

As she started back to her desk, she barely registered the familiar rumble of a semi. Holly Sykes took a quick step closer to the window, his sudden movement attracting her attention. She glanced out the window to identify the cause of his sudden interest and saw a semi hauling a flatbed trailer loaded with round hay bales.

The minute it passed, Holly abruptly pivoted away from the window and made a beeline for his desk. Dallas immediately guessed that the hay was destined for the Cee Bar. He picked up his phone and rapidly punched a set of numbers.

"It's Sykes. It just went by." That was the extent of his conversation.

There wasn't any doubt in her mind that he'd called the Slash R Ranch. The briefness of it was similar to the curt warning Holly had delivered when she showed up for work Monday morning.

"Stay away from that guy at the Cee Bar," he'd said. "You won't be told twice."

Dallas had a heavy feeling in the pit of her stomach when she thought of Quint. The odds were clearly stacked against him. She was suddenly angry and depressed, both at the same time.

Boone flipped the cell phone shut and sent a sidelong glance at the uniformed deputy behind the wheel of the patrol car. There was a dark glitter in his eyes that Deputy Joe Ed Krause found difficult to meet. And the smile that quirked Boone's mouth didn't make him feel any more comfortable.

"The truck just rolled into town," Boone told him. "You know what you're supposed to do."

Joe Ed bobbed his head in a quick nod and repeated the instructions, "I wait until after he's delivered the hay, let him get a mile or so down the road, then pull him over. In the meantime, I'm to stay out of sight."

Satisfied, Boone passed him some folded bills. "Just to show we appreciate the favor, take your wife out to dinner."

"You didn't have to do that." Joe Ed was quick to notice the top bill was a twenty and stuffed it all in his pocket. "You know I'm happy to oblige if I can."

"Like I said, we appreciate it," Boone said and climbed out of the car.

The deputy kept one eye on the rearview mirror, tracking Boone's progress as he made his way to the pickup parked behind the patrol car. The money felt good in his pocket. If he had any regrets, it was that there weren't more favors he could do for the Rutledges.

Less than a minute later, Boone swung his pickup around the patrol car and accelerated down the country road. Deciding that this was as good a place as any to kill time, Joe Ed settled back in the driver's seat, calculating that it would take the semi between fifteen and twenty minutes to reach the Cee Bar and somewhere around an hour to unload its hay.

Scant minutes after he arrived at the intersection a half mile down the road from the Cee Bar's entrance, Joe Ed spotted the semi coming down the ranch lane, its trailer empty. Waiting, he let it go past him, then pulled onto the road behind it. He followed for a good mile before he flipped on his lights. He smiled to himself, imagining the way the truck driver was cussing, certain there was no cause for getting pulled over.

Air brakes whooshed as the semi slowed and swung onto the shoulder. Joe Ed stopped behind him and took his time getting out of the patrol car, then dawdled at the rear of the trailer.

The driver swung down from the cab. Of average height and build, he looked to be in his early twenties.

"What's the problem, Officer?" His attempt to sound pleasant failed to mask the driver's underlying impatience.

"Your taillights kept blinking on and off," Joe Ed lied. "You probably have a short or loose connection somewhere."

The driver frowned in surprise. "They've been working fine." But there was new doubt in his voice.

"Didn't I just see you pull out of the Cee Bar Ranch?"

"Yeah, I dropped off a bunch of hay for them." The driver was already busy checking to make sure the connections were tight.

"As rough as that lane is, it wouldn't surprise me if something jiggled loose," the deputy remarked, then feigned nonchalance. "Say, does Red Parker still work there?"

"Couldn't say." The driver shrugged in indifference.

"I know he used to. He's hard to miss. His hair is as red as fire."

"Neither of the men I saw had red hair."

"They didn't." The deputy tried to sound disappointed. "The men you saw—what did they look like?"

"One was tall with black hair, maybe thirty. He's the one who signed for the hay. The other one was an old guy," the driver answered without any real interest.

"An old guy," Joe Ed repeated thoughtfully, then eyed the young driver. "What was he, forty? Fifty?"

"Hell, he looked seventy, if he was a day," the driver declared with a typical amusement of the young for the ancient. "But he sure knew how to work that tractor."

"Red isn't anywhere close to seventy. I guess it wasn't him. I wonder who the old guy is. You didn't happen to catch his name, did you?"

"No, we didn't get around to introductions. The other guy, though, he had an Indian name. Grayhawk or something like that." He paused, shooting the deputy a curious look. "Is it important?"

"Naw," he said with a quick shake of his head. "I was just curious." He flicked a hand at the trailer's taillights. "When you get down the road, you might want to have somebody make sure your lights are working right."

Back in the patrol car, Joe Ed pulled onto the road, eager to reach his prearranged meeting place with Boone Rutledge and relay the information he had gleaned from the truck driver. There was an excitement in knowing that there might be a way for him to earn more money. The question of whether it was ethical or not never arose. He didn't know of a single cop who didn't do some moonlighting during his off-duty hours.

*   *   *

The reds and golds of sunset streaked the western sky, tinting the Slash R's trademark white fences with a rosy hue. Evening's approach brought a natural slowing of activity. But any impression of calm was shattered by the roaring drone of a helicopter's powerful engine and the rhythmic chop of its rotary blades beating the air as it swooped out of the sky and took aim at the private helipad, located near the main house.

Boone clamped a hand on his hat and angled away from the powerful downdraft that preceded the helicopter's actual touchdown. It was a position he held until he heard the slowing whine of the engine shutting down and felt the abatement of its self-generated wind. He watched while the specially designed lift was rolled up to the passenger door.

The arrival scene was much too commonplace for Boone to marvel at the engineering that enabled his father to exit the aircraft onto a hoist that lowered his wheelchair to the ground, all with an absolute minimum of assistance from others. Impatience with the lift's slow descent was the only thing Boone felt as he waited for his father to join him.

At last the wheelchair came rolling toward him in its nearly noiseless glide, and Boone found himself under the scrutiny of his father's piercing gaze. As always it was difficult to hold. Boone lifted his chin a notch, girding himself with the knowledge that this time he had succeeded beyond his father's expectations. He couldn't possibly find fault with him.

"Well, well, well," Max Rutledge declared, his mouth twisting in a sardonic smile, "if it isn't my son on hand to greet me. That can only mean you have something of importance to tell me."

"I do," Boone acknowledged, irritated that he hadn't waited in the house.

"Spill it." Max gestured in annoyance at the delay. "Tell me this great news of yours."

Boone bristled at the ridicule in his father's voice and flicked an

113

irritated glance at Harold Barnett, his father's valet and full-time nurse, who now joined them. It galled him to have others hear the way his father spoke to him.

"I wouldn't call it great news—or even good news," Boone stated curtly. "But it is news."

There was a slight pause as Max's gaze sharpened on him, assessing the meaning of his statement. "You know who the hired man is."

"You aren't going to like it," Boone warned, secretly pleased about that. "It's Empty Garner."

"Garner," Max repeated, bitterness pinching his mouth. "That wiley old bastard. We can forget any thought of buying him off. And there isn't much chance of scaring him away either."

"Why would you want to? How much work can an old man like that do? Not much, I'll bet. Echohawk might as well not have anyone working for him as that old man. And that was the point, wasn't it?"

"It was originally," Max agreed, his brow furrowed in heavy thought. "But with Echohawk on the scene, it was time to change tactics."

"When did you decide that?" Boone frowned in surprise. "This is the first I've heard of it."

"There's a lot you don't know." The instant he issued the dismissive statement, Max engaged the control stick and sent the wheelchair spinning toward the side entrance to the house.

Boone stood flat-footed for an angry second, then strode after him. But the wheelchair's speed, the valet's presence, and the narrow walkway made it impossible for Boone to catch up with his father before he entered the house.

Simmering with resentment, he followed his father into the den and peeled off to the bar where he poured himself a straight shot of bourbon and tossed it down, welcoming the choking fire that closed off his throat. He refilled the glass, diluted the bourbon with water, and threw in some cubes.

After a galvanizing sip of it, Boone glared across the room at his father and challenged, "What about the hay?"

"What about it?" Max countered with annoyance.

"Since you're changing tactics," Boone began, his lip curling, "I thought that might go for the hay as well."

"As usual, you're wrong."

"I thought I'd better make sure. After all, the last I heard, you had issued standing orders that no one was to be allowed to work at Cee Bar for long. Since that's changed, I thought the one about the hay might have, too."

"It hasn't." Max removed some papers from the briefcase that Harold Barnett had placed on the desk, then issued a curt nod of dismissal to the man.

"Then what's different?" Boone demanded, unable to tolerate being kept in the dark.

"Echohawk. I don't like it that we're blind and deaf to what's going on over there." The troubled scowl Max wore gave credence to his statement. "The hay is a good example. If we had known who he was getting it from, there was a good chance we could have blocked the purchase. As it is, we're forced to react. We need somebody on the inside who can let us know Echohawk's intentions in advance. And there's only one way to do that—plant one of our own men. But we don't stand a chance of tricking Echohawk into hiring someone as long as Garner's in the picture."

"All you have to do is set back and wait for the old man to work himself to death," Boone said with a shrug.

"I have no intention of waiting that long," Max snapped in reply.

"Why not? You said yourself that Echohawk was suspicious," Boone reminded him. "If we lie low for a while, sooner or later the Calders will pull him out and send in someone else. We've waited this long to get that ranch. What's a few more months?"

"That's what you'd do, isn't it?" Max jeered. "You find yourself in a fight and you want to back off and wait until the going gets easier. This is when you have to get tough and clamp down hard."

"I just thought—"

"You thought," Max repeated in a voice thick with contempt. "That was your first mistake—thinking." He closed the briefcase with a snap and sank back in his wheelchair, propping an elbow on the armrest and rubbing a spot just above his eyebrow with three fingers. "Now shut up for a while so I can figure out what to do about Garner."

Smarting from the stream of insults, Boone retaliated, "As smart as you are I'm surprised you haven't already figured it out."

When his taunt failed to draw a response, he bolted down half of his drink and swung around to replenish it, his insides churning and his nerves raw. Needing to blame someone, Boone chose the first one that came to mind—the one who had sparked the heated exchange, that tough old bird Empty Garner.

Boone was certain that if he ever got his hands on that old man, he'd soon show his father that Garner wasn't so tough. There would be fear in the old rancher's eyes when he was done— enough that he would be too scared to tell anyone. Not even his granddaughter.

Boone lifted his head, letting his mind wrap around the thought that had just sprung into it. He turned, confidence once more surging through him as he again faced his father.

"There is a way." But his statement drew no response. Boone raised his voice in a demand to be heard. "I said there's a way to get to the old man."

"Really?" Max flicked him a jaundiced look.

"It's one you'll like."

Max released an exasperated sigh and demanded, "And what would that be?"

"Have you forgotten the old man has a granddaughter?"

# Chapter Eight

The sun was directly overhead, shrinking the shadows around the feed store to mere dark slits. Aided by the sun's warming influence, the thermometer mounted on the outside of the building registered a temperature in the low seventies.

An hour ago, Holly Sykes had taken advantage of the balmy weather and propped the front door open. Dallas welcomed the stimulating freshness of the air and ignored the dust that occasionally swirled in with it. The boost to her lagging energy had come at just the right time. She dragged in another deep breath of it and let it out in a weary sigh.

With only one more final exam to take, Dallas reminded herself that after tomorrow night, the stress and long hours would all be over. There would be no more classes until after the first of the year. Dallas suspected it might take that long to catch up on all her missed sleep.

With the printer chattering away in the background, Dallas continued the mindless task of paper-clipping the appropriate receipts to their invoice, ready for the check to be attached. This was one time when she was grateful for the tedious side of getting the payables done.

"I don't see how you can hear yourself think with that racket going on." The deep, male voice came from a point somewhere near her right shoulder.

Startled, Dallas jerked her head around and felt a jolt of shock when she saw Boone Rutledge looming tall next to her desk. Her gaze swept hastily up the muscled expanse of his chest and shoulders to the hard and manly angles of his face and halted when it encountered the steady regard of his dark eyes. For a split second, she felt oddly trapped.

"Sorry." Dallas hastily rolled her chair back from the desk and stood. "I guess I didn't hear you come in."

"How could you, as noisy as that thing is?" He nodded in the direction of the printer, busily spitting out checks.

"It is loud," she agreed and glanced at the empty chair in front of her boss's desk. "Were you looking for Holly? He was here just a minute ago. I'll—"

"I saw him outside," Boone interrupted. "I stopped in for a salt block, and he went to get it, said you'd write me a ticket to sign."

"Be happy to." Dallas immediately headed for the front counter, privately doubting that it was his sole purpose for coming in.

Ever since she had come to work at the feed store, whenever the Slash R wanted something it was either delivered or collected by a ranch hand. To her knowledge, Boone Rutledge had never picked up anything.

"You need to have Holly get you a new printer, one that's quieter." Boone sauntered up to the counter and leaned a hip against it inches from her, watching while she began filling out the ticket.

"I'll tell him—and mention that you said so," Dallas added, openly acknowledging the power of the Rutledge name but with a trace of reckless defiance in the look she gave him.

Boone smiled in response, but with a satisfaction that made Dallas uncomfortable. Or maybe it was the way his gaze traveled over her, taking note of the upswell of her breasts and the full curve of her lips.

"It's not often that beauty and brains are wrapped in the same package," he murmured. "But you seem to have both."

Dallas held her tongue with an effort and pushed the completed ticket over to him. "Sign anywhere."

He glanced at the ticket, then back at her. "Got a pen?"

With tension licking along her nerve ends, Dallas silently offered her ballpoint pen to him. He took it while seeming to make sure his fingers brushed hers. Dallas tried to convince herself that she only imagined the contact was deliberate. Yet it didn't diminish the urge to wash her hands.

As Boone scratched his name across the ticket, Holly Sykes walked through the door, mopping his forehead with a blue bandana. "Dallas got you all fixed up, did she?" he observed.

"She certainly did." Boone laid the pen aside and waited while Dallas separated his copy of the ticket from the rest. "I thought I'd swing by the Corner Café for lunch. Why don't you join me?"

She thought he was talking to Holly until she glanced up and discovered he was looking straight her. "Sorry, I wasn't paying attention. Did you say something to me?" she asked, to stall for time.

"I asked you to have lunch with me." But his tone was more of a command than a request.

Dallas took a chance just the same. "Thanks, but I brought mine."

He never blinked. "Save it for tomorrow."

Even as she searched for a plausible excuse to refuse, Dallas didn't fool herself into thinking his interest was personal—or, at least, not the man-woman kind.

"Now, you aren't still holding a grudge because your grandfather lost his ranch, are you?" Boone chided lightly.

"Of course not," she replied, unable to classify the strong distrust she felt as a grudge.

"Then quit your hemming and hawing around," Holly Sykes inserted, "and get going. I can handle the store while you're gone."

Seeing no way out, Dallas gave in to the inevitable. "It will take me a couple minutes to log off the computer and straighten my desk," she told Boone. "Why don't I meet you there?"

He hesitated, then nodded. "I'll be waiting."

His words seemed to carry a warning that if she didn't show up, he'd be back. Dallas had already figured that out for herself.

By the time Dallas parked her pickup in front of the Corner Café, she had reached the conclusion she had been wrong to think the warning from Sykes on Monday was the only one she would receive. Obviously Max Rutledge felt another one should be given to underscore the first, and he had sent Boone to deliver it. Although why Boone hadn't issued it at the feed store she didn't know.

"And the condemned ate a hearty meal," Dallas murmured under her breath as she walked into the café.

She faltered ever so slightly when she saw Boone seated at the table Quint always occupied. Had he known that? she wondered, then reminded herself that nothing happened in this town that the Rutledges didn't know about.

Her chin lifted a fraction of an inch as Dallas mentally steeled herself to get through this meeting without saying or doing something she would ultimately regret.

At her approach, Boone rose and pulled out the chair to his right. Dallas smiled a little stiffly and sat down, belatedly noticing that the nearest tables were empty of customers, providing an island of privacy in a public place. Something Boone had no doubt arranged.

The isolation added to the tension she already felt. Needing something to occupy her hands, she reached for the menu.

"You mean you don't have it memorized?" Boone remarked with amusement.

"Just checking to see what today's lunch special is," she replied.

Tension had robbed Dallas of her appetite, but when the waitress arrived, she ordered a bowl of homemade beef stew and coffee. Coffee probably wasn't the best choice of drink, she realized afterward, considering how tightly strung her nerves already were.

"A bowl of stew—that isn't much of a meal," Boone remarked.

"Too much food makes me sleepy, and I have a full afternoon's work ahead of me." Dallas propped the menu back against the napkin holder, aware that his gaze hadn't strayed from her.

"I'm sure Holly will appreciate that. He says you're good at your job."

"I try to be." Dallas was certain this small talk was simply a means to kill time until the waitress returned with their drink orders. She was impatient with it just the same.

"According to Holly, you succeeded." He stretched out one long leg and hooked an arm over a corner of the chair's backrest. "As warm as it is today, it's hard to believe Christmas is just around the corner. Do you have all your shopping done?"

"All the presents are bought, wrapped, and under the tree."

"I wish I could say the same." He rocked his chair onto its rear legs, making room for the returning waitress when she reached across him and set his mug of coffee on the table.

She placed another cup in front of Dallas and beamed a smile at Boone, promising, "Your order should be up shortly."

"We're in no hurry," Boone told her.

Dallas could have disputed that, but she reached for her coffee instead. Steam rose in curling wisps from the hot coffee. She blew lightly on its surface before taking a sip.

"Holly tells me you're taking night classes at Texas Christian," Boone said over the lip of his own coffee mug.

"That's right." Dallas was brief with her answer, eager to cut to the chase and get this ordeal over with.

"You're carrying quite a load on your shoulders—commuting to school, holding down a full-time job, and working here at the café on your free nights."

"I'm used to it." If he was attempting to remind her of all she stood to lose, Dallas could have told him it was unnecessary.

"It doesn't leave you much time for fun," Boone observed and flashed her a smile. "You know what they say about all work and no play."

"I have all the free time I want. Isn't that the reason you wanted to see me?" Dallas challenged, tired of all this dancing around the issue. "Because I had a drink with Quint Echohawk Saturday night?"

His eyes narrowed, but the amused smile remained. "What gave you that idea?"

"I wonder." There was a wealth of mockery in her dry response. "It couldn't be because Holly has already warned me about seeing him again."

"It's probably good advice, considering there wouldn't be much future in a relationship with him. Sooner or later he'll be on his way back to Montana."

It was a likelihood that hadn't occurred to Dallas before now. It left her feeling flat, even though she had already decided against seeing him again, aware that she had too much to lose.

For the first time, though, Dallas was confused. "If you didn't invite me to lunch to warn me about Quint, just why am I here?"

"Maybe I just wanted the pleasure of your company."

Again she felt the slow rake of his glance. "Everyone knows you want the pleasure of any woman's company, Boone." She was careful to keep any emotion out of her voice.

"Most men do," he countered smoothly and unhooked his arm off the backrest to lean forward and curve both hands around the mug. "But you're right. As much as I am enjoying your company, it wasn't the sole reason I asked you here."

"And that is?" Dallas prompted, both curious and wary.

"First, I think you should know how impressed my father is with the way you've dug in and started carving out a new life for yourself. There aren't many people willing to hold down two jobs, carry nearly a full load of college courses at night, and maintain a better than three-point-oh grade average. He feels such intelligence and determination should be rewarded."

"Really?" Dallas instantly doubled her guard.

"He's interested in providing you with a full ride. Tuition, books, a house in Fort Worth, all utilities paid, and a monthly allowance so you won't have to work, not to mention a vehicle to get you around. That old truck of yours can't have many more miles on it before it breaks down. In short, he's prepared to be very generous."

"Forgive me," Dallas began in a tightly controlled voice, an anger simmering, its origin unknown, "but everyone knows that your father is only generous when he's getting something in return. So what's the catch?"

Boone's smile widened a little. "Your grandfather."

"What about him?" She felt a lick of fear along her spine.

"Where is he now?"

"At home, of course." But Dallas was suddenly uncertain about that.

Boone took a cell phone from his pocket and handed it to her. "Call him."

Hesitating, she searched his face. He looked a little too smug and a lot too certain of himself for her peace of mind. Dallas didn't like jumping through the hoop he held, but there seemed to be few other choices. She punched in the phone number and pushed the Send button, then lifted the cell phone to her ear.

It rang once, twice, three times with still no answer. Dallas stole a glance at Boone while he calmly sipped his coffee. Four, five, six, seven times it rang. After the eighth, the answering machine clicked on and Dallas broke the connection.

"As nice as it is today, he's probably puttering outside," she said, more to convince herself than Boone.

"He's probably outside, all right," Boone agreed. "But you can bet he isn't anywhere near that old trailer you're living in."

What had been only a vague suspicion now became a full-blown certainty. "You knew he wasn't there, didn't you?" Dallas accused in a cold fury. "Where is he? What have you done with him? So help me, if you have laid one hand on Empty—"

"We have nothing to do with your grandfather being gone," Boone cut in, all cool and composed. "You're talking to the wrong person."

"Then where is he?" she demanded.

"Ask Echohawk," he replied with a shrug.

"Quint?" Dallas frowned in surprise. "What does he have to do with this?"

"Your grandfather works for him."

"That's a lie." Her denial was quick and heated, an instant reaction to the shock of his statement.

"Believe me, it's true," Boone stated.

"He couldn't—he wouldn't—" Dallas felt sick inside, knowing it was exactly the kind of thing her grandfather would do. Yet parts of it made no sense. "I don't understand. I mean, how—" She couldn't finish the question, finding it somehow disloyal.

Boone guessed at the question. "How did he get back and forth to the Cee Bar when you have the truck? Echohawk picks him up around eight o'clock in the morning after you've already left for work—and brings him back between four-thirty and five."

Dallas withheld any comment, her thoughts spinning so fast she couldn't separate them into anything coherent. The silence stretched a little longer as Boone waited, clearly expecting her to say something. But there was nothing she could say. And she certainly wasn't going to offer any apologies or excuses for her grandfather's actions, not to a Rutledge.

"Your grandfather is a very foolish old man," Boone said at last.

For all the ease in his voice, there was an unmistakable note of threat in it. Dallas felt cold to the bone. It was fear that gave birth to fury.


A long line of big, round bales stood caterpillar-like along the pasture fence, one hump flowing into the next. The length and bulk of them dominated the view from the Cee Bar's ranch yard.

The hay bales were the first thing Quint saw when he emerged from the barn, one arm hooked around the half dozen steel posts balanced on one shoulder. He crossed to the rear of the black pickup, hoisted the posts off his shoulder, and slid them across the lowered tailgate into the truck bed next to the roll of fence wire.

When he stepped back from the truck, the loud clanging of a rod being struck against an old iron triangle shattered the stillness. Quint automatically glanced toward the house, knowing it had to be Empty Garner. The minute the old rancher had come across the triangle hanging behind a half-rotted leather harness in the barn, he'd held it up triumphantly.

"I was getting danged tired of wearing myself out hollering for you to come eat," he'd declared. "You can be a mile away and still hear this."

Quint had yet to be a mile from the ranch yard, but, as loud as that clanging was, he was convinced the sound would carry that far.

He spotted the old rancher standing at the end of the porch. Before he could raise a hand, acknowledging that he'd heard the signal, Empty Garner cupped a hand to his mouth and shouted, "Soup's hot."

Answering with a wave, Quint turned and struck out for the house, absently tugging off his leather work gloves. Empty waited for him at the top of the porch steps, hands on his hips and a serenely pleased expression on his weathered face as he gazed at a point beyond Quint's shoulder.

"Pretty sight, isn't it?" Empty gestured at the hay when Quint joined him on the porch. "And just about as satisfying as watching those cows tear into the one I hauled out to them yesterday afternoon."

Automatically turning to survey the row of bales, Quint idly tucked his gloves in the rear pocket of his Wranglers. "We'll need more before the winter's over, but this gets us on our way."

"It sure enough does that," the rancher declared and grinned. "Don't you know Rutledge is over there in that big house of his gnashing his teeth in frustration?"

"Probably." Quint allowed a small smile of satisfaction to curve his mouth.

"Savor this while you can." Experience wiped the grin from the rancher's face. " 'Cause you've got to know Rutledge is over there cooking up something else. And chances are it won't be anything you'll expect."

Quint didn't dispute the truth in Empty's statement, aware that Max Rutledge wouldn't be quick to give up the fight. It would take him a while to realize that he had come up against somebody who wouldn't bow to pressure. It wasn't part of the Calder makeup to back down.

"Whatever it is, we'll handle it when it comes," Quint stated with certainty.

As he started to turn toward the house, he caught the distinctive rumble of a vehicle's engine. It sounded close, too close to be anything traveling on the road. His glance instantly swung to the ranch lane.

"I think we're about to have company," he said to Empty when the rumble grew louder.

"And coming fast, too," Empty added, like Quint, fixing his gaze on the bend in the lane that would offer their first view of their noonday visitor.

Within seconds, a battered white pickup, traveling a little too fast, careened around the curve, straightened itself out, and accelerated again toward the ranch yard, dust pluming behind it. Quint's eyes narrowed on it in a mixture of surprise and uncertainty.

He shot a questioning look at the old rancher. "That looks like your truck, Empty."

Empty hastily ducked his head and pivoted toward the door, muttering, "Better check on that soup 'fore it boils over."

Quint had little time to wonder why Empty was so eager to slip into the house. The white pickup had already reached the ranch yard. It made an initial swing toward the barn before the wheel was jerked, aiming the pickup at the house. As it plowed to a stop, kicking up more dust, Quint came down the steps to meet its occupant.

He halted in surprise when Dallas piled out of the cab and charged up the walk to him, her copper hair glinting in the sunlight, a crackling, contagious energy in her swift stride. There was a great swelling lift of emotion within him, something powerful and nameless.

"Dallas." He had barely uttered her name when the flat of her hand whacked against his jaw.

All of her weight was behind the swing, the impact of it sufficient to knock Quint off balance. She was on him in a flash, unleashing a torrent of abuse. Quint was too busy fending off the forceful blows aimed at his head to make sense of any of it.

His fingers finally closed around a slim wrist. Its capture made the snaring of its twin much easier. But it only intensified her fury as she struggled and kicked.

With his own anger growing, Quint twisted her arms behind her back, bringing her up hard against his body. "What the hell's going on?" he demanded, looking down at pale brown eyes that seemed to glitter with hatred.

"You dirty lying bastard." Her voice vibrated with bitter loathing. "All that talk about not wanting to cause trouble for anyone—it was nothing but a lie."

"What are you talking about?" he demanded again.

"Just let me go!" She struggled wildly, her voice rising. "You're no better than Rutledge. Do you hear? I swear I could kill you."

Hatred poured from her, the harshness of it at odds with the rounded feel of her body pressed so snugly against him. With her lips forming more vicious accusations, Quint had only one thought and that was to silence them.

He clamped his mouth across hers, smothering her gurgle of outrage. There was an anger of his own in the driving pressure of his mouth, an anger that it was her hatred she was heaping on him when it was something else he wanted. And a bitterness, too, that she would believe those things about him.

But the natural pliancy of her lips soon awakened needs of another kind. Quint felt the ache of it in his loins and in his chest. It was a regret that it was never likely to be between them that had him easing up on the pressure.

Only when he lifted his head did he notice that she stood motionless, no longer struggling to break free. In absolute silence, she stared back at him, all wide-eyed and a little stunned.

"That's a fast way of shutting her up when she blows her temper." Empty's marveling voice made Quint aware that they weren't alone.

Breathing a little heavier than normal, Quint released her wrists from his cuffing grip and stepped back from her. The separation seemed to allow his mind to return to its logical thought pattern.

"I take it Dallas is your granddaughter," he said to Empty without letting his gaze stray from her face.

"You didn't know?" she murmured, not at all certain she should believe that.

"How could I?" Quint countered. "I don't even know your last name. In case you've forgotten, we never got around to introductions."

"No, we didn't," she admitted, dropping her glance to a midway point on his chest. It snapped back to his face, with some of its previous fire. "How could you do it? Why on earth did you have to hire him to work here? For heaven's sake, he's an old man! He's been through enough!"

"You hold it right there, young lady," Empty cut in sharply. "Before you throw out any more accusations, you'd better get your facts straight. It was me that approached Quint about working here, not the other way around."

"It doesn't matter whose idea it was," Dallas retorted hotly. "It still ends up the same—you're working here. Didn't either of you think that Rutledge wouldn't find that out?"

"I expected it." But Quint hadn't expected that it would involve Dallas in any way.

Empty dragged in a deep breath and sighed it out, then arched a knowing look at Quint. "Like I said a minute ago, trouble never comes from the place where you think it will." With a certain grimness, he redirected his attention to Dallas. "It's for sure that you didn't accidentally find out I've been working here. I don't think you would've worked yourself up into such a lather all on your own."

"Boone came by the feed store and insisted I have lunch with him," Dallas replied with biting emphasis.

"Obviously there was more to it than that," Quint stated. "We were just about to sit down to lunch ourselves. You might as well come in and tell us what all he had to say."

Dallas hesitated an instant. "I promise you, none of it was good." The heaviness of defeat was in her voice, but she moved past him to the steps.

# Chapter Nine

Upon entering the kitchen of the old ranch house, Dallas immediately busied herself with the task of ladling soup into bowls while Quint washed up at the sink. He dried his hands on a towel and followed when she carried the bowls to the table where Empty was already seated.

Quint pulled out a chair and sat down, conscious that his awareness of her had doubled, adding its own brand of tension to the scene. And that awareness made it impossible for him not to notice the way she seemed to avoid looking at him. He wanted to blame it on the threats Boone Rutledge must have issued, but he had a feeling his rough kiss might have had just as much to do with it.

The instant she set the bowls down, Dallas moved away from the table, crossing to the counter where she poured herself a cup of coffee. She brought it back to the table with her and sat down opposite her grandfather.

Empty glanced at the cup. "Aren't you going to eat any soup?"

"I'm not hungry. And I couldn't eat and talk at the same time anyway." Dallas wrapped both hands around the cup as if fighting off a chill.

"Well, we can listen and eat at the same time, so you might as well tell us what he had to say." Empty crumbled a handful of saltine crackers into his bowl of vegetable beef soup.

After a short nod of agreement, Dallas paused to collect her thoughts, then began, "Like I said, Boone came by the feed store this morning. He used the pretext of picking up a salt block, but the minute he asked me to have lunch with him, I knew he was there to talk to me." Her glance skipped to Quint. "Right away I assumed it was because we had a drink together at Tillie's on Saturday night."

"You've been out with him?" Empty stared at her in surprise.

"He bought me a beer. I don't think that's quite the same as going out with someone," Dallas was quick to add, obviously uncomfortable with the phrase.

"You never mentioned anything about it to me." The rancher's statement bordered on an accusation.

"You were asleep when I got home."

"Wait a minute." Empty lost all interest in his soup and pointed a gnarled finger at Quint. "Saturday night is when those guys roughed you up." His gaze snapped back to Dallas. "Were you there then?"

"I never saw the fight itself," she replied while admitting, with some reluctance, her knowledge of it. "I went looking for him, saw a couple of men running off, and found him in the parking lot."

"And you never said one word about it to me," he said in sharp rebuke.

"If I had, you would have gotten yourself all worked up over Rutledge and the things he gets away with," Dallas said in her own defense. "There just didn't seem to be any point in telling you about it."

"It didn't do you much good. I got upset anyway when I saw his face." Empty flung up a hand, gesturing to indicate Quint and the faint bruises still visible along his cheekbone.

Seeking to end their somewhat heated exchange, Quint remarked,

"I've wondered several times if you'd had any repercussions from Saturday."

"On Monday morning, Sykes was quick to tell me that I'd better stay clear of you if I knew what was good for me. Which was exactly what I expected," Dallas replied, then paused a beat. "That's why I was a little confused when Boone showed up. I couldn't understand why he wanted to take me out to lunch just to repeat what Holly Sykes had already told me. I decided that there was something going on that made Rutledge believe it was necessary to emphasize it."

While she recounted her conversation with Boone Rutledge, Quint went through the motions of eating his soup, but he tasted little of what he put in his mouth. All of his attention was concentrated on Dallas. He had participated in too many interrogations not to know that a person's delivery, tone of voice, and body language often said more than the words.

Control was the strongest impression he had. He saw it in the stiff way she held herself, the care she took in choosing her words, and the tight restraint she kept on her emotions, allowing only hints of bitterness and anger to creep into her voice.

There were places where she hesitated, and each time she slid a quick glance at her grandfather. By the time she finished her story, Quint had the feeling that Dallas was holding something back. Something that she didn't want her grandfather to know. He suspected she was afraid for him, and seeking to hide that fear from her grandfather.

Empty Garner leaned back in his chair and hooked his thumbs through the belt loops on his jeans. "So all of Boone's talk boils down to one thing—if I don't quit working here, Rutledge is going to see that you lose your job and likely put our truck out of commission, probably by using that old trick of pouring sugar into the gas tank. Then, just to sweeten the pot, he tells you that if you talk me into quitting, his pa might be predisposed to paying for your college."

"It seems to me," Quint began, "the only thing missing is a veiled suggestion that some harm might come to Empty if he refused. Or did you just omit that part, Dallas?" He never altered the idle tone of his voice, letting all the challenge be in his words.

She shot him a look of sharp reproach, unaware of the glimmer of pain in her eyes. "He hinted that something might happen to him," Dallas admitted curtly, "then covered it by reminding me that my grandfather was an old man, well up in years."

"I'm shaking in my boots," Empty declared with thick scorn. "Just let them try something and they'll wish they hadn't."

Quint ignored the old man's boastful words. "What do you think your chances are of getting Boone to repeat the things he told you?"

Dallas eyed him warily. "Why?"

"Because it's extortion. I can arrange to have you miked and get it all on tape—with your agreement, of course," he added.

Her response was a wryly amused smile and a glance at her grandfather.

"Fat lot of good that'll do you." Empty snorted. "Even if you're lucky enough to get him arrested, the old man's got just about every judge in the state in his back pocket. You'll just get one delay on top of another until one day, lo and behold, the tape comes up missing and you've got nothing but your word against his. In the meantime, he's coming at you from a half dozen other directions."

"That sounds like the voice of experience," Quint guessed.

The old man nodded. "I thought I had that old bull Rutledge by the horns when I got his foreman on tape making threats about what might happen if I didn't sell. All charges against him were dismissed for lack of evidence. Even the copy of the tape I'd put in a safety deposit box disappeared. And you can be damned sure I never put it in any of the banks Rutledge owns, but he still managed to get to it. Mind you, I can't prove he did. But I know in my gut it was his doing."

"It might be different this time," Quint said and looked directly at Dallas. "But it's up to you since you're the one who would have to get Boone on tape."

"It would be a waste of time." Her shoulders moved in a vague shrug of dismissal. "After what happened the last time, he'll be suspicious if I try to get him to talk about it again. And you can bet his father will warn him about the last time."

"I guess that settles it then." Quint pushed his chair back from the table and stood up. "I'll write you a check for two weeks' pay, Empty. You can take it with you when you leave."

"Now you just haul back on the reins there, son," Empty said with high indignation. "I don't recall handing in my notice."

Quint smiled, touched by the gesture of loyalty, but it wasn't one he could accept. "The price to work here is a little too steep for you."

"That's for me to decide," the old man insisted.

"I think your granddaughter has a say in it, under the circumstances," Quint reminded him.

Empty never drew a breath. "If Dallas ends up getting fired, she can find herself another job. She's a smart girl and a hard worker. We'll manage."

Quint shook his head and turned away. "I'll get your check."

Dallas spoke up. "If you think that by paying him off, it will mean I'll keep my job, you're wrong."

He halted and made a slow turn to face the pair, leery of misconstruing her statement. "Why would I be wrong?"

There was a slightly combative tilt to her chin. "I guess I never got around to mentioning that I told Boone what he could do with his offer and his threat. Then, just for good measure, before I came out here, I swung by the feed store and officially quit."

Quint stared at her in angry disbelief. "Why the hell did you do that?"

"How should I know!" She flung up her hands and rose to her feet in sudden agitation. "Maybe I knew I'd never persuade Empty to quit. Maybe there's more of my grandfather in me than I thought. Or maybe I was just tired of the Rutledges always bribing and bullying people into doing what they want. And maybe I didn't want to be another one of those people who gave in to them."

"There were other ways of handling Boone's threat." Quint fought down the urge to grab her by the shoulders and shake some sense into her. "You could just as easily have told him that you needed some time to think. You didn't have to fly off the handle and quit!"

"Maybe not, but whether you like it or not, it's done. And there's no turning back from it now." Head up and chin high, Dallas was all defiance.

"There certainly isn't," Quint muttered grimly, then challenged, "Just what do you propose to do next?"

Dallas had a ready and decisive answer for that. "You and I both know that the best thing would be for me to work here at the Cee Bar. Empty can tell you that I'm as good as any man at ranch work. And it's obvious you need somebody to keep house and fix your meals," she added, casting a disparaging glance at the empty soup bowls on the table. "You can't keep opening soup cans or slapping a piece of meat between two slices of bread and calling it lunch."

But Quint noticed that Dallas made no mention of wanting to keep an eye on her grandfather, something he suspected was the true motivation behind her proposal. In her shoes, he'd feel the same.

"You're right. There would be safety in numbers," he conceded.

"I'm glad you see that." She relaxed a little, satisfaction easing some of her tension.

"Divide and conquer, that's always been one of Rutledge's favorite methods." The old man leaned back in his chair and grinned. "It sure isn't going to work this time."

But Quint wasn't so easily convinced that this particular problem was solved. "Just how far do you think Rutledge is prepared to go to carry out his threat, Empty?" he asked, recalling his own run-in with the three men in the parking lot.

The rancher was quick to follow his train of thought. "You're thinking that Rutledge might try something to get back at Dallas and me for going against him?"

"Would he?" On this, Quint had to rely to a certain extent on Empty's judgment and experiences with the Rutledges.

"He'd almost have to try something just to make sure nobody else around here got out of line." His expression turned thoughtful as he ran through the possibilities in his mind. "I suppose he could trash our trailer or catch us on some lonely stretch of road and try to run us off. He might even have some of his boys pay us a late-night visit. I can't see him doing anything more violent than that, though."

Quint hoped he was right. At the same time he didn't really want to take the chance that Empty was wrong.

"Then let's make it harder for Rutledge to get to you," he said.

"Just how do you propose to do that?" Dallas wondered.

"This house has three bedrooms. The two of you can stay here." He was quick to note the way her lips parted in surprise, but no objection came from them. "At least that way you wouldn't have to worry about leaving your grandfather alone when you go to class at night."

"No. No, I wouldn't," Dallas agreed on a slightly self-conscious note.

"You have to admit, Dallas," Empty inserted, "as old as this house is, it's bound to be better than that drafty excuse for a trailer we're living in. And it'll be good to wake up in the morning and hear the lowing of the cattle again."

Her expression visibly softened, a warm and tender light shining in her eyes as she gazed at her grandfather. Quint felt a trace of envy for the depth of feeling visible in her look.

"Is that your decision then?" he asked, subconsciously seeking to reclaim her attention. "You're moving in?"

"There doesn't seem to be any doubt about that." A wryly indulgent smile curved her mouth. "There isn't any place he'd rather live than on a ranch."

"In that case, let's not waste any more time," Quint stated.

"Between your truck and mine, we should be able to get you packed and moved before nightfall."

"We still got that section of fence to finish," Empty reminded him.

"It's waited this long. It can wait till tomorrow when Dallas can give us a hand with it." Deep down inside, Quint knew he was looking forward to having her around all the time, but he wasn't ready to examine the reason behind it. "As soon as I get my truck unloaded, I'll be ready to go."

The move required two trips. The first load was mainly the few pieces of personal furniture contained in the small trailer. All but the gun cabinet and Empty's favorite recliner were stored in a corner of the barn and covered with a protective tarp.

By the time Quint and Empty returned for the second load, Dallas had all their clothing and personal items from both the bedrooms packed in a mix of suitcases and boxes and had started emptying the kitchen cabinets. Leaving Empty to help her, Quint carried the boxes and suitcases out to the truck, then joined them when the last was loaded.

As usual, the old rancher kept up a steady run of chatter, but Quint noticed that Dallas had little to say. Any remark from her was either an instruction or an answer to a direct question. Her entire manner was one of brisk efficiency.

Yet Quint couldn't help noticing that she rarely made eye contact with him. He had the impression that, while she might agree with the practicality of the move, she wasn't comfortable with the idea of living in such close quarters with him.

The more he thought about it, he realized uncomfortable wasn't the right word. She was wary. Quint had only to remember how rough and angrily he'd kissed her to know that he had given her cause to be leery.

Twilight was purpling the hills when Quint carried the last of the boxes into the Cee Bar ranch house. Catching the sounds of boxes being moved around in the living room, he shoved his grocery-laden container onto the kitchen counter and headed for the living room.

Dallas stood among the stacks of boxes, busily sorting and separating. The old man had already collapsed in his recliner, the gray of exhaustion in his face.

"Which bedrooms do you want us to have?" Dallas asked as she picked up a box and kneed it higher in her arms.

"I've been using the one at the end of the hall," Quint told her. "There's one bedroom next to the bath and another across the hall from it. Both are about the same size."

"I'll take the one on the left and you can have the one on the right," she said to her grandfather.

"That's fine," he declared. "It doesn't matter much to me where I sleep."

She glanced at Quint and nodded at a suitcase lying atop a trio of boxes pushed together. "Those are Empty's things. Would you mind carrying them into his room?"

"Be glad to."

As she started for the stack, Dallas turned toward the bedrooms. "Better watch your step in the hall," Quint warned. "The floor's uneven. It can throw you off balance if you don't expect it."

"It can't be any worse than the trailer," Dallas replied in unconcern.

"How long before we eat?" Empty called after her. "My belly's so empty, I swear it's rubbing against my backbone."

"As soon as I get this stuff cleared out of the living room, I'll tackle supper," Dallas promised and headed down the hallway.

Quint hauled Empty's things into the bedroom he would occupy, crossing paths with Dallas only once. He paused in the doorway long enough to tell her where the clean sheets were stored, then went outside to do the evening chores.

When he returned to the house, Dallas was in the kitchen, stocking the shelves with the grocery items from their trailer. Two pots simmered on the stove, filling the room with a spicy aroma, and the table was set for three.

Without pausing in her task, she informed him, "Supper will be ready in a few minutes."

"It smells good." He shrugged out of his jacket and hung it on a hook by the door, then slipped his hat onto the shelf above it.

"Spaghetti and meat sauce. It was the fastest thing to make," she explained in an offhand way.

"Fast is good. I think we're all hungry tonight." He went to the sink to wash up, conscious that she never paused in her task. "Are you finding where everything goes all right?"

"Right now I'm just putting things wherever there's room. I can organize it later." She shoved a sack of sugar onto a shelf and pushed a container of cornmeal beside it. "I think Empty's snoozing in his chair. When you get through, would you go wake him up and tell him it's time to eat?"

"Sure." But Quint couldn't shake the feeling she was subtly pushing him away.

It persisted throughout the evening meal. Dallas was never cold or rude, but the studied indifference in her voice and attitude had its own way of holding him at arm's length. Justified or not, it annoyed Quint.

His plate slicked clean, Empty Garner leaned back in his chair and patted his full stomach. "That was a tasty meal, Dallas. You done good."

"Thanks." Rising, she reached for his plate. "Want some coffee?"

"Naw. My chair's calling me. I think I'll go in and watch some television," he replied and laid both hands on the tabletop to push himself upright.

As he hobbled toward the living room, Dallas glanced briefly at Quint. "How about you? Coffee?"

"No, thanks." Quint gathered up his own plate and silverware and carried them to the sink where he tightened the drain plug and turned on the hot water.

As he squeezed some dish soap into the water, Dallas arrived with the rest of the dirty dishes from the table. "Go watch TV with Empty. I can do these."

"So can I." Quint turned on the other faucet, adding cold water to the mix of steaming, billowing bubbles.

For an instant Dallas seemed on the verge of arguing the point, then shrugged. "Have it your way." She slid the dishes into the soapy water and went back to clear the rest of the items from the table.

By the time she finished, Quint was rinsing the silverware and adding them to the drain rack that already held the glasses and plates. Without a word, Dallas took a clean dish towel from the drawer and started drying the glasses.

"You aren't very comfortable with this arrangement, are you?" Quint remarked.

"Don't be silly. I don't care if you wash dishes," Dallas countered.

"That isn't what I meant. I was talking about you and your grandfather moving out here."

This time Dallas wasn't as quick with an answer. When she did offer one, Quint sensed again that she had chosen her words with care.

"It's the safest place right now."

"That isn't what I asked," he countered in a firm but gentle voice.

There was the smallest flare of defiance in the look she gave him. "With Rutledge's threats hanging over us, I wouldn't be comfortable anywhere."

"And maybe even less living under the same roof with me?" Quint suggested.

"It's nothing personal," Dallas insisted. "I just don't want you to get the idea that I'm interested in becoming romantically involved. That's all."

"I had a feeling you were concerned about that," Quint admitted. "But you can set your mind at ease on that score. I'm not going to force myself on you, and I apologize if my behavior earlier today gave you the wrong impression."

"Apology accepted." Yet she appeared far from reassured by it. If anything her tension had increased.

"Dallas—" he began.

She cut in quickly. "Let's just drop it, okay?" Her eyes were cool with challenge, a look that was more in keeping with the woman he remembered from past encounters.

"If that's the way you want it, then as far as I'm concerned, it never happened."

"That's the way it has to be," Dallas stated firmly and abruptly laid the towel aside. "I'll take care of the rest of these dishes in the morning. My last test is tomorrow, and I need to do some studying for it."

Quint didn't try to stop her. There wasn't any reason to try. Everything had already been said. Yet he sensed that nothing had changed.

How could it when he hadn't forgotten the feel of her warm lips against his or the sensation of her body pressed tightly to him?

That line had been crossed, and the memory of it would always be there to remind them of it every time they were in each other's company.

# Chapter Ten

Quint awoke to the smell of bacon frying. It took him a second to remember he was no longer the only one in the house. A check of the clock on the bedside table showed it would be another five minutes before the alarm would sound. Reaching over, he switched it off and rolled out of bed.

Realizing that the days of padding to the bathroom in his underwear were gone, Quint tugged on a pair of jeans before heading down the hall. The dampness of the two towels hanging on the bathroom rack indicated he was far from the first one in there, and the tepid temperature of the water coming from the shower nozzle confirmed it. In record time, he showered, shaved, and changed into a clean set of clothes.

When he entered the kitchen, Empty was already seated at the table, digging into a plate of bacon and eggs. Dallas stood by the stove, a spatula in hand and something sizzling in the skillet before her.

"You two are early risers," Quint remarked and walked straight to the coffeepot.

"Habit," Empty said just before he shoveled in another mouthful of fried egg.

"How do you like your eggs?" Dallas asked.

"I don't know. I've never had them this early in the morning," Quint told her. "I don't usually sit down to breakfast until after the morning chores are done."

"I have two here that are over easy," she told him, nodding to the skillet.

"You eat them," he said. "I'll fix my own after I've had this cup of coffee."

Taking him at his word, Dallas used the spatula to lift the eggs out of the skillet and onto a plate, then carried it to the table, pulled out a chair, and sat down. As she reached for the salt and pepper shakers, she glanced at her grandfather.

"You know we still have to drop the trailer key off and cancel the telephone and utilities," she said. "If I leave here no later than three-thirty, I should be able to get all of it done before I have to go to my class tonight."

"Might as well," Empty agreed and scooped strawberry jam onto his slice of toast. "No sense paying for a service we aren't using."

When Quint wandered over to the table, she glanced up, a sudden uncertainty flickering in her expression. "Sorry. I should have asked if it was all right with you if I left early."

"I don't have a problem with it," Quint replied.

"Right after breakfast, I'll put a roast in the slow cooker, along with some carrots and potatoes. You two can have that for supper tonight."

Quint wasn't ready to face the thought of breakfast and she was adding supper into the mix. Rather than comment on that, he asked instead, "How late will you be tonight?"

"I probably won't be back until around eleven or so. Just leave the door unlocked." Dallas snapped a slice of crisp bacon in two and sent a sharp glance at Empty. "Don't wait up for me. I don't want to walk in and find you sitting in the recliner with a shotgun on your lap."

"Those times you found me that way I had cause," Empty insisted.

The good-natured squabbling between the two reminded Quint of his own grandfather and his occasionally irascible ways. It made him smile.

"The shotgun's locked in the gun cabinet," Quint told her. "I'll see that it stays there, so you won't have any worries on that score."

With a loud harrumph Empty expressed his opinion of that. "You'll change your tune real fast the first time somebody comes snooping around here."

Privately Quint couldn't argue with that and responded with a noncommittal smile. But he knew his troubles with the Rutledges had only started.

A thin cloud drifted in front of the waning moon, dimming its light and intensifying the star-twinkle in the night sky. But Dallas took no notice of it, her senses dulled by a fatigue that was both physical and mental. At the moment all of her attention was focused on locating the Cee Bar's entrance gate.

But the truck's headlight beams were slow to separate the gate's tall posts from the roadside shadows. It suddenly loomed on the right, forcing Dallas to slam on the brakes. As the truck fishtailed nearly to a stop, Dallas swung the wheel and drove through the gate, sending up a silent prayer of gratitude that no one had been behind her.

With the rutted lane twisting before her, Dallas sagged against the seat and allowed her mind to wander back over the chaos of the last nearly forty-eight hours. When she threw in the pressure of final exams, she could easily see why she felt so dull and drained. She also knew the worst wasn't over. Not by a long shot.

She doubted, though, that Quint really believed that.

Quint. There was a big, hollow ache in her chest at the mere thought of him. Unconsciously she touched a fingertip to her lips, recalling the crush of his mouth on them, the anger that had been in it, along with the heat and the need. The memory of it stirred through her, livening her own desires.

Dallas sternly reminded herself that she could not become emotionally involved with Quint. Nothing could come from it but heartache. And her life was complicated enough right now, thanks to the threat Boone had made against her grandfather.

"Dear God," she murmured, a tightness gripping her throat, "I can't help it. I hate the Rutledges. I hate them."

Light bloomed in the darkness, spilling from the tall security light in the ranch yard, as Dallas rounded the last curve. The yellow gleam of the porch light beckoned her from the ranch house. With a deepening weariness of body and spirit, Dallas automatically set her sights on it.

Seconds after the truck rolled into the ranch yard, a muffled boom shattered the stillness. Certain it was made by a shotgun, she slammed on the brakes, alarm shooting through her as she jerked her head toward the barn that had almost simultaneously erupted with the panicked squawking of chickens.

In a flash, Dallas whipped the pickup toward the barn and tromped on the accelerator, the truck's fast-spinning tires spitting gravel. She barely gave it time to come to a full stop near the door before she charged out of it, leaving the lights on and the engine running.

"Empty, is that you?" Dallas yelled as two chickens fought to get through the partially opened barn door, wings flapping. "Are you all right?"

Before she reached the opening, Quint stepped out, hatless and holding the shotgun at his side, the muzzle pointed at the ground.

"It's only me," he said. "Sorry if I gave you a scare."

"You did. I was sure—" Her initial wave of relief was replaced with a new concern. "What were you shooting?"

"A raccoon," Quint replied and held up the lifeless body of a big male. "I heard the chickens making a racket and thought I'd better check it out in case the intruder was the two-footed kind. I'm glad it wasn't."

"So am I," Dallas murmured, feeling a bit like a yo-yo on its downward spin as she absently watched him lay the dead animal on a pile of wood next to the barn.

"I'll bury him in the morning—which isn't far away," Quint added, moving within range of the yard light when he turned toward her. The barn's shadows no longer concealed his slightly tousled hair. His denim jacket hung partially open, exposing a narrow wedge of chest hairs and a strip of tautly muscled flesh. Her heart started thumping crazily.

With an effort, Dallas dragged her gaze up to his face and was immediately mesmerized by the soft light in his eyes. More than four feet separated them, but it seemed slight, something easily spanned. And with each passing second of silence, the sense of intimacy swirling between them thickened.

Dallas tried to think of something to say and break the spell of it, but her mind was blank, and her feet were rooted to the spot.

"How did your test go?" The gentleness of his voice was like a caress.

"Fine, I guess—I hope," she corrected hastily and struggled to focus her thoughts.

A slow smile lifted the corners of his mouth. "If you're like me, by the time I finished the last exam, I was too tired to care how I did. That lasted about as long as it took for the results to be posted."

"I'm beat, that's for sure." Dallas was quick to seize the excuse he offered. "I'd better call it a night before I fall over."

She turned away, eager to escape from him while she could still deny that she felt anything more than a physical attraction. She climbed into the cab of the pickup and deliberately didn't offer him a ride to the house. The last thing Dallas wanted was to spend any more time alone with Quint, especially tonight.

For once, luck was on her side, and she reached the privacy of her bedroom as Quint walked into the living room to lock the shotgun back in its cabinet.

A midnight-blue Ferrari rolled to a stop in front of the Adolphus Hotel in Dallas. On a nearby street corner, a group of Dickens' costumed carolers broke into a rousing rendition of "God Rest Ye Merry Gentlemen." Boone Rutledge took no notice of them as he climbed out of the Ferrari and tossed the keys to the doorman at the curb.

"I shouldn't be more than five minutes. Keep it handy," he ordered and strode to the door.

He paused a few feet inside the hotel lobby for a quick scan of its occupants, totally ignoring the sweeps of evergreen boughs twinkling with Christmas lights. Within seconds, Boone spotted his father, dressed in an impeccably tailored black tuxedo with a white tie, gliding across the marbled lobby in his wheelchair, bound for the bank of elevators. As always, Harold Barnett accompanied him, walking directly behind the wheelchair.

Boone quickly crossed the lobby to intercept them. Both men stopped when they observed his approach, and Max angled his chair toward him and raked his glance over the suit Boone wore.

"Formal dress is required for tonight's dinner," Max curtly informed him.

"I have other plans this evening. I told you that this morning," Boone reminded him with cool stiffness.

"In Little Mexico, I suppose," Max replied with a small curl of contempt. "So why did you bother to come here at all?"

His nostrils flared slightly in anger, but Boone managed to keep his temper in check. "I thought you would want to know it's been confirmed. The Garners have moved onto the Cee Bar."

"You're certain of that?" Max demanded.

"Dallas arranged for the phone and utilities to the trailer to be turned off yesterday. Not a single possession was left in the trailer."

Max folded his hands together in his lap and digested this piece of news. "It never occurred to me that Echohawk would move them onto the ranch with him."

"I remember the Calders mentioning that Echohawk had a tendency to pick up strays."

"It's a pity you didn't remember that before," Max said in dry rebuke. "We could have anticipated the possibility if you had. Now it complicates things."

"I know," Boone agreed.

"We'll have to find a way to use it to our advantage," Max stated and shot a challenging look at his son. "What have you done about the hay?"

"Nothing yet."

"Why not?" Max asked in harsh demand.

"There's a new moon Sunday night," Boone replied. "That'll be the best time to take care of it."

"See that you do." Once again his hand was at the controls, sending the wheelchair toward the bank of elevators and leaving Boone standing there by himself.

Evergreen trees of varying heights and types were propped along the front of the grocery store, scenting the air with their pine smell. The minute he climbed out of the truck, Empty Garner walked over to survey the selection. Having just come from church, he was dressed in what he persisted in calling his Sunday-go-to-meeting clothes—a western-cut suit, a bolo tie, and a spotless black cowboy hat.

As Quint joined him, Empty pulled out a tree that stood about five feet tall. "This looks likes a good one."

Dallas veered away from the entrance when she noticed him inspecting the tree. "What are you doing, Empty?" She frowned.

"Exactly what it looks like," he retorted with a trace of impatience. "I'm picking out a tree. It won't be Christmas without one."

She darted a hesitant glance at Quint. "But it isn't our house, Empty," she reminded him.

"You're living in it. I think that makes it your house, too," Quint replied with a smile. "And I agree with Empty. It won't be Christmas without a tree."

"In that case, I guess we'll have a tree," Dallas said with a faint sigh of concession. "But it means we'll have to dig out those boxes with the tree stand and ornaments that we put in the barn."

"We haven't got anything better to do this afternoon, do we?" Empty countered in light challenge.

"I guess not." This time she managed a smile. "You two pick out the tree while I get the milk and bread and other items we need. But don't be long," she warned. "Because I won't be."

By late afternoon, the living room furniture had been rearranged to make a space for the tree. Six inches had been trimmed off the trunk to accommodate the room's low ceiling and the additional height the metal stand gave it.

It stood proudly in the corner, ready to be trimmed. Boxes of ornaments were scattered about the room. With one string of lights untangled, Empty was busy working on the second.

Quint sat on the floor, patiently searching for the burnt-out bulb or bulbs on a third string of multicolored lights plugged into the wall socket. From the kitchen came the sharp patter of corn popping.

The instant Quint switched out one bulb, the entire string lit up. "Found it."

"At least we got two strands that work now—maybe three if I ever get this one unsnarled," Empty muttered as he tugged loose another knot.

"Want some help?" Quint unplugged the light string and stood up.

Empty was on the verge of accepting his offer when the telephone rang. "You need to answer that. I can manage."

Quint slipped into the popcorn-scented kitchen and picked up the old rotary-style phone that sat on the oak desk, sliding a glance at Dallas as she emptied a pan of freshly popped corn into a large earthenware bowl.

"Cee Bar Ranch." The words had become automatic to him.

"Hi, Quint. It's your mom," came the answer.

"Hi. What's up?" Quint immediately pulled out the desk chair and sat down, certain the conversation wasn't likely to be a short one.

"Nothing much," his mother replied. "I just finished the last of the Christmas cards and thought I'd give you a call before I started wrapping presents. So what have you been doing?"

"We're in the middle of trimming the tree," he answered as Dallas returned to the stove, poured oil in the large pan, and measured more kernels into it, then set it on the burner.

"You're having a tree. How nice. Wait a minute, did you say 'we'?" she asked and immediately answered herself. "That's right. Jessy told me that your hired man had moved in with you, along with his granddaughter. You know, if I'm not mistaken, the Christmas decorations were always stowed in the attic at the Cee Bar. I'll bet they're still there."

"I'll check, but the Garners have plenty," he told her, then carefully changed the subject. "How's Gramps doing?"

"He's grumpy as usual."

Quint smiled at the description. "What's he complaining about this time?"

"We're having the Triple C Christmas party this coming weekend, and he thinks it should be closer to Christmas. I don't suppose you can come home for the party. Everybody would love to see you."

"I'll have to miss it this year, I'm afraid."

A faint sigh of resignation preceded her response. "I had a feeling you'd say that. As long as you're here for Christmas, that's what counts."

"I'm going to try." But Quint wasn't willing to promise anything beyond that.

"Now, Quint, there's no reason why you can't, especially now when your hired man is right there to do the chores and look after things while you're away."

"With any luck, that's the way it will work out." The first smattering of popping kernels rattled in the covered pot. Dallas immediately began moving it back and forth across the burner more vigorously.

"You'd better be here," Cat warned and would have said more on the subject, but there was an eruption of exploding kernels. "What is that noise, Quint?"

"Dallas is making popcorn."

"I thought you were trimming the tree."

"We are. The Garners have a tradition of stringing popcorn and draping it on the tree." Seeking to divert the conversation away from more talk of Christmas, he asked about Trey.

Fortunately his mother needed little urging to launch into other topics, bringing him up to date on family happenings as well as things at the Triple C. It was a good ten minutes before she wound the conversation to a close.

"Tell everyone hi for me," Quint said. "And let Jessy know things have been quiet here the last few days. Hopefully they'll stay that way."

"I'll tell her," she promised. "I love you, Quint. See you at Christmas."

"Love you, too," he said and hung up.

When Quint returned to the living room, the tree was a-twinkle with an array of red, blue, green, and yellow lights. Dallas was standing on the four-foot stepladder, rearranging the light strand around the top branches for a more visually appealing look. Empty was in his chair, a bowl of popcorn balanced on his lap, a long needle in one hand, and a piece of fluffy white popcorn in the other.

"I see you managed to get the lights untangled," Quint remarked. "The tree looks beautiful."

"It better," Empty grumbled and nodded to a second bowl of popcorn on the coffee table. "Grab yourself a needle and thread and some popcorn and start stringing." He shoved the needle through the popcorn and ran it down onto the thread. "Dallas got carried away with the popcorn. There won't be room on the tree for any ornaments."

"That's because I knew you'd eat most of it," she countered, sending him a knowing smile.

"It does smell good." Quint grabbed himself a handful on the way to the couch, pushed aside a box of ornaments, and sat down. "Is there any trick to this?" he asked and popped some kernels into his mouth.

"About the only trick is threading the needle," Empty replied, then glanced at him curiously. "Haven't you ever strung popcorn before?"

"Nope, never have," Quint admitted and reached for a long needle sticking out of a strawberry-shaped pincushion, noticing the spool of ultra-heavy-duty thread beside it.

"There's nothing to it," Dallas assured him. "Just make sure you don't jam the popcorn too closely together and accidentally push it off the end of the string."

"I know folks mostly use store-bought garlands these days, but I thought everybody had strung popcorn when they were kids," Empty declared.

"Not me. Although I remember one year cutting strips of colored construction paper and gluing them into a chain for the tree." Quint reeled off a length of thread. "How much do I need?"

With the lights arranged to her satisfaction, Dallas hopped off the step stool and crossed to the sofa to show him. As she bent to unroll more thread, her ponytail swung forward, brushing past his face. She automatically flipped it to the other side, but not before Quint caught a whiff of the strawberry-scented shampoo she used.

This was the first time Dallas had gotten this close to him since the day she arrived at the Cee Bar. And her nearness stimulated his senses, doubling his awareness of her and making it difficult for him to respond naturally.

"That should do it," she said after she had unrolled another foot of thread. Taking the scissors, she snipped it off the spool. "You shouldn't have any trouble threading it, big as the eye is on that needle."

When she remained close to observe the process, Quint had to check the urge to catch hold of her hand and draw her down to the sofa cushion beside him. Instead he concentrated on slipping the thread through the needle's eye, and succeeded on the first attempt.

"Very good." Her expression was a mixture of approval and surprise.

"I'm no stranger to a needle and thread," Quint informed her with a mild and jesting smugness. "My mother told me a long time ago that I had two choices—either find a reliable laundry that would faithfully restitch hems, sew on buttons, and mend torn pockets, or learn how to do it myself. I quickly discovered it was a handy skill for a bachelor to have, almost as necessary as cooking."

Her smile was quick and warm, and equally teasing. "A man who listens. That's even more amazing."

"I thought you'd be impressed." As he tossed her a teasing smile, Quint unwittingly let his glance slide down to her lips.

It lingered on their soft, full shape a few seconds too long. Immediately he sensed the cooling in her attitude toward him, and that easy camaraderie that had so briefly existed was gone.

Just like that, Dallas turned away. "I think I'll start hanging ornaments while you two work on the popcorn." Lending action to her statement, she picked up the nearest box and carried it to the tree.

Much of Quint's enjoyment of the moment left with her. But Empty was oblivious of all of it as his age-gnarled fingers continued to lengthen the amount of popcorn on his string.

"I seem to recollect that our kids made paper chains when they were small," Empty recalled. "Course back then, we made our own paste out of flour and water and glued them together with that. Paper chains and popcorn. Call me old-fashioned if you want, but that's the way a tree ought to be decorated. Nowadays they go to swooping wide ribbons all over the tree, and it ends up looking like a maypole."

"Now you sound like my dad," Quint said with a slight smile, recalling his father's aversion to the Victorian style of Christmas decorations.

"He doesn't like it either, huh?" Empty surmised.

"No." But Quint didn't correct his use of the present tense.

"Does your father work at the Triple C, too?" Dallas hooked an ornament on one of the higher branches.

"No, he was the local sheriff."

She swung around to face him, her eyes wide with question. "Was?"

Quint responded with a slow nod, then felt the need to speak bluntly. "He was killed this past summer when he stopped to get gas and walked into a robbery in progress."

"I'm sorry." Those two, softly murmured words carried a depth of feeling that seemed to reach across the room to offer comfort.

"You couldn't know," he said gently.

"Just the same . . ." Dallas let her voice trail off.

"It's a hard thing," Empty declared with a sad shake of his head. "Goes with the badge, I guess."

"It does," Quint agreed. "The irony is he planned to retire next year when his term was up, and start ranching full-time. We had a small spread, smaller than the Cee Bar," he explained. "But my dad never wanted anything bigger. He wanted to keep it a one-man operation, something he could handle by himself. There wasn't a tractor on the place. Everything was done with draft horses, from mowing hay to hauling it out to the cattle."

"You had to sell the place after he died, did you?" Empty guessed.

"No, my mom still has it, but she's got the Triple C running it for her."

The old man frowned. "How come she never turned it over to you?"

"Empty," Dallas said in sharp reproval. "It really isn't any of your business."

"Don't you be shushing me," Empty retorted, all indignant. "It's the most natural thing for a son to take over the running of things when his daddy passes."

"Since I work for the Triple C now, you could say I still do." As far as Quint was concerned, making that claim was easier than explaining his mother's ambition for him at the Triple C. Especially when he didn't share it. But that was a private matter between his mother and himself.

"And you got paid to do it," Empty realized, then remembered, "At least you did until you came down here." He paused and turned a thoughtful eye on Quint. "I reckon your daddy taught you a thing or two about the law and handling ruffians like the Rutledges. You aren't gonna be the kind to pack up when things get rough, are you?"

"No." It was a simple statement, made without boast or hesitation.

Empty chuckled to himself. "It could get interesting around here for a fact."

"Can we please talk about something other than the Rutledges?" Dallas protested in frustration. "It's a subject that doesn't exactly go with decorating a tree for Christmas."

"Dallas is right," Quint agreed.

Empty promptly lifted his hands in an exaggerated gesture of dismay. "Now why'd you have to go and say a thing like that? Now she'll start believing she's right about a whole bunch of other things, and there'll be no living with her. She already thinks she knows it all as it is."

"That's because I take after you," Dallas countered in sly mockery.

"See what I mean?" Empty declared. "There she goes mouthing off to me. Sometimes she just has no respect for her elders."

"Pooh," she scoffed. "Just because I don't agree with you all the time, that doesn't mean I don't respect you."

But the good-natured bickering succeeded in shifting the focus off the Rutledges, just as Dallas had wanted. Quint suspected he wasn't the only one aware of it.

But the lighter tone took root. Soon it wasn't something forced but came naturally—along with the smiles and the laughter.

By sundown, the tree was all decorated with a multitude of shiny ornaments, a white rope of popcorn, and brightly colored lights, all crowned by a silver star at the top. Leaving Dallas and her grandfather to stow the empty boxes in a bedroom closet, Quint headed outside to do the evening chores while there was still enough light to see. On his return, all three of them pitched in to fix a light supper.

After the dishes were done and they had drifted into the living room, the mood of friendly ease remained. As always Empty settled into his recliner and switched on the television. Quint stretched out on the couch. Dallas dug a magazine out of the wooden rack and curled up in the platform rocker.

Quint's glance strayed from the Christmas tree to the fireplace's dark maw. "A night like this seems to call for a crackling fire."

"It'd look pretty," Empty agreed. "But it's too warm tonight."

"If my cousin Laura were here, she'd turn on the air conditioner and then build a fire." Quint smiled at the thought, knowing it was exactly what she would do.

Empty reared back his head and stared at Quint in disbelief. "That's a blame fool thing to do."

"Laura wouldn't think so," Quint replied.

"Why, it's a plumb waste of money and fuel," Empty stated.

"That's the way you and I would look at it," Quint agreed and clasped his hands behind his neck, letting his attention wander back to the television and the truck commercial being aired.

A harrumph came from the direction of the recliner. "It's the only way to look at it."

The platform rocker creaked noisily as Dallas laid the magazine aside and pushed herself out of it. Quint's glance followed her as she crossed the room and disappeared into the back hall.

"That girl." Empty sighed in mild annoyance. "She never has been any good at sitting and doing nothing. That's not a bad thing, mind you, but sometimes I wish she'd park herself in one place and stay there."

Scuffling sounds came from the vicinity of the hallway, but with the television on, it was impossible for Quint to discern the cause for them. A few minutes later, Dallas reappeared, her arms wrapped around a large cardboard box.

Empty frowned when he saw it. "What are you doing lugging that back out here? We just put all those boxes away."

"I decided Quint was right. The fireplace needs something." She set the box on the floor in front of it and pulled loose its overlapping top flaps.

"Need some help?" Quint started to sit up.

"You look too comfortable. Don't get up. I can manage easily," she assured him and dragged a section of artificial pine garland out of the box, laying it aside.

When she began lifting out snowy white pillar candles, Quint understood her plan. Soon a half dozen candles of varying height filled the fireplace opening, some sitting on the hearth itself and the rest on a flat board lying on the andirons.

Off to the kitchen she went and came back with a box of kitchen matches. One by one, Dallas lit the wicks until there were a half dozen individual flames burning high and bright.

"How does it look?" She stepped back to survey the result.

"Perfect. Absolutely perfect," Quint announced.

"If you ask me, it's a waste of good candles," Empty countered.

Dallas threw him a chiding look, full of amusement and affection. "And a 'bah, humbug' to you, too." Again she turned to the fireplace and studied it with a critical eye. "It still needs something," she murmured and picked up the pine garland.

With practiced skill, Dallas arranged the garland across the mantelpiece, anchored it at each end with two more pillar candles, and added a few sprigs of fake berries.

"How's it look?" Dallas stepped back to survey the result with a critical eye.

"Looks good," Quint said.

"I think so too," she said and picked up the nearly empty box.

Again she disappeared into the hallway with it and returned a short time later empty-handed. Empty eyed her narrowly. "Are you done with this decorating business?"

"You started it by insisting we get a tree," Dallas reminded him. "But, yes, I am done—at least for the time being. Why?"

" 'Cause it would be nice to watch television instead of you walking back and forth in front of it," he retorted.

"You don't have to worry. I'm going out to the kitchen and fix some cocoa. Anyone interested in a cup?"

"It sounds good, but only if you sit down and drink yours," Empty replied with pseudo gruffness. When she left the room, he slid a glance at Quint. "See what I mean? She's never still for two minutes."

Noises came from the kitchen as cupboard drawers and doors were opened and closed, water was run in the sink, and items were set atop the counter. Mixed in with all of it was the beeping of the microwave.

A few minutes later, Dallas entered the living room, carrying a tray with three mugs of steaming cocoa, each topped with a marshmallow. Quint sat up to take his from the tray she placed on the coffee table.

When Dallas picked up hers, Empty pointed to the platform rocker. "Now sit down and drink it."

"I planned to." Again she curled up in the rocker, both hands holding the cup.

Yet for all her relaxed pose, Quint sensed her restlessness. "Are you having a hard time adjusting to the idea that you don't have books to crack?"

Her quick smile was an admission in itself. "No books to crack, no racing off to wait tables at the café, no rushing to get to the feed store, then hurrying home to throw a meal together before dashing off to class. And all of it stopped. Yet I still have the feeling that there's some place I have to be, something I have to do. It makes it hard to sit and do nothing."

Empty's solution was a simple one. "Just sit there and stop thinking about it."

"I wish it was that easy," she said and took a sip of her cocoa, then picked up the magazine again and began flipping through its pages.

Even after the last of the cocoa was consumed, Dallas was still in her chair. Empty was the first to stir, reaching up to stifle a big yawn.

"Mmmm." He shook his head as if to clear away its grogginess and released the catch to lower the recliner's footrest. "That dang cocoa always makes me sleepy. Guess I'd better call it a night."

He stood up, passed the remote to Quint, and ambled toward the bedroom with a parting admonition to Dallas. "Don't forget to unplug the tree and blow out them candles before you come to bed."

"I won't," she promised.

Empty's departure marked the end of her idleness. The instant the bedroom door closed behind her grandfather, Dallas sat forward and reached for his empty cocoa mug. Quint picked it up before she could, and slid it onto the serving tray with his own.

Tray in hand, he stood up as she came to her feet as well. "Want to set yours on the tray and I'll take it out to the kitchen?"

Instead she reached for the tray. "That's all right. I can manage it."

"So can I," Quint replied with a smile, recalling the time at the feed store when she had answered him with the same phrase.

"I know that." For once there was no trace of self-consciousness or unease in the glance she sent him. "But it always feels awkward to let someone else do something that's usually your job."

"In that case you bring yours, and I'll take these." Before she could remind him the task didn't require two people to accomplish, Quint headed for the kitchen.

But Dallas was too amused by his solution to do more than smile and fall in behind him. She studied the breadth of his shoulders, finding it difficult as always not to be conscious of his leanly muscled physique.

In truth, she knew of few men more handsome than Quint, and none who weren't totally aware of it. Yet Quint didn't seem to be one of them. Or if he was, he attached very little, if any, importance to his looks. Yet "modest" wasn't an adjective she would ascribe to him, especially when there were so many that suited him better like steady, strong, competent, solid, and caring.

Even as she ran through the list of his attributes, Dallas wondered if they were the reason she felt safe when Quint was around despite the fact that she was far from it. But safe didn't describe the high sense of ease she experienced in his presence, a feeling that ran strong and deep, so deep it left her a little breathless at times.

It was the first time Dallas had allowed herself to explore her reaction to him, and the result was a bit disturbing.

Ahead of her, Quint slipped the tray onto the counter. "Just set the cups in the sink," Dallas told him. "I'll wash them with the breakfast dishes in the morning."

"You know," Quint began, filling both mugs with tap water before placing them in the sink, "putting up the tree reminded me that I haven't done any Christmas shopping yet. Any suggestions on what I can get my mom?"

"If she's like most mothers," Dallas replied as she placed her cup in the sink, "she'll like anything you buy her."

Quint cocked an eyebrow at her and smiled. "That's no help."

"I suppose not." She grinned and allowed herself to become captivated by the unusual smoke-gray color of his eyes.

"You should do that more often. You have a beautiful smile," he murmured.

His gaze darkened on her, the starkness of want in it. It stirred up all her closely held feelings for him.

Dallas knew she should say something—do something to break the moment.

Instead it was Quint who turned away. "I think I'll follow Empty's lead and call it a night."

Alone in the kitchen, Dallas gripped the edge of the sink counter with a fierceness that turned her knuckles white, stunned to discover how very much she had wanted to feel the warmth of his kiss and experience the hunger she had seen his eyes. She called herself every kind of fool, but it didn't change the truth.

# Chapter Eleven

Sleep was elusive. The old house was far from soundproof. Yet tonight, more than any other night, Quint was aware of every sound Dallas made, even to the squeaking of bedsprings when she finally slipped between the covers. He rolled onto his side and tried to block out the image of her lying in bed, but he couldn't shut off so easily the wish that she were there with him.

For a long time Quint drifted between wakefulness and slumber. Sleep, when it came, wasn't the deep and restful kind, which made it easy for a sudden, hard thud to pierce its shallow layers.

Stirring, Quint raised his head and listened. A second later, he became aware of a faint drumming sound. As he struggled to identify its source, Quint heard the distinctive whinny of alarm from one of the horses in the corral. A chicken squawked an echo of it.

Certain it was another coon raiding the barn, Quint threw back the covers and climbed out of bed, automatically reaching for his jeans. He stepped into them one leg at a time, fastened them around the middle, pulled up the zipper, and tugged on his boots.

Leaving the bedroom, he walked straight to the gun cabinet in the living room. He took out the shotgun and fed a couple of shells into it.

The instant he turned toward the door, Quint noticed the unnatural glow beyond the front windows. The sight of it jolted through him like a bolt of electricity.

"Fire!" he shouted and ran out the door, disregarding the shotgun he still carried.

But the wavering glow hadn't prepared him for the sight of flames running along the entire length of the row of round bales, greedily licking over the dried hay. It halted him long enough for his side vision to register another glow near the barn.

He swung his attention to it and saw a quick rush of flames curling over the bale in the corral as well. Beyond its light were the shadowy outlines of the horses milling about in panic.

Getting the horses away from the fire became the top priority as Quint took off toward the corral. He was halfway across the yard when he glimpsed a hatted figure silhouetted against the tan earth of the driveway. There wasn't a doubt in his mind that this was the culprit who had started the fires.

A cold and raging anger had Quint skidding to a stop, snapping the shotgun to his shoulder, and squeezing both triggers, even though he knew his target was out of range. But he had the satisfaction of seeing the figure crouch low before the night's darkness swallowed him.

Quint was half tempted to pursue the man, but the shotgun blast had ignited a fresh panic among the trapped horses. He had no choice but to rescue them before they injured themselves.

By the time he got the pasture gate open and succeeded in driving the crazed and wild-eyed horses through it to safety, Empty was using a hose to pour water on the corral's round bale and Dallas was stabbing a pitchfork into the burning edges of the tightly rolled hay in an attempt to separate it from the unburned portions.

All Quint saw in the roll of smoke and hiss of stubborn flames was the loose swing of her coppery hair when she turned her face away from the fire's heat. He jerked the pitchfork out of her hands and shoved her aside.

"Get out of here and get that hair under a hat," he ordered and attacked the bale, resuming her efforts without any illusion that it might be successful. To her credit, Dallas hesitated only an instant before she sprinted for the house. Quint spared a glance at Empty. "Did you get the fire department called?"

Empty responded with a curt nod and aimed the hose at the top of the bale. "They're supposed to be on their way. Not that it's going to do much good," he added with a short glance at the bales along the fence line that were now a solid wall of flames. "I suppose it's too much to hope that you got the bastard that started this."

"He was too far away."

"I was afraid of that," Empty muttered, then added bitterly, "Wanna bet the fire trucks will take their time getting here?"

"No, thanks."

When Dallas came running back to join them, Quint was quick to note the feed store cap on her head and the absence of hair falling loose about her shoulders. Half out of breath, she pointed to burning bales along the fence row.

"The grass caught fire." The alarm in her voice lent its own urgency to her words.

Quint threw a quick look in that direction, his gaze scouring the area beyond the billowing smoke and fire, and located the yellow line of fast-creeping flames. He didn't need to be reminded that the winter grass was tinder dry.

"Forget this," he told Empty and tossed the pitchfork aside. "Give me a hand getting the plow hitched to the tractor." As he turned for the barn, he pushed Dallas toward the house. "Get any blankets you can find, throw them in the truck along with some shovels and all the buckets of water you can haul."

No time was wasted acknowledging his instructions. All knew time was the fire's ally, not theirs. While Dallas ran to get the blankets, Quint vaulted the corral fence and shoved open the double doors to the barn where the tractor was housed. Empty hauled himself onto the tractor seat and cranked up the engine. Quint climbed on behind him, holding tight to the seat as the tractor lurched out of the barn and roared over to the plow that sat next to the building. With an expert swing of the wheel, Empty backed the tractor up to the plow and Quint hopped down to secure the ball hitch. The instant he was back on board, Empty took off.

The entire process took only scant minutes. And in that same period of time, the flames had advanced another fifty yards across the tinder-dry grass. Fanned by its own powerful draft, the fire was picking up speed.

It was like a living thing, leaping to devour anything in its path, its appetite never satisfied. Smoke rolled ahead of it, lit by flying embers that looked like so many devil-red eyes in the darkness.

As the tractor chugged out of the ranch yard at full throttle, the plow rattling behind it, Quint caught a glimpse of Dallas sprinting from the house, bundled cloth clasped in her arms. Then the tractor was shooting onto the ranch lane, taking advantage of the natural firebreak it provided on the east side to skirt the racing flames and charge ahead of them into the obscuring wall of smoke.

Empty kept his foot to the pedal, never slackening the tractor's headlong pace through the smoke. At last the sting of it was no longer in their eyes.

Holding on tightly, Quint leaned close and shouted in the old man's ear, "The dry wash up here on the right—we'll try to stop it there."

Empty's answer was a short nod that signaled he had heard and understood.

The shallow wash was one that nature had carved near the base of a hill to handle the runoff from heavy rains. At its widest point it was no more than three feet across, its bed a mix of bare soil and stones of varying sizes. The wash itself didn't reach all the way to the ranch lane, but rather started at a point some one hundred feet from it.

As the tractor approached the imaginary point of intersection, Empty slowed its speed and braked to a stop with its nose pointed at the fence. He pulled a pair of wire cutters out of his jacket pocket and passed them to Quint.

Cutters in hand, Quint swung down from the tractor and hurried to the fence post on his right. Standing to one side to avoid the whip of the wire, he cut through the top strand, heard the sharp *whang* of its release, and moved to the second, then the third. Careful to avoid the barbed points, he dragged all three strands out of the way, clearing a path for the tractor.

"I'll wait here for Dallas," he shouted to make himself heard above the revving of the tractor's motor.

Empty waved an acknowledging hand and started through the gap in the fence, lowering the plow blades when he was nearly through.

Quint observed the struggle of the blades to dig into the hard-packed ground. The first smoke was already showing above the hilltop. For a moment he doubted that he had picked an area far enough in advance of the flames to give them a chance of stopping them. He'd know soon enough.

By the time Dallas arrived in the pickup, the tractor's headlight beams were past the midway point in the wide swale between the two hills, and a black line of smoke showed above the rise of the first one. Once the fire crested the hill, Quint knew the wind would whip it down the slope at lightning speed.

Off in the distance, he caught the wail of the fire trucks. The sound offered confirmation that help was on the way, but he couldn't wait for it to arrive, not with the smoke smell growing stronger every minute. As soon as the pickup rolled to a stop alongside him, Quint opened the door and hustled Dallas out of the cab.

"Did you bring some gas?" he asked as he slid behind the wheel.

"There's a two-gallon can in the back. It was all I could find."

"It'll have to do." He handed her the flashlight that he kept stowed under the front seat and directed her to wait there for the fire trucks.

He pulled the door shut, effectively cutting off any objections before Dallas could make them, and drove off into the pasture. She stood alone on the darkened ranch lane, conscious of the steadily advancing smoke cloud.

Soon the black pickup blended into the night shapes, its form no longer distinguishable. She had only its red taillights and the outward sweep of its headlight beams to track its passage. Her grandfather was out there somewhere. She could hear the growl of the tractor, but she couldn't see it.

Turning, Dallas threw a searching glance down the lane, her attention drawn to the full-throated cry of sirens. But the fire trucks had yet to roll into view.

Stars dotted the sky to the south. Their glitter was a contrast to the smoke-darkened sky above and behind her. But it was the low ominous sound the approaching fire made, a sound that reminded Dallas of a howling wind, that had her anxiety level rising.

The metallic slam of the pickup door had Dallas swinging back around to face the pasture. She quickly located the lights from the pickup, noticing they were no longer moving. Seconds later, Quint passed in front of the their beams, toting the red gasoline can, before the shadows swallowed him.

As she scanned the darkness in search of him, she became aware of a dim glow in her side vision. It was from the fire, backlighting the hill. Dallas threw another anxious glance down the lane, focusing on the undulating sirens in an effort to judge how close they were.

In the next second, she was startled by the sudden whoosh of flames leaping to life very close to her. A long, yellow line of them ran along the entire base of the hill, stretching to a point well beyond it. The moment she saw them, Dallas realized that Quint had used the gasoline to start a backfire and slow the red flames that now crowned the hill. But it was traveling fast, so very fast.

The sirens' loud wail almost drowned out the screech of brakes that came from the state road, but Dallas caught it and hastily turned on the flashlight as she ran forward to meet the arriving fire engines.

The wind was in the wrong direction to carry the smell of smoke to the Slash R Ranch, yet lights blazed from a half dozen windows in the main house. All shone from the private quarters of its occupants.

Clad in a burgundy silk robe, Max Rutledge shoved open the door to his son's bedroom and maneuvered his wheelchair through the opening as the heirloom clock on the room's fireplace mantel struck the two o'clock hour. His black gaze skipped over his terry-robed manservant and personal nurse, Harold Barnett, and fastened on Boone, seated on a chair, his back to the door and the male nurse.

"Just what in hell is going on here?" Max glowered at Boone as he rolled his chair closer.

Boone tossed him a backward glance. "Exactly what it looks like," he retorted in a hard, tight voice. "Barnett's digging buckshot out of my back."

"It's nothing serious," Barnett said with calm assurance. "Only one is lodged very deeply. The rest barely penetrated the skin." Using surgical tweezers, he plucked one out, drawing a wince from Boone, and added it to the three lead pellets already nestled on a saucer.

Max was close enough to see for himself the blood that lightly seeped from a dozen or so holes across the right side of Boone's muscled back. "Who did it?"

"I didn't hang around to see who was holding the shotgun," Boone answered with sarcasm and grimaced when Barnett probed another hole. "Probably old man Garner. A shotgun's always been his weapon of choice."

Max leaned forward, nearly choking on the rage that reddened his face. "Good God, are you telling me that you went to the Cee Bar tonight?"

Boone nodded, unable to explain why he had chosen to go himself rather than send one of the ranch hands. At the time it had seemed a wise decision, eliminating any chance of loose talk. But that reasoning was now colored by the thrill of the almost overwhelming sense of power he'd experienced slipping through the night, setting the fire.

And when that shotgun had gone off and he'd felt the sting of the blast, there had been a rush unlike anything he'd ever known. But it wasn't something Boone could put into words, not the kind his father would understand. So he didn't try.

"That hay made the biggest bonfire you've ever seen," Boone said, still seeing it in his mind's eye. "It was the slickest thing. I just walked along that row of big bales, touching the flame from the portable butane torch to each one until they were all on fire. I probably should have left it at that," he added. "But I saw a round bale over in the horse corral. So I went over and torched it, too. The fire spooked the horses, though. Old man Garner must have heard the fuss they raised and come out to see what was going on. Another couple of minutes and I would have been long gone."

"My God, what an utter fool you are," Max muttered thickly. "Don't you have enough brains to realize you could have been caught?"

Boone bristled at the anger and derision in his father's voice. "I could have been killed, too, but I wasn't. So quit your bitching and consider that you're getting off easy. You can bet if it was one of the ranch hands sitting here, he'd be squawking big time about getting peppered by a shotgun. And you'd end up paying him a fistful of money to keep his mouth shut. Just look how much I saved you."

"Don't talk to me about the money you saved!" Max exploded in temper. "Not when you could have cost us everything!"

"And just how could I have done that?" Boone taunted as another shotgun pellet plinked into the saucer.

Max stared at him for a long second, his expression a mixture of incredulity and rage. "My God, you really don't have the brains to figure it out, do you?" There was a trace of loathing in the curl of his lip. "It turns my stomach that I have to explain something so obvious to my own son."

"Then don't bother," Boone jeered in retaliation, then grunted sharply in pain and jerked away from Barnett.

"Sorry, sir," Barnett offered in bland apology. "That one's embedded a bit deeper than I thought. It'll take some probing to reach it."

"Then do it," Boone ordered curtly. "But next time give a man some warning."

Coldly silent, Max Rutledge looked on while Barnett switched instruments and resumed his search for the buckshot buried in Boone's back. Sweat beaded on Boone's forehead, but it was the only outward indication of discomfort as he sat unmoving, not a sound coming from his throat, not a single muscle twitching in pain. Once the foreign object was extracted, Barnett was quick to press a gauze pad on the area and stanch the fresh flow of blood from the wound.

"For your information," Max began in an icy-hot voice, "the use of a third party for such tasks as tonight's provides deniability if he should have the misfortune of being caught in the act. It makes it a matter of his word against ours."

"So you've said before." Boone's anger simmered closer to the surface as he lifted his head in challenge. "Have you ever considered how many third parties are out there, scattered over the country? If one starts talking, what's to stop the rest from speaking up? Suddenly it's *their* word against ours."

"Don't be stupid. That will never happen." Max dismissed the notion out of hand.

"Probably not," Boone agreed with reluctance. "If any tried, you'd just hire a bunch more third parties and harass them until they broke, just like you always do."

"Nobody will ever cross me and get away with it." The flat, hard statement was its own warning.

Boone knew it was true, but he felt nothing but disgust for the gutless methods employed by his father. He looked away and muttered, "Why don't you go back to bed and leave me alone? You got what you wanted tonight. The hay's been destroyed."

"I'll leave when I'm ready." The answer came back hot and quick. "In case you've forgotten, I own this house!"

"How can I forget when you constantly ram it down my throat?" Boone fired back, then muttered, more to himself, "Sometimes I wonder why I'm still here."

"You're here because you don't have the brains to make it on your own," Max retorted. "You'd fall flat on your face if you tried."

Goaded by the scathing rebuke, Boone challenged, "If that's true, then how come I know there's a quicker way to put the Cee Bar out of business than the way you're going about it?"

"And just what bright idea have you come up with?" The question was riddled with contempt for its answer.

"I certainly wouldn't waste my time setting fire to a bunch of hay," Boone sneered. "I'd burn the whole damned place down and poison the cattle—"

"And have it splashed across the front page of every newspaper in the state while you're at it. There'd be reporters all over the place. Wouldn't that be an intelligent move?" Max declared in open disparagement. "Don't do any more thinking. Just do what I tell you. And *only* what I tell you," he added in emphasis. "And try not to screw that up."

With a flip of the controls, Max swung the wheelchair in a half circle and rolled out of the bedroom while Boone glared holes in his back. As soon as the door closed, he twisted his head around to throw an impatient glance at Barnett.

"Aren't you finished yet?" he muttered.

"I'll only be a few more moments, sir." The placid Barnett never looked up from his task as he methodically swabbed antiseptic on the first wound and placed a small bandage over it.

"Hurry it up," Boone grumbled and bowed his head once more, but he was smarting too much from his father's cutting remarks to notice the sting inflicted by the antiseptic solution Barnett used. "I'm tired of all his bitching. Every time I turn around he's crawling up my ass about something. It doesn't matter what I say or do, you can bet he'll find fault with it. And I'm getting damned tired of it."

Fully aware that no comment was expected, Barnett withheld any, although he was privately of the opinion that Max Rutledge's judgment of his son was an accurate one.

"All he wants from me are my legs," Boone said in a vindictive mutter. "One of these days he's going to push me too far and, crippled or not, I'll haul him out of that wheelchair and throw him across the room." He paused and laughed to himself. It had a cold, ugly sound. "I can just see him crawling on the floor. Don't you know he'd hate that?"

Barnett smoothed the last bandage in place and straightened up. "There you are, sir. All finished."

"It's about time." Boone pushed out of the chair with the swiftness of an animal that had been too long restrained.

"I'll need to change those dressings tomorrow evening. As slight as your wounds are, we don't want to risk infection setting in," Barnett stated as he gathered together his assortment of instruments, bandages, and antiseptic bottles and returned them to his personal medical bag.

"Yeah, whatever," Boone murmured in absentminded agreement as he scooped the whiskey decanter off the drink tray on his dresser and splashed some in a glass. Too consumed by his own thoughts, he never noticed when Barnett exited the room.

"I get shot. But does he get mad and start ranting about getting even with the man who hurt his son? Hell no. Instead he chews me out for going there in the first place." Boone gulped down a swallow of straight whiskey, the searing fire of it fueling his own anger. "And not because he cared whether something happened to me. No, it was only because the trail would have led straight back to him."

Boone downed another swallow of whiskey, but the anger he felt wasn't the kind that could be washed away.

Smoke swirled among the line of firefighters like a thick fog, blurring shapes and making it impossible for Dallas to identify the men working only yards from her. Now and then a flame would leap high enough to reveal the blackened stretch of fire-scorched earth on the opposite side of the dry wash. But she searched only for the tiny tongues of fire that sprang up on her side.

Rivulets of sweat ran down her neck, partly from the physical exertion of fighting the blaze and partly from its blistering heat. Soot and ash mixed in with the perspiration to leave muddy streaks on her face. But Dallas was oblivious of them.

Not far from her, water from a fire hose arced across the wash and hit a section of flames on the other side. There was a whoosh and a sizzle, and an instant eruption of steam and smoke, littered with sparks.

Enveloped in a thick, hot cloud, Dallas automatically turned away and clamped a hand over her mouth and nose to avoid breathing in too much of the choking smoke while she retreated from the dense haze.

Speed was impossible over the newly plowed ground. She stumbled over a hard clod and would have fallen if a pair of hands hadn't steadied her.

"Careful." The quiet-voiced warning was muffled by a dingy white handkerchief tied across the lower half of her rescuer's face. But Dallas would have recognized Quint's voice and those gray eyes anywhere.

"Thanks," she murmured, not at all surprised to find Quint at her side.

Several times since the fire trucks arrived, she'd caught glimpses of him, moving up and down the fire line, pitching in to help where the flames threatened to jump the wash and run wild again.

"Are you all right?" A supporting hand remained on her.

Dallas tried to nod in answer and started coughing instead. His grip shifted to her waist. "Let's get you out of here," Quint said and proceeded to half carry and half guide her clear of the thick smoke. He turned her to face him and pulled down the masking kerchief. "Can you breathe okay now?" he asked, tipping his head toward her.

She smothered a last, low cough and nodded. "I'm fine."

The lines around his eyes crinkled in a smile. "Good." His glance immediately darted back to the fire line. "I think the worst is over. We've almost got it under control."

The words were barely out of his mouth when flames shot into the air, soaring twenty feet high or more some distance to the west. Dallas breathed in a sharp gasp of alarm at the size and suddenness of them.

"The hay bale Empty put out for the cattle," Quint said in explanation. "I figured it would be going up any second now. I was right."

Reassured by his lack of concern, Dallas felt her pulse settle back into its normal rhythm and pulled her gaze away from the fiery yellow tower, bringing it back to Quint. His face was in profile, the ridges and hollows of his lean features lit by the brilliant glow of the distant flames.

There was no weariness or worry in his expression. The impression he gave was one of alertness and determination. But Dallas recalled it had been that way from the moment the fire was first discovered, showing haste but never panic or indecision.

"Empty should be coming along with the tractor any minute now," Quint said, once more bringing his attention back to her. "When he does, have him take you back to the ranch house." Before Dallas could insist again that she was fine, Quint added, "Make sure he goes with you. He looked like he was about to collapse when I last saw him. But you know Empty. He's too proud to admit that."

"But even if he takes me back, he'll never stay." Concern for her grandfather had Dallas searching for an excuse he might believe.

Quint was quick to provide one. "He can help you throw together some sandwiches and coffee for the firefighters. It'll be his job to bring them back here as soon as they're all made and packed up. But take your time and keep him out of this smoke for as long as you can."

"I'll find a way," she promised.

His gray eyes crinkled at the corners again. The chug of the tractor reached them, and Quint turned in the direction of the sound. "Here he comes now," he said as the tractor's headlights became visible in the smoky darkness. "Good luck."

When he headed for the fire line, Dallas called after him, "Be careful."

She couldn't tell whether Quint had heard her. At the same time, she knew her words of caution were unnecessary. She had the feeling Quint could handle anything that came his way.

Except Rutledge, of course.

# PART THREE

*A shining star,*
*A rainy night,*
*A Calder loves,*
*But something's not right.*

# Chapter Twelve

S hortly after dawn the fire was out, and the exodus of the fire-fighting units began as the focus shifted to searching out hot spots and hosing down the still-smoldering hay bales next to the ranch yard, a task that required the services of only a single fire truck and its crew.

Standing at a kitchen window, Dallas had a clear view of the charred landscape to the south. Where the hay bales had been, there was a long, black heap of ash and cinder with only an occasional golden scrap of unburned hay glinting in the morning sunlight.

With no more wisps of smoke coming from the hay pile, one of the firemen was busy stowing the hose in the truck. A second man had already shed his protective gear and stood talking to Quint.

But it was the tired slouch of Quint's shoulders that claimed her attention. There were smudges of soot and ash on his jeans and denim jacket. Dallas suspected that a closer inspection of his clothes would reveal a collection of burn marks where sparks had landed.

After an exchange of parting words, Quint backed a step, then turned and headed toward the house in a slow, leg-weary walk.

When she heard the clump of a booted foot on the porch planks, Dallas moved away from the window and crossed to the kitchen cupboards.

The back door opened and Quint walked in, bringing with him the smell of smoke and wet ash. His glance traveled around the kitchen and came to a stop on her.

"I hope you still have some coffee left." Half turning, he closed the door, shutting out the rumble of the fire truck's motor as it started up.

"Just made a fresh pot." Dallas reached into the upper cabinet for a clean cup. "The fire truck's leaving, is it?"

"Yeah." Some of his fatigue crept into Quint's voice. "There's still a couple of guys on the fire line, making sure there's nothing smoldering. They'll hang around most of the morning, just to play it safe."

Quint shrugged out of his jean jacket and gave it a halfhearted toss onto one of the kitchen chairs. He was shirtless beneath it. Just for an instant Dallas was unnerved by the unobstructed view she had of his lean-muscled torso as he walked over to the sink. But one glimpse of the contrast between the bare flesh across his back and the grimy color of his face, neck, forearms, and a long swath down the front of his chest, and Dallas understood the practicality of his actions.

"I guess the fire marshal will be out either this afternoon or to-morrow," Quint said as he turned on the faucets and adjusted the water temperature.

"I suppose that's standard procedure." She filled his cup with coffee and tried to ignore the distraction of all that hard, bare skin. It was impossible. "You did tell them about the man you saw running away."

"I told the fire chief." Quint soaped his hands and forearms all the way up to his elbows until a gray lather covered them, then rinsed it off under the faucet. "You and I both know it was arson. Proving it might be something else, though. More than likely it will simply be labeled 'suspicious.' "

Dallas stared at him in surprise. "Why only 'suspicious'?"

"Without any evidence of cause or some type of accelerant, arson becomes difficult to prove." Bending, Quint splashed water on his face and neck, then reached again for the soap bar. "As dry as that hay was, a cigarette lighter is all it would have taken. We can only hope the arsonist was stupid enough to leave it behind— assuming that's what he used. Although it could just as easily have been one of those small portable torches they make nowadays."

"If they found something like that, then that would be proof, wouldn't it?" But Dallas didn't have much hope that it would occur.

"It would be proof, and evidence that a crime lab could trace." Eyes closed against the stinging lather, Quint scrubbed at his face and neck.

"I wouldn't hold my breath if I were you." Dallas removed a clean hand towel from one of the lower drawers. "Rutledge would never allow any of his men to make such a foolish mistake."

Quint nodded an agreement and ducked his whole head under the faucet to rinse off the soap, not caring that he got his hair wet. When he straightened up and started to grope for a towel, Dallas placed the fresh one in his hand.

"Thanks," he said and pressed it first to his face, then down and over his neck, and lastly wiped his hands and arms. The sooty grime was gone from his face, exposing the fatigue that pulled at him. He dragged in a deep breath, then sighed it out. "That's better. At least now I feel halfway human."

"You look it too," Dallas retorted in light jest, although there was nothing remotely amusing about her response to the sight of him standing there, his skin gleaming with a lingering dampness, moisture making black spikes of his eyelashes and emphasizing the gray of his eyes.

Quint made a last swipe at the wetness along one side of his neck and glanced curiously around the kitchen. "Where's Empty?"

"He fell asleep in his chair about two hours ago. He went to have a relaxing cup of coffee before heading out to do the morning chores and fell asleep almost the minute he tipped his head back."

"I forgot all about the chores," Quint muttered in irritation.

"Don't worry. They're already done." Dallas found it difficult to keep her glance from sliding down to his tanned chest and the crown of dark hair in its center.

"Thanks." His eyes warmed on her. A slow smile curved his mouth as he turned at right angles to her and leaned a hip against the sink counter, the towel still clasped between his hands. "Speaking of thanks, the chief asked me to pass along his. The men really appreciated the sandwiches and coffee you carted out to them last night."

"I can hardly take credit for that. It wasn't even my idea." There really wasn't any reason for her to continue standing there, but her feet seemed rooted to the floor. "While we're on the subject of coffee, though, I already poured you some." She gestured to the cup on the counter.

"Thanks." Quint twisted the towel over his hands in a final wipe and started to set it aside, then hesitated and lifted it close to his face before laying it aside. "It smells of smoke now."

"Everything does," Dallas countered.

"You don't." His gaze returned to her, something darkening his eyes, something that had her pulse skipping. "You smell of strawberries." He reached over and lifted the lock of hair that rested on the front of her shoulder, fingering it lightly. "It seems right—a strawberry scent for a strawberry blonde."

"Does it?" Her voice was suddenly husky, and it wasn't from the effects of the smoke.

"Yes." His response was little more than a low murmur. He swayed closer to her, then paused, a wistful smile edging the curve of his mouth. "You don't know how tempting you look, Dallas. Or how tempted I am to—"

He never finished the sentence. Instead, his head made a slow dip toward hers, his hands staying at his side, making no move to gather her into his arms. An inner voice warned Dallas to step away—now—while she still could, but she didn't listen to it.

Her lashes fluttered shut as his mouth moved over her lips, warm and exquisitely tender, yet full of aching need.

Thrilling to it, Dallas melted against him, a desire of her own clamoring within.

Her hands slid over the tapered firmness of the back she had longed to touch, exploring the complex roping of muscle and sinew. Then, and only then, did she feel the circling of his arms draw her more fully against him.

The kiss deepened seemingly of its own accord into something hot and wet and greedy. Everything swirled together, arching and straining, striving for something more. When his mouth rolled off hers to travel hungrily over her cheeks, eyes, and brow, Dallas pulled in a trembling breath that seemed to lodge somewhere in her throat.

"This is something I've wanted to do," Quint admitted, "almost from the moment I laid eyes on you."

"What stopped you?" But Dallas knew she had, at least in the beginning. A man worth having needs encouragement, and she hadn't shown him any, even though the attraction had been there from the start.

Quint raised his head, his fingers tunneling into her hair as his gaze wandered over her face in a kind of visual caress. "It didn't seem fair to get you caught up in this battle with Rutledge." He smiled crookedly. "Then you went and involved yourself anyway. I'll never forget how you stormed out here that day."

She remembered it, too—the fury, the frustration, and the anguish—but for an entirely different reason. "Why did you kiss me that day?" Needing to renew contact with him and shut out the fear, Dallas rubbed her lips over his chin, ignoring the scrape of his whiskers.

"I don't know," Quint murmured. "I guess I was hurt and mad. Anger was all I ever seemed to arouse in you, and I wanted exactly the opposite."

"You definitely got your message across," Dallas declared. "Coming out of nowhere like that, it scared me a little."

It still did when she tried to think beyond this moment. But there would be time enough to consider what tomorrow might hold. It was enough to savor the here and now.

"I knew I'd scared you with that kiss. I—"

"Shhh." She pressed two fingers to his lips. "None of that matters. Not now."

Her lips were quick to take the place of her silencing fingers. His arms tightened around her as his mouth opened moistly on her lips, taking them whole.

Everything quickened and rose inside her, blood rushing hotly through her veins and all her senses sharply intensifying. The invasion of his tongue brought with it a bold sensuality and something else—a kind of keening sweetness that had its own brand of glory. Dallas arched closer to the hard length of his body, letting it burn its impression on her.

Desire and discovery reigned, making them both oblivious of the muffled slam of a door and the faint thud of footsteps across the porch. They were absorbed too much in each other and the power of what they shared.


On the porch, Boone cast a backward look at the charred remains of the round bales and the fire-scorched landscape that stretched beyond it. His glance lingered there. He derived a sense of satisfaction from knowing that it had been his hand that caused all this devastation.

He felt strangely empowered by the sight. It was there in the gleam of his eyes when he turned back to the door.

The screen door squeaked in protest when he opened it. As he lifted a hand to rap on the door, Boone automatically glanced through the windowed upper portion of the door. He paused at the sight of the pair, locked in an embrace that could only be described as passionate. The gleam in his eyes took on an interested glitter.

The voyeuristic side of him was tempted to watch, aware that, in Echohawk's place, he would be tugging off the redhead's clothes and spreading her across the kitchen table in another minute. Before his imagination reached the point where Echohawk plunged into her, irritation surfaced that he hadn't suspected there was that much wildness beneath the Garner woman's cool poise.

Boone rapped sharply on the door and watched them pull apart before giving the knob a turn. As he stepped inside, the two separated to face him. Echohawk's expression instantly hardened at the sight of him while Dallas stared at him in open shock. Boone rather liked the glimmer of fear in her eyes.

Echohawk never gave him a chance to speak, demanding, "What are you doing here, Rutledge?"

"Max asked me to come." Actually he had ordered him, but Boone wasn't about to admit that. "We heard about your fire last night." He let his glance stray over his shoulder to the door's windowed top and the blackened area visible beyond the ranch yard. "It burned a big chunk of your range. Looks like it must have covered a good three or four hundred acres."

"Closer to five," Quint confirmed, his gaze never losing its steely look.

"That much?" Dallas murmured in surprise, slashing Quint a look of concern.

Boone ignored that, his curiosity shifting to something else. "What about your cattle? Did you suffer any losses there?"

"Considering the last fire crew pulled out less than twenty minutes ago, I haven't had a chance to check on the stock. But all the gates were open. As long as they weren't trapped against a fence, they should have been able to escape the flames."

"You never know," Boone said, deliberately countering Quint's optimism. "Cows can be dumb creatures, especially when they panic. And a fire would cause that. As dry as it's been around here, I'm surprised we haven't had more fires. It wouldn't take much of a spark to ignite one, and once it starts burning, it can spread rapidly."

"It was no accidental spark that started this one." The flat, hard statement teetered close to an accusation.

Boone feigned surprise. "How do you know that?"

"About the same time I discovered the fire, I saw a man running away." Quint paused. Something that wasn't amusement curved his mouth. "I even managed to get off a shot at him."

Surprise splintered through Boone at the news that it hadn't been old man Garner wielding the shotgun. The discovery that it had been Echohawk rankled.

But Boone had played too many hands of poker to let his reaction creep into his expression. "I hope you hit him."

"Unfortunately he was out of shotgun range," Quint replied.

Boone knew better; he had the bandages on his back to prove it. "Too bad. The sheriff might have had a chance of catching him then. Now he'll have to make do with just a description of your arsonist. You did get a good look at him, didn't you?"

Quint cocked his head to one side. "Is that why Max sent you over here? To find out if I got a good enough look at your man to identify him?"

Boone shook his head and smiled broadly. "You've got us all wrong. I think you've been listening to her grandfather too much," he said, indicating Dallas with a nod. "That isn't why I'm here at all."

"Then why are you here?" Dallas said in quick challenge, using anger to mask the fear that lurked around the edges.

"Because Max learned that the fire destroyed your hay," Boone replied smoothly. "Along with passing on his regrets for the loss of it, I'm to tell you that we're sending some hay to tide you over until you can get more delivered."

"That's generous," Quint murmured dryly.

"In Texas, neighbors help neighbors," Boone responded, shrugging it off while secretly relishing the irony of the gesture.

On the heels of his remark, there was a movement in his side vision. Boone glanced around as Empty Garner padded into the kitchen in his stockinged feet, looking all mussed and sleepy-eyed.

"Any time a Rutledge helps a neighbor, you can bet he'll stab him in the back before he's done." The accusation was accompanied by a layer of loathing. "Don't let him fool you," Empty said, issuing the warning to Quint. "Him sending you over hay, it's all for show, and to fool people into thinking he didn't have anything to do with your hay getting burned."

"His motives for sending it don't really matter," Quint replied with a touch of grim resignation. "We need the hay."

"Echohawk is more pragmatic than you are, Garner," Boone observed with a complacent smile. "He knows better than to look a gift horse in the mouth."

The old man snorted. "Might be smarter if he did. Look what happened at Troy."

Boone gave him a puzzled look, failing to make the connection between Troy and the Trojan horse. Rather than admit his lack of knowledge, he switched back to the original subject. "Like I said, we'll be bringing the hay over some time today." He paused a beat. "I can't say for sure when it will be, but probably this afternoon. You might want to let Dallas know where you want it stored. That way you won't have to hang around here waiting for it to show up. I imagine you have a lot of other things you need to get done."

Quint made no reply to that, saying instead, "I'll expect to receive a bill for the hay."

Boone shrugged his indifference. "If that's what you want."

"I do."

Boone reached behind him for the door. "Let us know if there's anything else we can do to help."

"It'd be a big help if you'd just leave the Cee Bar alone," Empty retorted. "But it's not likely you'll do that."

Boone shot a look at Dallas as he opened the door. "I'll be seeing you."

When the door closed behind Boone, Dallas turned away in agitation, fighting the turmoil inside, angry and scared both at the same time.

"I wouldn't be surprised if Rutledge sends over hay that's been treated with something that will make the livestock sick," Empty grumbled behind her.

"He wouldn't," Quint stated. "Not on hay that could be traced directly back to him."

"Maybe not," Empty conceded with reluctance. "Where'd I put my damned boots?"

"I think you left them in the bathroom," Dallas answered. "At least they were there when I took my shower."

"That's right. I forgot I took them off in there," he murmured. "I would've remembered if I hadn't got so mad at how righteous that Boone was acting. Hell, he just came over here to look at the damage and gloat."

He all but stomped out of the kitchen. Dallas glanced after him. There was a light touch on her shoulder, and she turned with a jerk, finding herself the subject of Quint's probing gaze.

"What's wrong?"

After a quick, stiff shake of her head, she sighed in frustration. "Boone. The Rutledges." Her voice was tight with the bitterness and anger. "Somehow, in some dirty underhanded way, they always get what they want."

"Not this time." The calm certainty in his voice brought a twist to the line of her mouth.

"I know you think it will be different this time, but it won't," Dallas said. "They don't care how long it takes. That's the advantage they have. And during all that time, it will be just one hassle on top of another. Machinery sabotaged, hay burned, hired men scared off, cattle auctions rigged, credit refused. And that's just a small part of the trouble they'll cause. How long do you think it will take before the Calders decide this ranch isn't worth all the trouble and grief it's given them and throw in the towel? One year? Two? Five?" she challenged, pain and anger mixing together. "I had a front-row seat when they broke my grandfather—broke his heart and his spirit. I don't want to see that happen to you."

"It won't, Dallas," Quint insisted, smiling in easy assurance.

"You'll fight to the bitter end, won't you?" Dallas saw it in his face. That knowledge only added to the turmoil ripping through her. "Why?" she demanded in frustration. "It won't change anything. I know this is your job, but you'd be better off to convince the Calders to cut their losses and unload the ranch now."

"That will never happen." Some of the gentleness went out of his expression, his features setting in resolute lines.

"In time it will. The Calders won't have any choice." Her statement was forceful in an attempt to press home the reality of the situation to him.

A coolness entered his gray eyes. "You don't know the Calders."

"Neither do you," Dallas countered with impatience. "You said yourself that you've only worked for them a few months."

Quint never blinked an eye. "I'm a Calder; that's how I know. My grandfather is Chase Calder," he stated and moved past her.

For a split second Dallas was too stunned to react. Turning, she reached for his arm, stopping him before he could leave the room.

"I'm sorry." The phrase came automatically to her lips.

But Quint was unmoved by it. "About what?" he challenged coolly. "That I'm a Calder?"

"I wasn't referring to that at all," Dallas denied, annoyed that he would even think she was.

"Then what?" he repeated, but never gave her a chance to respond. "When you threw your lot in with the Cee Bar, you said it was because you didn't want to see the Rutledges win. And here you are, trying to convince me to give up. I think you need to make up your mind whose side you're on."

His point was inarguable, but it stung. "Just because I don't want them to win, it doesn't mean that I don't think they will. And I take back my apology. Whether you like it or not, I'm not sorry for anything I said. For your information, I care what happens to you!"

A sudden smile curved his mouth, and that intimate light was back in his eyes. "You did make that very clear a few minutes ago," he murmured and cupped a hand to her cheek, stroking his thumb across her lips and igniting a fresh disturbance.

"Quint," she began, only to hear the solid thud of approaching footsteps signal her grandfather's return to the kitchen.

Regret flashed in her expression at the inopportune loss of privacy, and she stepped back, away from his hand.

"We always seem to get interrupted," Quint murmured. A wry smile tugged at a corner of his mouth as he brought his hand down to his side.

Dallas nodded in agreement a second before Empty Garner appeared in the kitchen doorway. He paused at the sight of them and directed a frowning glance at Dallas.

"How come you're still standing around? I thought you'd be fixing this poor man some breakfast by now." Empty gestured at Quint. "After working all night, he needs some food in his belly."

Seizing on his suggestion, Dallas walked directly to the refrigerator. "Over easy on the eggs?" she asked over her shoulder.

"Sounds fine," Quint replied and started toward the kitchen table.

The action drew a quick frown of disapproval from Empty. "Don't you think you better put a shirt on first?" To his old-fashioned way of thinking, a man didn't sit down to eat half clothed.

"You're right," Quint agreed with a faint trace of chagrin.

Empty watched him leave the kitchen, then headed for the coffeepot and poured himself a cup. In the true, asbestos-mouthed tradition of a longtime cowman, he downed a healthy swallow of the hot liquid, then turned a curious eye on Dallas when she set a carton of eggs and a package of bacon on the counter next to the range top.

"What's going on between you two?" Empty wandered over to the stove.

"What do you mean?" She slid him a brief, uncommunicative glance.

"I heard you two arguing just now."

"We weren't arguing. Just disagreeing." Dallas turned on the burner underneath the cast iron skillet. "We worked it out. Every-thing's fine now."

"Good." He nodded in satisfaction. "The Rutledges are giving him enough grief without you pouring more on him."

Dallas knew that better than he did, but she chose not to say so. "Did you know Quint is a grandson of the Calders?" she asked instead.

"Is that a fact?" Empty murmured, eyebrows raised. "Says some-thing about the Calders, that they'd send one of their own."

"How?" Dallas gave him a puzzled look.

"When they've got trouble, they don't send somebody else to deal with it; they handle it themselves. You don't see that too often nowadays," he added thoughtfully. "It's kind of nice to know there are still people like that around."

A faint smile curved her mouth. His words were an echo of one of the old codes of conduct that decreed a man should fight his own battles. Considering how strongly rooted her grandfather's beliefs were in the old traditions, Dallas wasn't surprised that this decision of the Calders to send Quint had found favor in his eyes.

After adding a final strip of bacon to the skillet, Dallas started to reseal the package. Empty peered over her shoulder.

"Don't be so stingy with the bacon."

Dallas stared at the six strips in the skillet and frowned. "Six isn't stingy, unless you plan on having some."

"I already had my breakfast," he reminded her. "But Quint's got a man's appetite. He'd probably eat the whole package if you fried it."

She added two more slices to the large skillet. "How's that?"

"It'll do," Empty declared.

The aroma of frying bacon filled the kitchen, banishing the smoke smell, when Quint returned to it, a blue chambray work shirt tucked inside his jeans and a belt fastened around his middle. A smile edged the corners of his mouth at the sight of Dallas standing at the stove, her long coppery blond hair flipped forward to fall over one shoul-der, baring the curve of her neck.

The urge was strong to walk up behind her, slide his arms around her waist, and nibble along that curve. It was only Empty's presence in the room that prevented Quint from taking such a liberty. It was enough that he knew Dallas would have welcomed it if he had. The knowledge brought a deep contentment that warmed and buoyed him. The shine of it was in his eyes when he met her over-the-shoulder glance.

"Excellent timing," Dallas said. "Your eggs will be ready in a minute."

"Good. I didn't realize how hungry I was until I smelled that bacon." After pouring a fresh cup of coffee, Quint carried it to the table, pulled out a chair, and sat down.

Empty occupied the chair across the table from him, his gnarled and sun-leathered hands clasped around an empty cup. "Dallas tells me that all the firemen pulled out except for a handful. I gotta admit I'm not looking forward to going out there and surveying the extent of the damage."

Earlier Quint had been dreading it, too. But the prospect no longer bothered him in the least. Those moments with Dallas had changed that—and the brief taste they'd given him of the glory a man and woman could know, the kind that evoked an emotion older than time. It was something he had unknowingly sought for years.

It wasn't a man's way to question that it was too soon or too sudden for such certainty; he simply accepted it as fact.

"The fire accomplished one thing." Quint took a sip of his coffee. "I planned on doing some winter seeding to improve the graze. And the fire provided a clean slate for that."

"That's one way of looking at it." But Empty's view wasn't as positive. "To tell you the truth, I don't think we could have stopped those flames if the fire trucks hadn't shown up when they did. A hundred years ago we wouldn't have had a prayer of halting it."

"There might have been a way," Quint said. "I remember a story my grandfather told me about a prairie fire that threatened to sweep across half or more of the Triple C range back in the ranch's early days. To stop it, they killed a couple of steers, skinned them, and used ropes to stretch the carcasses between two riders, then dragged them over the fire until they smothered it."

"How gruesome," Dallas said with an expressive little shudder and transferred the fried eggs from the skillet to a plate.

"I never heard of doing such a thing . . . but I can see how it could work," Empty declared with a slow, affirming nod of his head.

Dallas crossed to the table and set a plate of eggs, bacon, and toast in front of Quint. A smile accompanied his upward glance, the warm light in his eyes conveying more than mere gratitude.

"Thanks." Quint was aware of the way her gaze clung to him for an instant, then skittered self-consciously to her grandfather before sliding away altogether.

She bypassed the empty chair next to him and headed straight for the coffeepot. "Are you ready for another cup, Empty?"

"Sure." He pulled one hand away from his cup and sat back to give her room to fill it. "So, what are your plans?" Empty directed the question to Quint. "Do you want to drive out and look around after you finish breakfast or are you going to call the Triple C first and give them a heads-up on the fire?"

Quint shook his head and used his fork to cut off a bite of egg. "I'll let them know about the fire after I've determined the full scope of the damage."

"It'll save you making two phone calls," Empty said in approval. "There's not much they can do clear up in Montana anyway. I guess you already figured that out."

"Where do you want the hay stacked?" Dallas asked, returning to the table with the coffeepot.

"In one of the barn stalls. It doesn't matter which one," Quint answered between bites.

The sun's morning rays streamed through the barn's wide opening, bringing light to its cavernous alleyway and darkening its shadowy corners. A few yards inside the barn, Dallas stood next to one of the stalls, fingertips tucked in the hip pockets of her jeans.

It was a casual pose that disguised the high tension she felt as she watched another Slash R ranch hand walk past her, holding a square bale in front of him by its twine. A fresh swirl of dust motes danced in his wake.

Her gaze followed him to the open stall where the hay was being stored. There, it switched to John Earl Tandy as he emerged to retrace his steps to the stock trailer parked outside the barn doors.

The two men passed each other without speaking. The only sounds to be heard were the rustle of hay, booted footsteps on the barn's cement floor, and the occasional grunted breath of exertion.

Dallas knew both men, but neither had addressed a single word to her, and merely acknowledged her presence with a slight nod on their arrival. She suspected they held their silence for the same reason she did—the presence of the man beside her, Boone Rutledge.

In her side vision, she could make out the long shape of him, leaning against the stall gate, one leg cocked, a near smirk on his lips. Dallas knew every time his dark glance drifted over her, making a man's slow, raking study of her. The touch of it was enough to make her skin crawl.

John Earl poked his head inside the stock trailer, then swung back around and looked directly at Boone.

"That was the last of them," he announced.

Boone made a languid show of straightening himself away from the stall. "I'll see you and Rivers back at the ranch then." His dark glance encompassed both men in its dismissal of them.

"Right." John Earl pulled the trailer gate closed, double-checked to make sure it was securely latched, then sent a glance at his partner to verify he was on his way.

Using their departure as an excuse to move, Dallas crossed the alleyway and paused outside the stall with the hay as if inspecting it. Boone followed while, outside, there was the twin thud of pickup doors being pulled shut, followed by the revving of its engine.

When the pickup pulled away from the barn, the empty stock trailer rattling behind it, Boone rested a hand on the top of her shoulder. "What do you think Echohawk's going to say when he finds out the hay came this morning instead of this afternoon?" he wondered, sounding almost smug.

"Probably nothing." She made an abrupt right-angle turn to shrug off the loose weight of his hand.

Boone simply transferred it to the opposite shoulder. But this time he shifted it forward, fingertips sliding under the neckline of her blouse. Dallas immediately seized his hand and attempted to push it away. But she was no match for his strength.

"Keep your hands off me." Her voice trembled with the depth of her loathing.

"Take it easy." His grin was wide and taunting. "I'm just making sure there aren't any bugs on you," he said, putting a light stress on the word *bug*.

Dallas knew at once that Boone was referring to a recording device. "You don't have to worry about that. I'm not wearing any," she said curtly.

"Just to be safe, I'd better check—whether you like it or not." The smiling glitter in his eyes showed a desire that seemed to welcome any attempt to resist a search.

Dallas had no difficulty imagining the pleasure he would get out of a forcible search. Fighting it would prolong the inevitable.

Steeling herself to endure the touch of his hands, she swung to face him. "Then let's get it over with."

"That's a sensible attitude to take." Boone stepped closer. "But you are a sensible woman, aren't you?"

Any thought of responding to his comment fled the instant he cupped his hands over her breasts, fingers feeling around as if searching for the telltale ridge of a wire or small microphone, and taking their own sweet time about it.

"Satisfied?" Dallas challenged, fighting the bitter gall in her throat.

"Not quite," he said as his hands moved to her waist, fingers gliding inside the waistband of her jeans, touching bare skin and following all the way around to her spine.

Dallas maintained a rigid stance, not moving an inch even when his arms virtually encircled her, bringing her face against his shirtfront. Just when she thought she couldn't tolerate his touch another second, Boone stepped back and crouched down to run his hands down the length of her leg and back up again. Her control lasted right up to the moment when a hand cupped her crotch. At that point she jerked back from him and retreated a step.

"You're enjoying this too much," she accused.

"It's your fault," Boone countered. "I can't seem to get it out of my mind—that picture you made when I caught you two together this morning." His voice was all low and lazy, but not his eyes. They had an avid interest. "You were crawling all over Echohawk, eating his mouth like a starving woman. And all along I thought the only thing hot about you was your temper. I was obviously wrong about that."

His hand glided onto the side of her neck with insidious ease. Dallas reacted with a swift and hard swing of her arm, knocking his hand away.

"That's my job, isn't it?" Dallas challenged, her voice thick with revulsion—for Boone and this whole business. "To win his confidence? Get Quint to tell me his plans?"

"I didn't know you could do it so well. You're just full of hidden talents."

"Stop making it sound like something dirty. It wasn't like that." Dallas was stiff with resentment and sickened by his attitude.

"My, aren't we testy?" Boone mocked in amusement and cocked his head to one side. "Could it be that you're starting to like him a little?"

Her chin came up high in defiance. "I like him a lot better than I like you."

"That tongue of yours hasn't lost its sharpness, has it?" Boone laughed in his throat.

"Not when it comes to you, it hasn't," Dallas retorted.

But the gibe never fazed him. "So what have you managed to find out so far?"

"I've learned that you have a real fight on your hands." Dallas took pleasure in telling him that. "You aren't going to find it easy to make Quint knuckle under."

"He will, though." Boone oozed with confidence. "It's only a matter of time. But you know that."

Loath to admit that she knew it was too bitterly true, Dallas said instead, "I suppose you already know he's a grandson of the Calders."

"Naturally."

"You could have told me. I thought he was just another hired man."

"What difference does it make?" Boone countered in smooth dismissal.

"None, I suppose," Dallas admitted reluctantly. "It's just that . . . his family owns this land. It will make him even more determined to hang on to it." She paused, then couldn't resist the dig. "Maybe this time you won't win."

His gaze sharpened on her, eyes narrowing. "Now that's dangerous thinking. It tells me you might have enjoyed kissing him a little too much." His statement was too accurate for comfort, making it difficult for Dallas to hold his steady regard. "Maybe it's given you the idea that you could catch yourself a Calder if you play your cards right."

"You don't know what you're talking about." Dallas turned away in a show of anger and disgust. "For your information, marriage is the furthest thing from my mind."

"That's right. You have your sights set on a college degree," Boone recalled thoughtfully. "You keep them there because a little Miss Nobody from Texas like you doesn't have a chance in hell of getting Echohawk to the altar—especially when you consider that his cousin just married an English lord. As the old saying goes, he might bed you, but he'll never wed you."

"You've made your point," Dallas flashed.

"I hope so." Boone continued to study her. "Because it's your grandfather you need to be thinking about, and what might happen to him if you are foolish enough to change sides."

She raged inwardly, but it was the impotent kind. All she could do was glare. "I'll keep my side of the bargain. You'd better keep yours. Because if anything happens to Empty, even accidentally, I'll find a way to make you pay."

"Issuing threats, are you?" he said with amusement.

"Surely you're not surprised," Dallas countered, acid in her voice. "I learned it from you."

Boone smiled. "But I never make threats I can't carry out. You need to remember that."

It galled her to let Boone have the last word on the subject, but Dallas had no counter to his statement. "Can we get to the point of this meeting?" she challenged instead.

"You know you really should be nicer to me," he murmured.

"That wasn't part of the deal," she reminded him coolly.

"It can always be changed."

When his hand moved toward her cheek, Dallas struck it aside before it could reach its target, her eyes ablaze with temper. "It'll stay just as it is, thank you," she snapped and moved a cautious step back.

Anger flickered in his expression, then faded into something vaguely cunning and determined. "As smart as you are, you'll change your mind once you've had time to think about it."

"Don't count on it."

Boone smiled and turned to face the stall, stacked with square bales. "This hay isn't going to last Echohawk up a short hill. He'll have to buy more. The question is, where and from whom? I'll expect a call from you as soon as you know."

"You'll get it," Dallas stated, all too conscious of the bad taste the words left in her mouth.

# Chapter Thirteen

The sun sat atop the western horizon. The red glare of it poured through the driver's-side window when a dusty and ash-coated pickup pulled up at the fence gate. At the cessation of movement, Empty Garner roused himself and groped to locate the door handle on the cab's passenger side.

"Where is the damned thing?" Empty grumbled in annoyance.

Quint took one look at the old man's face, hollow-eyed with fatigue, and threw the gearshift into Park. "I'll open the gate."

Empty subsided against the seat back without protest, a statement in itself of his bone-tiredness. Quint's own legs felt wooden beneath him when he stepped to the ground. As he advanced to the gate, his gaze made an automatic sweep of the charred landscape, empty of any living creature. It was an all-too-familiar sight.

He unlatched the gate and dragged it open wide, then climbed back in the idling pickup. Without turning his head, Empty sent him a weary look.

"I wouldn't bother to close it if I were you," he said. "No cow's going to venture across all that burned ground to get to it."

"You're probably right," Quint agreed and drove through the

opening, but the habit of closing a gate behind him was too deeply ingrained. He stopped the truck, got out, and shut the gate.

When he parked in front of the low ranch house, Empty declared, "It's been a long damned day. I don't mind telling you I'm glad to see the end of it."

Quint switched off the engine and reached for the door. "I keep telling myself it could have been worse, but it was bad enough."

As he swung out of the cab, the door to the kitchen opened and Dallas stepped onto the porch. A moment ago Quint had been so tired that he felt half drunk, but the sight of her standing there, tall and slim, coppery pale hair catching fire in the sun's waning light, lifted some of the weariness from him.

"There's someone on the phone for you, Quint," she called. "It's Jessy Calder."

"Coming," he said in answer and forced his legs to quicken their pace.

Behind him, Empty called to Dallas, "Did you get the chores done?"

"All done," she confirmed and moved to one side of the doorway, allowing room for Quint to pass.

Once in the kitchen, Quint walked straight to the corner desk and picked up the receiver lying next to the phone. "Hi, Jess. It's Quint." Knowing the conversation could turn into a long one, he sat down in the old wooden office chair.

"You're working late tonight." Her familiar voice sounded in his ear, registering above Empty's grumbling voice as he trooped ahead of Dallas into the house.

"I guess you could say that," Quint replied and let out a sigh. "We've had some trouble here."

"It's the hay, isn't it?" she guessed. "Chase has been worrying about it."

"He had cause," Quint admitted and absently watched when Dallas took her grandfather's jacket and hat from him and hung them on the iron hooks near the door. "It's gone. Burned. Every bit of it. Along with nearly five hundred acres of grass."

"How? When?" The questions came rapid-fire.

Quint wasn't surprised that Jessy would seek the facts first. There was a lesson to be learned from the way she dealt with things.

Details she wanted, and details he provided, everything from his discovery of the fire and the man he'd seen running away to the shot he'd fired and their efforts to check the blaze prior to the arrival of the firefighting crews. Through it all a part of him registered the other activity going on in the kitchen, water gushing from the faucets, Empty standing at the sink, washing his hands, Dallas collecting plates and silverware and placing them around the table, the vague hum of their voices.

"Most of the stock managed to escape the fire, but we did find three cows that were cut up pretty bad. They had some burns around the hocks and singed skin. More than likely they went through the barbed wire fence to get away from the flames." Quint rubbed a hand against his forehead and struggled to organize the damages into a coherent list, but nearly thirty-six hours without sleep was having its effect on him. "Right now none of their injuries look to be serious, although one of the cows did abort her calf. The fire weakened nearly all of the wooden posts along the inner fencing," he continued. "So all of it will have to be replaced."

At the stove, Dallas turned the burner down under a pot of corn and strained to catch Quint's words. A chair leg scraped across the floor, cutting across the sound of his voice. She darted an irritated glance at her grandfather when he took a seat at the table. Her annoyance vanished the instant her glance fell on the haggard lines etched in his face.

Yet exhausted as he was, Empty Garner had been a rancher too long, and nighttime had always been when the next day's work was planned. "First thing tomorrow morning we need to get that burned hay out of the corral," he stated. "It's the smell of it that's probably spooking the horses and keeping them from coming back in. We'll need to catch them so we can ride out and check the cattle. It's hard to get close to them in a truck."

Unaware that Dallas had overheard Quint's account of the injured cows, Empty went on to tell her about them, describing the wounds they'd doctored and which salve had been applied on the burns, his forceful, semiloud voice almost completely drowning out Quint's more quietly pitched one. Dallas managed to snatch bits of Quint's conversation, something about Rutledge, morning, and bales, enough for Dallas to assume it was about the hay that had been delivered.

But mostly she couldn't piece it together into anything that made sense. There was frustration in that. At the same time a part of her was glad.

Not until the end of the phone conversation did Empty fall silent and Quint's voice was the only one in the room. "Sounds good, Jess. I'll talk to you then," he said and hung up.

His hand stayed on the receiver for a thoughtful moment. Then he rolled to his feet and went to the sink to wash up, a tired and distracted look to his expression. Dallas busied herself dishing up the evening meal and transferring it to the table, setting the platter of roast beef in front of her grandfather to carve. By the time Quint joined them at the table, all was in readiness.

"So what's the word?" As always, Empty came straight to the point. "Are you going to order more hay from the same outfit that sold you the last bunch?"

"By now Rutledge is bound to have done some arm-twisting to cut off that source." Quint reached for his napkin and absently draped it across his lap.

"You're probably right there." Empty spooned a helping of corn onto his plate. "Likely you'll have to buy it from another outfit."

"We're still talking about it and mulling over a couple ideas. Jessy's going to get back with me tomorrow night. We'll know more then," Quint stated and took the platter of carved beef Dallas passed to him. He slid her an appreciative smile. "Dinner looks good."

"Ah, but can you stay awake long enough to eat it?" she teased lightly, oddly relieved that as yet she had nothing to report.

"Now there's the question," Quint agreed with an easy grin.

Conversation was minimal during the meal as both men centered their attention on the food before them. Dallas suspected she was the only one uneasy with the long stretches of silence. She blamed her meeting with Boone for making it difficult to ignore the reason she was really there.

At meal's end, Quint and Empty leaned back in their chairs and replayed the day's events over a cup of coffee while Dallas transferred the leftovers to individual containers and stored them in the refrigerator. When she returned to the table to clear off the dirty dishes, Empty heaved a big sigh.

"I think I'm going to call it a day. I'm whupped," he declared.

"The bed's the best place for you," Dallas said. "Not that easy chair."

"And bed is where I'm going, too." He flattened both hands on the table and used them to lever himself out of the chair.

When he shuffled out of the kitchen, Quint stirred. "I'll give you a hand with these dishes."

"I can do them myself tonight." Dallas piled the dirty silverware atop the stack of the dinner plates. "You look like you're out on your feet, too."

"I feel a bit like that as well." Quint collected the cups and drink glasses and followed Dallas to the sink. "But you're bound to be as tired as I am."

"Not really. I cheated and grabbed a nap this afternoon." She suddenly found it difficult to respond naturally to Quint, discovering that she was no longer sure why that was. As a consequence, she chose to keep it light. "So, go hit the shower, then the sack, in that order."

"Always looking after someone, aren't you?" His arm brushed hers when he set the items in the sink along with the rest of the dishes. Bone-tired he might be, but not so much that the contact and her nearness didn't stimulate his male impulses.

"It's a habit, I guess." Her easy dismissal of it was delivered with a smile.

"It's one that I like." Quint studied her upturned face and the light sparkle in her sherry-colored eyes. But it was the slightly parted line of her lips that drew him. "But there are a lot of things I like about you."

Turning, he slid his hand onto the opposite curve of her waist, drawing her toward him. He ignored the surprise that flashed in her expression and the startled tightening of her body in automatic resistance, fully aware she hadn't anticipated his move and confident she didn't really object.

"More than like," he murmured an instant before his mouth settled onto her lips. They were motionless for an instant, then turned pliant and giving as his enfolding arms gathered her to him.

The kiss was languid and long, yet never quite losing its gently insistent quality and deepening into something more raw. Then her fingers were there, their pressure light near a corner of his mouth as she pulled her lips away from his, the moist warmth of a tremulous sigh feathering across his skin.

A part of him didn't want the kiss to end, but Quint felt the heaviness of his limbs that warned of flagging strength. When she tipped her head down, he lightly kissed the top of it.

"Good night, Quint," she murmured.

"Good night," he echoed and moved reluctantly toward the door. He was halfway through the living room before he heard water gush from the kitchen sink's faucets.

The noonday sky was clear blue, crisscrossed with slowly dissipating contrails left by high-flying jets. With the sun at its zenith, the temperature hovered at the seventy-degree mark. On the west side of the ranch house, a pair of white sheets and pillowcases flapped in the south breeze.

Another set of sheets, straight from the washing machine, filled the large wicker basket Dallas carried as she crossed to the kitchen door. Pausing, she shifted the basket to the side, propping it on her hip, and reached for the doorknob. She pushed open the screen door, glancing to see Quint and Empty coming up the walk.

"Lunch is on the stove," she told them. "Hot beef sandwiches. You're welcome to help yourself or wait until I come back."

The phone rang in a shrill punctuation of her announcement. Automatically she swung away from the door to answer it.

"I'll get it." Quint loped up the porch steps, and Dallas stepped back to let him through.

With Empty not far behind him, Dallas held the door for him. Ten hours of sleep had removed the shadows from under his eyes and put some of the spring back in his step. Truthfully Dallas hadn't expected him to bounce back so quickly, but she was glad he had.

"Cee Bar Ranch." Quint's voice followed when she stepped onto the porch with the basket. "Jessy. I didn't expect to hear from you until tonight."

Everything inside her tightened up. For an instant Dallas was torn between staying and going, pretending there was no significance to this call. But she knew better.

She set the wicker basket on the porch's planked flooring and crouched down, going through the motions of rearranging the wet sheets for better balance and using the delay to eavesdrop on Quint's phone call.

"I'm glad you agree with my suggestion, Jessy," he said. "In the long run, I think it'll be the wisest move we can make." There was a rather lengthy pause, and Dallas gripped the basket by its handles while pushing to her feet. "I'll work out all the arrangements on my end. If I run into any snags, I'll let you know."

There was a finality to his voice that signaled further discussion was at an end. Dallas immediately headed down the steps and struck out for the clothesline.

A gusting breeze snapped the sheets already hanging on the first strand of wire stretched between the tall posts. Dallas hauled the basket to an empty stretch of line and set it on the ground near her feet.

Clothespins in hand, she matched together two corners of one sheet, welcoming the mindless task that required little of her attention. It left her time to wonder how long it would take before she became used to this tension and the sense of duplicity that nagged her. Never once had she thought it would be easy or without some feeling of guilt. At the same time she'd never expected to have any type of close relationship with Quint.

The screen door slammed. Dallas cast an idle glance over her shoulder, but the front of the house was beyond her view. Quint came around the corner, heading in her direction. Self-conscious and uneasy, Dallas briskly resumed the task of pinning the wet sheet to the line.

"What happened?" Quint stopped beside her, a slight frown creasing his forehead. "Did the dryer quit on you?"

"No, it's working fine." She scooped up a trailing corner of the sheet before it could touch the ground. "It would have been quicker to throw the sheets in the dryer, but there's nothing like the smell of sheets that have dried in the sun."

A naughty gleam sprang into his eyes. "I could think of one or two things that might be better."

Her pulse skittered with her own awareness of those things, but the need to protect herself from them was stronger.

"Spoken just like a man," she chided to keep him at arm's length. "Was that Jessy on the phone just now? I thought I heard you say her name."

"It was." The frank admission only increased her unease. When she reached to pick up the next sheet, Quint bent down to the basket. "I'll help you with that. It's easier with two people."

"So what's the decision?" Dallas worked to inject a casual note to the question. "Did she find out where you can buy more hay?"

"She never tried." He gathered up one end of the sheet and deftly fitted the corners together. "Jessy agreed with me. Buying more hay would only play into Rutledge's hands. There's no way we can maintain a twenty-four-seven watch over the hay and prevent him from burning it again. At the same time, it would be too costly to install a sophisticated security system around it."

"But what's the alternative?" Dallas frowned. "You need hay to feed the cattle. They won't make it through the winter without it."

"They could if we cut down the size of the herd and keep only what the remaining land can support."

It was a logical solution, yet it raised more questions for Dallas. Questions that required answers.

"So what will you do? Send the cattle to market? Or run them through one of the local auction barns?"

"Probably not." Holding the wet sheet by its opposite corners, Quint kept it off the ground while Dallas pinned it to the line. "It would be too easy for Rutledge to get wind of it. The same would be true with hiring a local hauler."

"What, then? Will you hire someone from out of state like you did with the hay?"

"You're just full of questions this morning."

Her heart leaped into her throat as she threw him a startled look. His expression was one of amusement with no trace of suspicion, but it did little to ease the guilt she felt. Dallas looked away.

"I can't help it," she said with a stiff little shrug. "By nature I'm a detail person. Any time I hear a decision, my mind automatically jumps to the steps that have to be taken to carry it out."

"Spoken like a true bean counter." Quint grinned and passed her the ends of the sheet he held. "In this case, before any steps can be taken, other questions have to be answered first. And a hard look needs to be taken at the grazing land that's left. From that we can make a determination of the number it can support. That number will tell us—"

"How many have to be sold," Dallas inserted, quick to follow his line of thinking. "Which tells us how many have to be shipped to market, and the number of trucks to haul them."

"Now you've got the idea." Quint smiled in approval.

But Dallas found little pleasure to be taken from that. For the first time she wished she wasn't intelligent enough to ask the right questions.

*   *   *

Boone Rutledge stared out the window of the granite-and-glass-skinned building, headquarters for the conglomerate known as Maresco, but his gaze failed to take in the view of Fort Worth that the executive office suite provided. His expression had a look of brooding impatience to it. It was echoed by the agitated and intermittent jangling of the keys in his right hand.

In a surge of restlessness Boone swung away from the window and threw an irritated glance at the connecting door to the meeting room. The impulse was there to walk over and fling it open. He dragged his gaze from it before he could succumb to the urge. Instead he crossed to the sleekly contemporary desk. Reaching across it, he punched the phone's intercom button.

"Yes, Mr. Rutledge?" Despite its slight drawl, the female voice that answered projected a note of businesslike efficiency.

Boone had no trouble picturing the brunette on the other end. The onetime Miss Texas runner-up was little more than a glorified waitress/receptionist, hired to provide his father's cronies something to ogle when they stopped by. Some months ago Boone had discovered that her sole ambition was to land herself a wealthy husband; young or old, she didn't particularly care which. Failing to snare him, she had moved on to richer pastures.

"You did inform my father I needed to see him right away, didn't you, Miss Bridges?" he demanded curtly.

Her voice turned cool. "I passed your message to Mr. Edwards," she replied, referring to Max's chief secretary and personal assistant. "He assured me that Mr. Rutledge would be informed that you were waiting in his office. But I did warn you that Mr. Rutledge doesn't like to be disturbed when he's in a board meeting."

"Disturb him anyway. I've cooled my heels long enough." Boone broke off the connection and stalked back to the window, muttering, "Bitch."

Behind him there was the snick of a latch releasing. Boone swung from the window as Max maneuvered his wheelchair through the doorway.

He fastened a stony look on Boone. "This better be important."

"Yeah, like I'd drive all the way here just to find out how your day has been," Boone jeered, then pulled in his anger. "No, Echohawk's thrown us a curve."

"You heard from the Garner woman," Max surmised instantly.

Boone nodded. "An hour or more ago. She said Echohawk isn't planning to buy more hay. He plans to sell off some of the cattle instead."

"When? Where?"

"She doesn't know. According to her, those decisions haven't been made yet," Boone replied. "Supposedly he isn't even sure how he's going to get rid of them."

"Good. That gives us time," Max murmured, his attention turning inward.

Boone had already considered that. "I can't see how it would give us much more than three days. Four at the outside. And he could be ready to ship that soon. It depends on who he hires to haul them and whether they have trucks available right away. It's unlikely he'll run them through any of the local sale rings." He paused and grinned. "She claims he's leery of using them for fear we'll catch wind of his plans. Imagine that."

"I told you having a set of eyes and ears on that ranch would come in handy." Max idly tossed out the reminder that the suggestion had come from him.

"But Dallas can find out more than any of our men ever could." Boone was quick to claim credit for choosing her. "There's nothing like a redhead to get a man to say more than he should."

"I'm sure you know that from your own experience." Max's sidelong glance was riddled with disgust.

Boone bristled in ready denial. "Damn it, I never—"

Max cut across his words. "You wouldn't admit it if you had, and we both know it. It's irrelevant anyway. I don't particularly care how the girl pumps the information from Echohawk, whether it's in bed or out of it, just so long as she isn't fool enough to start caring about him and double-cross us."

"She knows what would happen if she did. Besides, I've already warned her about thinking she'd ever be any more to Echohawk than a piece of ass."

"Let's hope she remembers that," Max replied absently.

"She will," Boone asserted, then paused a beat. "So what do you want me to do? It would be a waste of time to call any local haulers or sale barns to put them on notice to get a hold of us if they hear from Echohawk. He'll probably get someone from out of state like he did with the hay."

"Don't do anything. Just leave it to me." There was a smug curve to Max's smile. "I think I can guarantee Echohawk won't be shipping cattle any time soon."

"What have you got up your sleeve?" Boone knew his father had a plan, and it grated him that he wasn't being informed of it.

"Publicity. With the Cee Bar at the center of it—just like you were so ready to do the other night. With a different story line, though." On that enigmatic note, Max sent the wheelchair gliding to the meeting room's connecting door.

Boone waited, certain that any second Max would swing his chair around and announce his intentions—like a word coming from on high. Instead Max hit the remote and the door opened, allowing his wheelchair to pass through without pause.

For a stunned instant Boone was too furious at being kept in the dark to do more than glare at the closed door. Then he spun on his heel and strode from the office, slamming the door behind him.

# Chapter Fourteen

⟨∽⟩

Thunder rumbled in the distance, an accompaniment to the soft patter of rain on the roof. Quint sat at the old desk in the kitchen, his feet propped on a corner of it, the telephone to his ear, and his body angled toward the window that looked onto the front porch. In the living room, a sitcom's laugh track competed with the loud, sawing breaths of a snoozing Empty.

Quint paid little attention to any of it, not even the sound of his mother's voice in his ear, catching him up on all the current happenings at the Triple C. He was too distracted by the vague shape of Dallas, standing outside by the porch rail.

Occasional lightning flashes would show her silhouette, sometimes with both hands braced against the railing, or one resting on an upright post. A heavy sweatshirt gave the illusion of bulk to her slim figure, yet it seemed to emphasize the downward slope of her shoulders, a posture that gave the impression she was in a pensive, almost melancholy mood. It was a sight that aroused all of his protective male instincts, filling him with a need to make the world right for her.

"Quint, are you listening to me?" The rather strong hint of reproach in his mother's voice commanded his attention.

"Sorry, Mom. I'm afraid my mind wandered," Quint admitted. "It's been a long day, and I've had a bunch of them in a row."

And it had been rare that he'd spent more than a few minutes alone with Dallas. It seemed that whenever he wasn't occupied with something, she was.

"Tell me again, what did you say?" he asked.

"It doesn't matter," Cat replied. "It wasn't important anyway. You probably have a dozen things you need to do tonight, so I won't keep you from them. Try to get some rest, though. You need your sleep, too."

"I will." Quint swung his feet off the desk and sat forward, the chair squeaking at the shifting of his weight.

"Be careful, dear. And remember I love you."

"Love you back, Mom." With those parting words, Quint slipped the receiver back on its cradle and rose to his feet.

In the living room a car salesman bragged about the savings available at his lot, but his voice marked the only change of sound coming from the room. After an idle glance in its direction, Quint crossed to the back door, lifted his windbreaker off the wall hook, and slipped it on as he opened the door and stepped onto the porch.

Light from the kitchen penetrated the shadows, brushing over the smoothness of her cheek when Dallas glanced over her shoulder. Her hair was pulled back from her face, the dim light glinting on the gold clasp at her nape. His glimpse of her face was a brief one as she turned to gaze again into the night and the soft falling rain.

Quint eased the screen door closed and crossed to the railing to stand next to her. He pushed his hands into the side pockets of his windbreaker and surveyed the view that seemed to absorb her interest.

A faraway flash of lightning briefly lit the undersides of the low clouds and reflected off the surface of the gathering puddles of water scattered around the ranch yard. Then all was still again, marked by the whisper of the falling rain and the trickling of water in the downsprouts.

"Nice night," Quint remarked, finding the moisture-laden air not as cool as he had expected it to be. But the only response from Dallas was a nod of agreement. "A steady, soaking rain like this makes me wish that we already had seeded that burned ground."

"I like gentle rains like this," Dallas remarked in a musing voice. "There's something soothing about them."

"Are you in particular need of soothing tonight?" Quint made a sideways study of her profile—the smooth sweep of her forehead, the straight line of her nose, and the strong jut of her chin.

"Doesn't everybody need to unwind at the end of a busy day?" Dallas challenged lightly in return, but Quint detected something self-conscious in the glance she darted at him.

"I suppose." The desire was there to curve an arm around her, establish contact, yet there was something in her manner that made Quint hesitate.

"Was that your mom on the phone just now?" The question had all the earmarks of an idle one, but there was an interested lilt to her voice that seemed to genuinely seek verification of the assumption.

"It was," he confirmed, wondering why it mattered to Dallas.

"I thought so."

"I noticed you out here on the porch. You looked a little blue."

"Really?" She turned at right angles to the railing and leaned her back against a wooden post, a smile curving her lips. "Is that why you came out? To cheer me up?"

The movement created more space between them, which was the last thing Quint wanted. Unhurried, he swung toward her, simultaneously shortening the distance between them and reaching up to brace a hand against the post a few inches above her head.

"Does that mean you think I can?" he asked with a slight grin.

"I suppose it would depend on how you went about it." Again there was a trace of uncertainty, a kind of drawing back that seemed to push him away, but her gaze slid almost unwillingly to his mouth and that pushed him closer.

"I was always taught that a kiss makes everything better." He followed his words with a downward dip of his head and claimed her lips.

The night air had chilled their surface, making his first taste of them cool. He warmed every inch of them with a nuzzling heat that soon coaxed the responsive pressure he sought. The quickening ardor of her lips burned through the restraint he had placed on himself. And the kiss became something that was no longer warm and persuasive, but one that was hot with need, demanding contact with her body.

But the minute his hand gripped her waist to draw her against him, Dallas ripped herself away from his lips and turned into the railing, all in one twisting motion.

"Is that how you usually go about cheering someone up?" The disturbed breathiness in her voice took much of its stiff demand away from it, and offered its own kind of reassurance to Quint.

"I saved it for you." Standing behind her, he wound his arms around her, drawing her back against him and bending his head to nuzzle the side of her neck. "I admit I got a bit carried away," he murmured against her skin. "It's been a little too long since I held you in my arms, and the desire just builds up."

"I could tell."

"Obvious, wasn't it?" He smiled, but he could feel the tension in her body that kept her from relaxing against him.

"Quint," she began, a wealth of hesitation and reluctance in her voice. "I think we should slow it down."

Quint sensed again this figurative pulling away from him, and it was totally at odds with the passion that had been in her kiss a moment ago. Puzzled by her conflicting signals, Quint turned her around, needing to see her face.

"Are you saying I've been rushing things?" he asked.

Her glance bounced off his face and centered on his shirt collar. "We both have," she replied somewhat stiffly.

"And that's bad," he guessed; yet he was oddly reassured by her comment.

"Not necessarily. I just think it would be too easy to let ourselves get carried by the heat of the moment and find ourselves in a situation that we might have cause to regret."

Quint smiled at her tactful choice of phrases. "I might as well be honest, Dallas. An affair isn't what I want at all."

"Good. I don't think it would be wise either," she agreed quickly.

"You misunderstand." He tucked a finger under her chin, lifting it to force her to look at him. "I'm hoping for something more permanent."

Something else was mixed in with the shock and disbelief in her, but the dim light made it impossible for Quint to identify it.

"We hardly know each other," Dallas said in confused protest.

He smoothed the hair back from her face. "I wouldn't be surprised that, even after a lifetime together, there would still be things we don't know about each other."

There wasn't an ounce of doubt in his mind that it was a lifetime he wanted to spend with her. The certainty of it filled him. But it was the expressions chasing across her face—surprise, joy, doubt, and something akin to panic—that made Quint laugh softly. "There goes that mind of yours again, processing all the data and searching out potential problem areas."

"How can you ignore them?" Dallas countered, her gaze clinging to him in uncertainty. "You don't know me at all."

Unconcerned, Quint smiled. "You'd be surprised at what I know about you."

She stiffened instantly, her hands flattening across his chest, ready to push. "I suppose you hired a private investigator to check me out."

"Not hardly." His smile widened. "He could only supply me with a lot of useless facts and little about you as a person."

"Which, of course, you know." There was something defensive about the hint of scorn in her voice, but her hands had eased their pressure against his chest.

But it was the lingering doubt in her eyes that made Quint patient. "Do you need to be told how warm and caring you are? Not to mention intelligent and proud, not afraid of hard work. Or the deep sense of family loyalty you have." Again Dallas avoided his eyes, and again he tipped up her chin to force the contact. "And it goes without saying that you're beautiful and have the most kissable lips."

To prove it, he covered them with a warm and fiercely tender kiss. Victory came when she leaned into it, a wanting and needing in her response that echoed his own feelings.

Quint knew then he could take her beyond where she wanted to go. Yet there was a risk of later regret, and it wasn't one he wanted to run. He eased the pressure and shifted his interest to the curve of her cheek and along the side of her temple.

She sagged against him, her head dipping to rest again on his chest, a hand balling into a fist near her chin. "You don't know me, Quint," she murmured. "You only think you do. I'm not—"

"Perfect, I suppose," he guessed. "I've never met anyone who was." His arms circled her in a loose, undemanding embrace. "At first I had a hard time dealing with your pessimism until I realized that your thinking wasn't really negative. It's just your nature to analyze every aspect of a situation and identify its weaknesses. It's your method of problem solving. Your biggest fault isn't that you think too much. Most of the time, you do what your head tells you, not your heart."

"That isn't wrong," Dallas insisted.

He idly rubbed his chin over the silken strands of her hair. "Not always," Quint agreed. "But a good many years ago my dad gave me some advice. He said if you ever find yourself in a situation where everything seems fine, yet your gut tells you differently, listen to your instincts and forget what your head is saying. That's what you need to do, Dallas, trust your feelings."

He felt the negative, denying movement of her head. In a rare loss of patience, Quint dug his fingers into her shoulders and held her away from him. The roughness of his action showed in her look of shocked surprise.

"Right now, Dallas. Be honest with me and with yourself." The rawness of need was in his demand. "Tell me what your heart is saying. Not your head, but your heart."

Wordless, she looked at him, a thousand uncertainties in her gaze. The gnawing ache in his chest grew with the lengthening silence

"Good God, Dallas." His voice was thick with emotion. "Nobody knows what will happen tomorrow. My father's death taught me that. Right now—tonight—may be all we ever have. Are you going to deny us that and wait instead until you can get your head to line up with your heart?"

She closed her eyes, making a tight line of her lashes. He dug his fingers into her flesh, but the truth was inescapable: an answer unwillingly given was no answer at all.

Exerting iron control, Quint uncurled his fingers, spreading them wide, and took a step back from her. But there was a certain hardness in his voice when he said, "Let me know when you've made up your mind."

The slight emphasis on the last word was designed to cut, and it did. Her wince was small, but it was there.

Quint pivoted away from her and went back inside, shedding his windbreaker at the door and jamming it onto the wall hook. There was no lingering, no glancing back for any signs of regret from Dallas. He walked straight from the door to the living room.

In the recliner, Empty snorted and stirred, awakened by the sharp sound of Quint's strides. "What time is it?" he mumbled, throwing a dazed and sleepy look around the room.

"A little after nine." Quint's pace slackened only slightly as he continued across the room.

"Making an early night of it, are you?" Empty surmised.

"Might as well." But fatigue had nothing to do with the decision. Pain and anger and a dozen other emotions roiled too close to the surface. Quint didn't trust himself to see Dallas again that night.

"Think I will, too." Empty lowered the footrest. "Where's Dallas?"

"Out on the porch." Quint's answer was curt, but it left no mark on Empty.

His mind was on other things as he pushed out of the chair and noted Quint's disappearance into the hallway with an absent glance in that direction. The stiffness in his joints gave him a hobbling gait when he crossed to the living room's front door. His gnarled fingers closed around the knob and swung the door open, letting in the soft, steady sound of falling rain.

It was a moment before his eyes adjusted to the shadowed darkness of the porch and located Dallas standing near the rail. "Quint and me are calling it a night. You'll need to lock up when you come in."

"I will."

The low-voiced answer reached him. As Empty gave the door a closing push, he caught the reflection of multicolored lights on a windowpane and pulled it open again. "Don't forget to unplug the tree lights, too," he added.

Her response was muffled, yet it had an affirmative ring that satisfied Empty. This time he closed the door tight and shuffled off to his bedroom.


Lightning flashed outside Quint's bedroom window, briefly illuminating its interior. Quint lay on his back, staring at the ceiling with one arm flung across the pillow under his head, and the bedcovers pulled halfway up his bare chest. His jaw was clenched against the annoying and incessant drip of water from the eaves.

A troubled sigh came from him. He tried closing his eyes again, but his mind wouldn't rest. In irritation, Quint rolled onto his side, his glance sliding to the luminescent face of the alarm clock that sat on the bedside table. Its hands were positioned at eight minutes after midnight.

"So much for an early night," he muttered and gave the pillow a punch, using more force than necessary to bunch it under his head.

Thunder rumbled long and low, almost muffling the faint scrape of a releasing door latch. But his nerves were strung too fine, sharpening his senses too keenly for Quint to miss it. With a quick, turning lift of his head, he glanced at the door and watched it swing inward.

For a split second he stared at the woman's shape in the doorway, backlit by the glow from the bathroom's night-light. An oversized T-shirt stopped near midthigh, revealing a familiar pair of long legs.

Something leaped inside him, but he'd already been burned once tonight. Quint sat upright, the covers slipping down to his hips.

"What are you doing here?" he demanded in a low, half-angry voice.

"I couldn't sleep." Dallas's voice was soft and hesitant.

But Quint found no satisfaction in knowing that sleep had been equally elusive for her. "Unless you've made up your mind, you'd better turn around and leave right now."

It was a warning, generated by the raw desire that ripped through him at the sight of her briefly clad body, when it was obvious she was wearing nothing underneath that thin cotton shirt.

"I have. That's why I'm here." Dallas closed the door behind her and crossed to the side of the bed where he was, the fabric falling in a soft drape from the pointed roundness of her breasts. "Quint, there's something you need to know."

But it was the dip of the mattress under the weight of the knee she placed on it and not her words that snapped the thing that had held Quint motionless.

He reached out and pulled her onto the bed with him. "There

isn't anything I need to know." He pressed her back onto the sheets, his body following to pin her there. "You're here. That's enough."

"You don't understand." Her head moved in protest, a plea in her eyes.

"No, you don't understand." All the hunger and torment of being without her rose up inside Quint as his hand spread itself across her ribcage just beneath the swell of her breasts. "I love you. There's nothing you can say or do that will ever change that."

"I wish I could believe that," Dallas whispered.

The doubt in her voice momentarily froze him, forcing him to question the assumptions he had made. "Tell me one thing, Dallas, do you love me?"

"Yes, b—"

The single word was all he needed to hear. His mouth came down to smother the unnecessary ones in a kiss rough with need. There was an instant when he thought she was going to resist him. Then her arms wound around him, her hands pressing and urgent in their caress.

Gone was the steady calm that had always ruled him, its place taken by something primitive and demanding. Her lips parted under the insistence of his, allowing him to mate with her tongue. But it wasn't enough. Not nearly enough.

The T-shirt's thin material became an irritating barrier, denying him the sensation of skin against skin. A hand tunneled under its hem and rolled it up while it explored the smooth bend of a hip, the quivering flatness of her stomach, and the button-hard peak of a round breast. The need surfaced to take it into his mouth and taste it.

But with the first dragging movement away from her lips, he encountered the shirt's bunched cloth. Impatient hands pushed at it even as hers reached down to pull it off.

Then there was nothing between them, nothing to block the heat of her body from burning its impression along the length of him. The contact with it, the motion of it, wanting and eager, banished all else from his consciousness except the knowledge that her need matched the fierceness of his.

The hot urgency of it turned them both wild as they hungrily sought all the pleasure that can exist between a man and a woman. Time stood still, without a yesterday or tomorrow—only this night, this moment, together.

There was no patience, no gentleness. The strain of waiting, wondering, wanting, allowed no room for it. There was only the desperate hunger that drove each of them relentlessly and ruthlessly with its urgent demands.

As wave after wave of awesome pleasure shuddered through Quint, an awareness swept through him that one night would never be enough to satisfy his desire for this woman. For that he would need a lifetime.

Filled with a high sense of ease, Quint pulled in a long contented breath as he lay in a loose-limbed sprawl on the bed, one arm hooked around Dallas. She was curled against him, using his chest for a pillow. The heat and the weight of her along his length felt right, the way a night in bed should be.

He idly studied the shadow patterns on the ceiling, slow to absorb anything beyond feeling Dallas against him and remembering the satisfaction they had shared. Even as he listened to the steadying sound of her breathing, he noticed the absence of that annoying drip of water from the eaves.

"I think the rain's stopped," he murmured.

She stirred, her head lifting fractionally as if to listen, then settled back against him, snuggling closer, a soft sound of agreement coming from her throat.

His arm tightened to keep her close while his hand made slow strokes over the firm flesh along her waist and hip.

Quint had lived too close to the land for too many years for his mind not to wander to the rain, so crucial to all ranchers.

"I wonder how much we got," he mused idly.

"However much it was, it isn't enough," she replied, echoing his absent tone.

A smile burst across his face, and he rolled toward her, the movement shifting her head onto the pillow.

"Are you sure you're talking about the rain?" he asked, a provocative amusement dancing in his eyes.

Her answering laugh was low and breathy. "That's definitely a leading question."

"I know." Quint bent his head to nuzzle at the already kiss-swollen curves of her mouth.

Her hand came up, fingers brushing his jaw and tunneling into the thickness of his black hair. "I know I didn't actually say the words before, Quint," she murmured, their breaths mingling. "But I do love you."

It was the note of regret in her voice that prompted Quint to tease her. "You almost sound sorry about that."

Her head moved in denial. "I'm sorry about a lot of things, but loving you isn't one of them . . . no matter what happens."

"There you go—borrowing trouble again," Quint said in light reproval. "Don't we have troubles enough right now?"

She drew back from his kiss, a wariness in her expression. "Like what?"

"Like getting enough of you."

A glow softened her whole face. It was a look that told Quint everything he needed to know. He covered her mouth in a long, drugging kiss that ignited more flames.

Quint made love to her again, but this time with all the finesse and tenderness that had been lacking in the first.


Quint forced his eyes open, not at all sure what had awakened him. Before he could identify it, his attention became riveted on the woman's shape pressed spoon-fashion along his length, the round breast that his hand familiarly cupped, and the stray strands of hair tickling his chin.

From the hallway came the muffled sound of a door closing. Quint stole a glance at the alarm clock. With regret, he drew his hand away from her breast and levered himself onto an elbow.

Tempted by the bare curve of her shoulder, he nibbled lightly on it and murmured, "I hate to tell you this, but it's morning. Time to wake up."

There was a sleepy lift of her lashes, accompanied by a faint sound of protest. Then awareness sank in, and she shifted onto her back, one hand making an idle cruise up his arm, her mouth curving in a drowsy smile of remembrance and contentment.

"It can't be morning already." Her voice was husky and low, slurring a little with leftover sleepiness.

"I'm afraid it is," Quint confirmed with reluctance.

Her smile faded and her gaze drifted down to his chest. "There's something I need to tell you, Quint."

"I think it'll have to wait. Empty's up and stirring about," Quint explained. "In another few minutes he'll discover the coffee isn't made and check to see why you aren't up."

Alarm skittered through her expression, the look reinforced by the sound of water running in the bathroom. "I've got to get up."

Lending impetus to her words, Dallas rolled away from him and scrambled out of bed. A scouring search quickly located her sleep shirt. She scooped it up and hurriedly pulled it over her head, but not before Quint had a chance to enjoy the unobstructed view of her.

She threw a last smiling and somewhat self-conscious look at him before crossing to the door. But any thought Dallas had of slipping into her bedroom unobserved vanished when she stepped into the hall and encountered her grandfather exiting the bathroom.

There was an instant narrowing of his eyes, first on her, then on the door to Quint's room before they fastened on her. A certain grimness claimed his expression.

"That's the way it is, is it?" It was more of an accusation than a question.

Dallas answered it just the same. "Yes." She made no attempt to defend or justify her actions.

He studied her for a long, assessing second, then turned and gave a short and sharp decisive nod of his head. "It's time I had a talk with that boy."

She caught hold of his arm. "Grandpa, don't."

Empty turned in surprise, unable to recall the last time she had called him that. He was even more surprised to see that her eyes had the anxious and uncertain look of a little girl.

"What's wrong, Dallas?" he asked in concern.

"Nothing," she said quickly. "It's just that . . . I'd like to get a couple things straight with Quint first. When I do, there may not be any reason for you to talk to him."

Empty was old-fashioned enough in his ways that there were some things that he plain didn't want to know. Even though her explanation was far from informative, he didn't press for specifics.

"I'll wait," he said and continued across the hall to his bedroom door.

# Chapter Fifteen

The microwave beeped, signaling the end of its timed cycle. A quick check of the pancakes on the griddle confirmed they weren't ready to flip. Leaving them, Dallas crossed to the microwave and removed a jug of maple syrup, careful not to glance in Quint's direction.

She already knew he was talking on the phone to Jessy. This was one time when she refused to listen and glean what information she could from his side of the conversation. It was a matter of tuning out the sound of his voice and tuning in the chirp of the birds outside the window and the noisy clumpings coming from the porch, noises that her grandfather made removing boots muddy from morning chores. For the most part she succeeded.

Back at the stove, Dallas turned the pancakes and transferred the sausage patties onto a plate covered with a paper towel to absorb their excess grease. As she carried the plate to the table, her grandfather walked in his stocking feet, toting the egg bucket.

He set the bucket on the floor and sliced a glance at Quint as he paused to shed his hat and coat. "Who's he talking to?" As usual Empty made no attempt to lower his voice.

"Jessy," Dallas told him. "Better wash up. Breakfast is ready. Will two pancakes be enough?"

"Should do it," Empty agreed and went to the sink to wash up.

But the running water failed to drown out the sound of Quint's voice. "I'll give you a call tomorrow after the semi pulls out. Let me know if he runs into any delays."

The response was obviously in the affirmative. After a final parting word, Quint hung up and walked over to the kitchen table, arriving just as Empty did.

"Sounds like you found an outfit to haul the cattle," Empty surmised, taking a seat. "Who'd you end up hiring?"

As she retrieved the platter of pancakes, kept warm in the oven, Dallas longed to cover her ears to shut out Quint's answer, then smiled, realizing it no longer mattered if she heard it.

"The same company who ships most of the cattle for the Triple C," Quint replied.

"A Montana outfit," Empty said in approval. "Rutledge will have a hard time getting to them. Are you going to sell the cows up there, too?"

Free of inner tension, Dallas brought the pancakes and sausage to the table and set them near her grandfather. Returning the smiling glance Quint directed her way suddenly became easy.

"We won't be selling them," Quint announced. "We'll ship them up to the Triple C instead."

"That's bound to get old Rutledge's goat when he hears about it," Empty declared. "It's for dang sure that it won't sit well with him. If you'd tried selling the cattle, you know he would have been looking for a way to make that sale hurt your pocket."

Dallas was briefly tempted to relay this information to Boone, just for the pleasure of knowing this was one move they couldn't use against Quint.

With an utterly free conscience, she asked, "When will the truck arrive?"

"Around midday tomorrow." Quint forked a stack of pancakes onto his plate. "Which means we'll make our gather and sort today.

That way the ones we're shipping north will only have to be penned overnight. Thanks to Rutledge we have enough hay to feed them," he added, his gray eyes twinkling with the irony of that.

Empty grinned. "I never quite looked at it that way, but you know—you're right." Empty picked up the jug of syrup and drowned his pancakes in it. "Where are you figuring on starting this gather?"

"We'll start with the south pasture and sort as we go. Much of that area was burned so we should make short work of it." He slid a warmly intimate glance at Dallas. "Think you're up to a long day in the saddle?"

She smiled at his ever so subtle reference to the previous night. "I can handle it as easy as you."

Quint chose not to comment on that. "We won't be breaking for lunch so you'd better throw together some cold sandwiches after breakfast. Empty and I will get the horses saddled and ready."

Last night's rain had softened the parched ground, making it muddy in the low areas where the runoff had collected. No clouds lingered to mar the blue of the wide sky, but there was a touch of coolness in the fresh-smelling breeze.

Quint noticed little of it, his attention focused on the eight head of cattle, mostly heifers, trotting through the open gate into the west pasture. Dallas waited for them at a discreet distance from the gate, her presence on horseback applying an oblique pressure to turn them north.

When the last cow showed signs of balking, Quint pushed his horse forward to drive the animal through the gate, then rode through himself, preceded by his shadow. He glanced back at Empty and waited for him to draw abreast.

"I'll ride over and see what I can find on the other side of the river," Quint told him with a nod toward the tree-lined banks a hundred yards from them. "You check out this side."

Empty responded with an acknowledging nod, and Quint split

away from him, pointing his horse toward the river and lifting into an easy lope. He noted with approval that Dallas had already moved her horse after the loosely bunched cattle, maintaining their northward drift.

Ahead of him, the river made a sweeping curve. Quint followed it until he came to a place where the bank sloped gently to the water's edge and a well-worn path identified it as a favored crossing point of the cattle. Reining in, he slowed his horse to a walk and swung it onto the cattle trail.

An earsplitting whistle pierced the morning air. Instantly Quint turned his horse away from the river, a frown gathering on his face. Empty Garner was the only one Quint had ever heard make a sound that shrill. And it wasn't a signal the canny old rancher would issue without cause.

Quickly he rode clear of the obstructing trees and spotted Empty some distance away. The old man motioned for him to come, then dismounted to inspect something on the ground.

It wasn't until Quint rode closer that he saw the dead cow. Empty knelt on one knee beside the bloated carcass. When Quint halted up next to Empty's ground-hitched horse, the old man straightened up.

"What happened? Was it struck by lighting?" Quint asked, voicing his first thought.

"I wish," Empty replied grimly and continued his visual study of the dead animal.

"What do you mean?" Quint frowned and walked his horse closer.

"Take a look at that crusty discharge around the nose and the scoury look to the rump," he directed. "There's a dark bloody look to both. If I'm right about what killed it, you won't be shipping cattle anywhere for a while."

Quint immediately grasped the significance of the two symptoms. "You think it could be anthrax?"

Every cattleman had knowledge of it, although in Quint's case it wasn't firsthand. While the disease wasn't as common as it once had been, nearly every year isolated cases were reported somewhere in the country.

"It looks like anthrax to me." There was a certain gravity to Empty's expression. "Fifteen or twenty years back, the Barlow place lost nearly a dozen head of cattle to anthrax. He told me one day they were fine, and the next they were dead. And I know for sure that I never noticed any sick cows—except those fence-cut ones—when we checked this area the other day."

"I've heard anthrax can take them quick." Automatically Quint's attention shifted to the handful of cows within his range of vision, his mind already considering the possibility that others in the herd might have contracted it. "We'd better get the vet out here."

Dallas rode into view, pulling up a good distance from them. "What's wrong?" she called.

"Dead cow," Quint answered. "Ride back to the house and phone the vet, have him come out as soon as he can."

"Do you want me to call the rendering truck, too?" She had the horse on the bit, ready to ride away.

"No." Quint gave a firm shake of his head, recalling that care had to be taken in disposal of an infected carcass. "But tell the vet it looks like anthrax."

"Anthrax." Like Quint, an instant after she assimilated the word, Dallas shot a look at the trio of cows grazing near the tree line, alert for any sign of illness or distress, leaving little doubt she had been raised on a cattle ranch.

"You might as well stay at the house and bring the vet out when he comes," Quint told her.

With an acknowledging lift of her hand, Dallas swung her horse toward the house and sent it forward at an easy, ground-eating lope. Quint watched her leave, then glanced at Empty.

"I'm going to check the rest of the pasture and make sure there aren't any others that are sick or dead. Give a whistle if I'm not back when the vet gets here."

"Good luck," was all Empty said.

But luck wasn't with him. Twenty minutes later Quint came

upon the bloated remains of a second cow with the same bloody discharge around the body openings and a lack of significant rigor mortis. Quint marked the location in his mind and crossed the river to check the other side.

Roughly an hour later, Empty's piercing whistle summoned Quint back to the site of the first cow. When Quint rode up, the vet's mud-splattered pickup was parked at the scene. Dallas stood slim and straight near its hood, her attention on the big man crouched next to the carcass, making a thorough visual inspection of it. She turned at Quint's approach.

"What did you find?" she asked, searching his face.

"There's one more dead." Quint swung to the ground and let the reins trail. "Looks just like this one."

With a straightening turn, the vet came erect and squared around to face Quint. "Where's that one?"

"Along the south fence line on this side of the river, fifty yards or so from the cross fence," Quint replied and sized up the man before him out of habit.

Somewhere in his early thirties, the local veterinarian was a tall, huskily built man with the stout neck and shoulders of a bull-dogger, an image that was reinforced by the cowboy hat, yoked-front shirt, and blue jeans he wore. The only part of his costume that didn't ring true to a bulldogger was the absence of cowboy boots with underslung heels. Instead, he had on a set of heavy-duty rubber boots, coated with mud and excrement.

"I'll need to examine it when I'm done with this one," he told Quint.

"I figured that," Quint replied and introduced himself. "The name's Quint Echohawk. I'm running the Cee Bar for the Calders."

"Dan Weber." He didn't offer to shake hands, but Quint hadn't expected him to make the gesture when he noticed the rubber gloves the vet was wearing.

"Thanks for coming out so quickly."

"If it is anthrax as you suspect—and I agree the cow presents all the classic signs of it—the quicker we can get a jump on it, the better off you'll be. I was just getting ready to draw a blood sample so I can get it sent off to the lab. They'll have to run their test to verify whether we're dealing with anthrax or not." He paused a beat. "Does this ranch have a history of anthrax occurring?"

"Not to my knowledge," Quint replied. "But the Calders purchased this particular parcel of land only ten or twelve years ago. So it isn't likely anyone would know whether there had been previous cases of anthrax."

"It was a thought," the vet said with an idle shrug. "Once the bacteria forms into spores, it can remain in the soil for years. Estimates range from thirty to as much as a hundred years, and it could be more. Usually heavy rains or floods bring it to the surface, but last night's rain hardly qualifies as that. Although . . ." He paused, a reflective look to his expression. "On the way here, I remember driving over a strip of ground that looked like it had been plowed up recently. That might be your source. Anything that disturbs the ground can scatter any spores that were present."

The ground had been plowed to create a firebreak, but the means used to stop one destructive force had potentially unearthed another one. And the irony of that was not lost on Quint. Yet given the same set of circumstances, it was a decision he would make again.

Using a syringe, the vet collected a blood sample from the animal's jugular vein. "Have either of you touched the carcass?" he asked.

"I did," Empty replied. "But I was wearing my gloves."

"Play it safe and burn them when you take them off. Make sure you disinfect your clothes, too." The vet stowed the blood sample in a sealed container and scratched the necessary information on it. "You should be all right, but if you notice any skin lesions or flulike symptoms, call your family doc right away. It wouldn't hurt to contact him anyway and have him prescribe a course of antibiotics as a preventive measure."

"We'll see about getting that done," Quint agreed. "What about the carcass?"

"It needs to be buried as soon as possible, but that's something the state authorities have to supervise. I'll get a hold of them as soon as I get back to the office and see if they can't get someone out here today—before any scavengers have a chance to rip into the carcass," he said and explained, "Right now the bacteria is in an active state. Any tearing of the flesh could unleash billions of spores." He turned to Quint as he snapped off his rubber gloves. "I'm through here. Want to show me where the other one is?"

Quint rode along with him to the second carcass where the same procedure was repeated. During the ride back to the first, the vet tossed a sidelong glance at Quint.

"I've got to be honest, I've only seen three cases of anthrax before, and two of those were when I was still in vet school," he said. "But if this isn't anthrax, I will be very surprised."

"Can you give me a heads-up on what the procedure will be once it's confirmed?"

"First, all the cattle will have to be removed from the contaminated pasture and kept isolated from the rest of your livestock. Any that look like they might be sick will need to be treated with antibiotics, and the rest will be vaccinated for anthrax. It's hard to say how long your cattle will be quarantined. It could be a month or more. If I remember right, it takes roughly four weeks for the vaccinations to be effective."

Most of what the veterinarian told him merely confirmed Quint's recollections of things he'd heard in the past. But it gave him the advantage of anticipating what would be required and planning for it.

"There's a preliminary test the lab can run that takes only a few minutes," the vet told him in parting. "But it can provide a fairly solid indication whether or not it's anthrax. It can't be confirmed until they grow a culture, and that can take twelve to twenty-four hours. I'll pass along any news as soon as I get it."

"I appreciate that." Quint climbed out of the cab and let Dallas take his place in the passenger seat. "We'll be following you to the house."

As the vet drove off toward the ranch house, Empty eyed him with a watchful interest. "What now?" he asked. "Are we gonna sit on our hands and wait to learn the test results?"

"No, I think we have to operate from the assumption it will be positive for anthrax." Reins in hand, Quint gripped the saddle horn and swung into the seat. "If we have to isolate the cattle, we might as well decide now where we want to hold them. It will need to be somewhere with easy access to water."

The availability of water dictated his final choice—the burned area adjacent to the ranch yard with its metal-legged windmill and water tank, undamaged in the fire. Loss of the pasture had already made it a given that hay would be needed to feed the cattle, so it mattered little there was no grass for grazing. And there was the bonus that the fire would have killed any anthrax spores in the soil.

Once the choice was made, they immediately went to work stringing electric fencing to pen off a fifteen-acre section that would allow them to keep the potentially infected items under close observation at all times.

Less than two hours after the vet left, he called Quint on his cell phone. The preliminary test result indicated anthrax. A representative from the state would be there no later than two-thirty to supervise the disposal of the carcasses. Before he hung up, he provided Quint with the name and telephone number of a backhoe operator.

The backhoe operator and the state worker arrived within minutes of each other, the latter accompanied by a team sent to gather soil samples. Quint left Empty and Dallas to finish installing the electric fencing and went with the new arrivals to the carcass locations.

A deep burial pit was dug, and the carcasses were dragged to it and covered with quicklime before the pit was filled with dirt.

More quicklime was applied to the areas where the carcasses had lain to inactivate any bacterium still present. Twilight had set in before the entire process was complete.

Quint returned to the ranch yard in time to give Empty a hand with the evening chores. A purpling shadowed the buildings when they finally headed for the house and the welcoming gleam of light from its windows.

The sharp ring of the telephone greeted Quint when he walked in. Automatically he headed for the desk to answer it. Dallas turned from the refrigerator, clutching a gallon of milk and a bowl of fruit salad.

"You might want to let that ring, Quint," she warned. "Somehow the media found out about the possibility of anthrax. The phone hasn't stopped ringing since I came in. There must be at least a half dozen messages on the answering machine—all from newspaper and television reporters."

A certain grim acceptance thinned the line of his mouth as he turned away, letting the machine take the call. "They'll probably show up here tomorrow." Quint hung his hat and jacket on the rack by the door. "When they do, just refer all their questions to me."

Neither Dallas nor Empty raised any objections to that.

By necessity, dinner was mainly thinly disguised leftovers from previous meals. Dallas helped herself to some home fries and set the bowl by her grandfather's plate, then noticed he had yet to put any food on it.

She darted a questioning look at his morose and vaguely distracted expression. "Aren't you hungry, Empty?"

He made a small grimace of disgust. "It's this anthrax business. It's put me off my feed." Almost grudgingly, Empty picked up the bowl and spooned a helping of potatoes onto his plate. "Don't you know Rutledge will be wearing a big smirk when he hears about it? You can bet if he's sorry about anything, it's that he didn't think of it."

"He'll try to find some way to use it to his advantage, though."

Quint took the bowl from Empty. "It could be that we have Rutledge to thank for all the calls from the media. It would be like him to leak the news to them as soon as he heard about it. And with his connections, he could have heard about it two minutes after we called the vet. My guess is that he'll do his best to ensure that it becomes a big story."

"He can make it as big as he wants," Empty declared with contemptuous unconcern. "I can't see how that will cause us any trouble."

Quint smiled wryly. "You've never had a horde of reporters flocking around you like vultures, pointing cameras and sticking microphones in your face, or you wouldn't say that."

Empty responded with a harrumph. "The first time a reporter sticks a microphone in my face, I'll stick the muzzle of a shotgun in his and escort him off the premises."

"That's a fast and sure way of making an enemy of the press—and convincing them that you have something to hide," Quint said, although he knew it was one his own grandfather would favor. "No, we'll give them free rein, show them how cooperative we are. If there are any restrictions placed on them, they'll come from state officials. Not us."

Before her grandfather could take issue with that decision, Dallas sought to change the subject. "What did the state guys have to say when they were here?"

"Like I already told Empty while we were finishing chores, they're recommending that we remove all the cattle from both the south and west pastures. Right now their thinking is that the strip we plowed for a firebreak may be the source of anthrax. Until they can determine otherwise, they want to keep all livestock away from it."

"That makes sense." Empty nodded in rare agreement. "A couple years back there was a big outbreak of anthrax over around Uvalde. There are a lot of old cattle trails in that area, going back to the days of the big drives north. Back then, if an animal got sick, they just left it along the trail to die. Some claim the ground there is thick with anthrax spores. A hard rain was blamed for causing the spores to migrate to the surface this last time." He paused a moment. "Somewhere close to sixteen hundred animals died." He shot a challenging glance at Quint. "A measly two dead cows can't be such a big story when there's been a lot worse cases in the past."

"Unfortunately terrorism has made anthrax a hot news topic," Quint replied. "And the media seldom make a distinction between the manufactured anthrax strains created for germ warfare and the bacteria that exists in practically every corner of the world. The only thing we can to do is catch tonight's late newscast and see what kind of slant they're taking on this."


"Anthrax is back in the news," the news anchor announced, and Quint sat forward on the couch, the whole of his attention focused on the television screen. "This time it's in connection with the famed Calder Ranch in Montana. We have confirmed that state authorities suspect anthrax caused the deaths of two cows at the Cee Bar Ranch southwest of the city. The Cee Bar is the Texas branch of the Calder Cattle Company, owned by the Calder family."

Stock footage of a dead cow rolled across the screen, accompanied by an explanation of the deadly swiftness with which anthrax can strike a herd. Then the camera was once again on the news anchor.

"The authorities have not yet determined the extent of the current outbreak at the Cee Bar," he continued. "But there is much speculation about the effect this will have on the renowned auction of breeding stock held by the Calders. Buyers are often reluctant to purchase cattle from ranches with a history of anthrax. And the Calder ranch now falls into that category." After a slight pause, he added, "We will keep you informed of this developing story."

Quint pulled in a long, deep breath and let it out in an irritated rush. "Now we know how Rutledge intends to exert some financial pressure."

Empty punched the power button on the remote and the screen went dark. "Trouble is some buyers do fight shy of ranches that have lost cattle to anthrax." There was a curl of disgust to his mouth. "It doesn't matter to them that there's no record of any healthy animal from a ranch that's had anthrax, carrying it with him to another. But some buyers are just spooky that way."

"What's worse," Dallas inserted in a tight, angry voice, "Rutledge wants to make anthrax synonymous with all Calder cattle, not just the ones here on the Cee Bar. It's another one of his plots to force a sale—get rid of the Cee Bar and the Calders lose the taint of anthrax. It's an obscenely brilliant strategy."

Quint pushed off the sofa. "I'd better call Jessy and let her know what's being said. She'll be getting calls about it tomorrow if she hasn't already."

"Isn't there something we can do?" Dallas demanded, rising from her chair in agitation.

Quint took one look at her battle-bright eyes and smiled. "Those sound like fighting words," he said, recalling all the times when she had advocated otherwise.

"They are." Her chin lifted a notch.

"Keep that attitude," he said, still smiling. "But right now, the best thing to do is go to bed and get as much rest as you can. You're going to need every bit you can get these next couple of days."

# Chapter Sixteen

Early the next morning the media swarmed onto the Cee Bar, television crews in vans and satellite trucks as well as reporters and photographers from local newspapers or stringers for national publications. Anticipating their arrival, Quint had made sure that Empty and Dallas had ridden out at first light, before any reporters were on the scene.

Promptly at eight-thirty, Quint stepped before the phalanx of microphones, cameras, and reporters gathered at the porch steps, and issued a brief statement that admitted little, other than that they were awaiting lab results on the deaths of two animals and cooperating fully with the authorities.

A barrage of questions followed, but Quint answered only one that exaggerated the health risk to the ranch employees and implied a lack of concern by the Calders.

"Anthrax is an occupational hazard for everyone who works with livestock," he stated. "All proper precautions are being taken."

Ignoring a fresh onslaught of questions, Quint stepped off the porch and moved through the throng of camera lenses and microphones pointed his way, responding to any and all with a shake of his head and a firm "No comment."

Undeterred, they followed him to the barn and waited while he saddled his horse.

One asked to be shown where the dead cattle had been found. Quint informed him that permission to do that would have to come from state authorities.

By the time he swung into the saddle, the throng had begun to divide into smaller groups. Soon they would disperse to track down the veterinarian, state officials, and neighboring ranchers for comments.

Quint rode out of the ranch yard, confident that he had gotten rid of the media, at least temporarily. About midmorning he learned how wrong he was when a helicopter swooped low, scattering the cattle they had gathered.

The camera lens pointed from the side of the helicopter captured the scramble of the three riders to gather the cattle back into a bunch—as well as the discovery of a third dead cow, this time along the west fence line. The helicopter it subsequently hovered above the scene to record the arrival of the vet and the eventual burial of the carcass.

News of the third dead cow spread quickly, along with a bulletin from the lab confirming anthrax as the cause of death. The media returned to the ranch yard in force.

Their presence complicated the work of driving cattle, already spooked by the helicopter, into the makeshift holding pen. Shortly after the gate closed behind them, the vet arrived to examine each cow, as the state required, providing more fodder for the cameras.

Any hope Quint had that the state officials would insist that the media keep their distance was soon proved wrong. In fact, they appeared to welcome the opportunity to show the public the extent of their diligence. It was after sundown before any of them called it a day, forcing evening chores to be done in the dark.

Come morning, Quint, Dallas, and Empty were back in the saddle again, this time to round up the rest of the cattle from unaffected areas and bring them in for the vet to examine and inoculate for anthrax.

Streaks of coral ranged across the western sky when Quint led his horse into the barn. The clop of its hooves on the alleyway's cement floor echoed through the barn. Empty was there ahead of him, dragging the saddle off his horse. He set it on the floor and draped the damp saddle blanket over a stall partition, then spared a glance for Quint.

"I sure was glad to see the last of those nosy reporters pull out a minute ago." The gruffness in his voice made his opinion of them clear. "I'd already made up my mind that if that helicopter showed up again today, I was getting my shotgun and shooting it out of the sky."

"I think that might have been a bit drastic," Quint suggested dryly and hooked a stirrup on the saddle horn before reaching down to loosen the cinch strap.

"Maybe so, but we would have been done with this work in half the time if it wasn't for those nosey parkers," he grumbled. "Darned near every time I'd get a cow headed into the chute, some fool would climb on the rail. There was many a time today when I wished I still chewed, just so I could have the satisfaction of spitting on the lens of one of their cameras."

Rustling noises, accompanied by the grating slide of a metal lid settling into place, were heard from the combination tack and feed room. A hen clucked and strutted away from its door as Dallas shouldered it open, lugging a five-gallon bucket of grain for the horses. Quint's bay gelding swung its head toward her, ears pricking, nickering softly.

Quint's glance tracked her progress across the alleyway to the stalls while he removed the saddle and used the blanket to wipe the gelding's sweaty back. His expression softened when he noticed the smudge on her cheek and the wisps of hair that had escaped from the French braid.

She stopped at the first stall and scooped a portion of grain into its feed bunk. Chickens pecked in the straw near her feet, then scattered when Empty gave his horse a slap on the rump, sending it into the stall.

The instant Quint stripped the bridle off the bay, the gelding trotted eagerly into its stall. Out of the corner of his eye, Quint saw Empty stoop to pick up his saddle, his movements slow and stiff.

"I'll put your gear away for you, Empty," Quint told him. "You go make sure there's plenty of water in the horse trough."

"You won't get any argument from me," the old man replied and trekked out of the barn.

When Quint hefted one saddle onto his shoulder and picked up the other, Dallas threw him a brief glance. "Grab some scratch for the chickens while you're in there."

"Sure," Quint agreed, his stride never slackening as he crossed to the tack room.

Once the saddles were placed on their individual racks, the bridles hung on a wall peg, and the blankets and pads set out to dry, Quint scooped some scratch into a can and scattered it along the alleyway to lure the rest of the chickens into the barn. After the last chicken darted into the barn, he slid the wide door closed to shut them in for the night.

He turned as Dallas tossed hay squares into the last manger, then stepped to one side, leaning a shoulder against a stall post in a vague gesture of weariness. Drawn by the sight of her, he moved closer.

With her face bare of makeup, there was nothing to distract his gaze from its strong, pure lines. Rust-colored lashes outlined the unusual tan of her eyes and the rounded ridges of her cheekbones stood out cleanly. Her wide lips lay comfortably together, warmly curved and generous.

Her glance lifted to his face. "This is one day I'm glad to see end."

"Tired?" Quint guessed.

"Tired and sore." The admission brought the ghost of a smile to her lips. "Nothing that a long, hot shower won't cure, though."

"A shower has a definite appeal right now." But it was the vision of her under its spray that lived in his mind. He leaned closer and braced a gloved hand on the rough post near her head. "It doesn't seem like we've had a moment to call our own these last couple of days."

A smile deepened the corners of her mouth. "Or if there was, we were too tired to care."

Quint chuckled softly. "That, too. The worst should be over after today, though. With any luck, things will start getting back to normal."

Dallas shook her head in mild skepticism and declared with amusement, "There hasn't been anything normal about my life since that night you walked into the café." And there was very little about it that she would have changed if she could; in fact, there was only one thing she would have done differently. The thought of it pushed at her. "Quint," she began on a serious note.

The side door to the barn swung open and sunset's rosy light flooded in. Then Empty's bandy-legged frame was silhouetted. "The horse trough's full," he announced. "Did you get the chickens fed?"

Straightening up from the post, Quint turned, angling toward Empty. "All done."

"Then what are we standing around here for?" Empty wanted to know, frowning. "Let's head to the house. What are we having for supper anyway?" He addressed the question to Dallas.

"I don't know." She released a heavy breath. "Spaghetti would be the quickest, I guess."

"Tell you what," Quint said, falling in step with her as she moved toward the door, "I'll fix the spaghetti tonight and you can go take that long, hot shower you were talking about."

"You've got a deal."

But the plan went quickly awry. Within seconds after entering the house, the phone rang. The garage in Fort Worth called to inform Quint that the repairs were complete on the ranch pickup. Arrangements were made for Quint to go in the following afternoon, return the leased truck, and collect the repaired one.

The minute he hung up, the phone rang again. This time it was Jessy, and the conversation gave every indication of being a lengthy one. At which point, Dallas gave in to the inevitable and fixed the evening meal.

By the time the table was cleared, the dishes washed and put away, it was after nine o'clock when she finally found time for a shower. In no hurry, she stood beneath the spray letting the steam and pulsating jets loosen stiff, sore muscles and wash away the day's tension.

When she emerged from the bathroom, clad in a terry robe, and absently toweling her wet hair, she felt refreshed and relaxed. She glanced in surprise at the darkened living room and the silent television.

The only light still on in the house came from the kitchen. Assuming Quint and her grandfather were in their rooms, Dallas went to turn off the kitchen lights.

When she came through the doorway, she saw Quint sitting at the desk. "I thought you and Empty had both gone to bed." She crossed to the desk and laid a hand on his shoulder.

Her touch, as much as her comment, roused him. There was something distracted in the way Quint looked up, taking in the rumpled wetness of her hair and the robe she wore.

"How was the shower?" That slightly absent air remained when he caught hold of her hand and drew her down to sit crossways on his lap.

Dallas settled comfortably against him, liking the casual intimacy that came so easily between them. "The shower was wonderful." She took advantage of the closeness to toy with the hair along the back of his neck. "I almost feel like a new person."

"That's good."

Again Dallas sensed she didn't have the whole of his attention even as his hand idly rubbed over her hip.

"What have you been working on?"

"Nothing really. Just going over some things." His glance flicked to the papers on his desk, a troubled light entering his eyes.

But Dallas could tell that those "things" continued to claim the whole of his attention. "Is something wrong?"

A hint of a frown flickered over his features. "I don't know about wrong, but definitely curious." Quint nodded to the papers on the desk. "According to that, the number of cattle the vet examined these last two days is the same number Empty and I came up with in the tally we made close to three weeks ago. Yet . . . we have three dead cows."

It took a second for the significance of his statement to register.

"You're saying that counting those dead cows, you would have three more head than you thought you had?"

"Curious, isn't it?" But there was no amusement in his crooked smile.

"But all three of the dead cows carried Cee Bar brands and ear tags," Dallas reminded him.

"That's what bothers me." Quint continued to stare at the papers. "It's possible we could have missed one cow when we made our tally. Even two. But I find it very hard to believe that we could have overlooked three."

Dallas had to agree. The ranch wasn't that large and the number of places where a cow might escape detection were very few.

"How could it happen?" she wondered aloud.

"A better question might be—where were those three cows when we made our count?" Quint countered. "We came up twenty-seven head short of the number the ranch was carrying on its books. I assumed they'd been stolen. But it does make me wonder if those three dead cows were part of the stolen twenty-seven. And it also makes me wonder who stole them—and why they didn't get rid of them right away."

"Surely you don't think Rutledge is behind this." The minute the words were out of her mouth, the possibility didn't seem as far-fetched as Dallas first thought. "He might have kept them if he was planning to infect them with anthrax and run them back on Cee Bar land to die. All of it—the quarantine, the vet bills, the publicity—fits right into his plans," she said. "He could have orchestrated this whole thing."

"Proving it is another matter."

In a sudden surge of restlessness, Dallas moved off his lap and paced away from the desk, then swung back.

"The Slash R land borders the west pasture where all the dead cows were found. It wouldn't surprise me if he had kept the stolen cattle there. That way he could have claimed they simply strayed onto his land if anyone noticed them."

"True, but opportunity and motive aren't enough." Quint remained in the chair, his expression never losing its look of deep thought.

Dallas frowned. "But how could he infect your cattle without running the risk of infecting his own?"

"It wouldn't have been all that difficult," Quint told her. "All he needed to do was pour some grain in a feed pan, contaminate it with the bacteria, give it to the cattle, then torch the pan and anything that might have fallen on the ground. He's already shown how adept he can be with a torch," he added dryly. "If he played it safe, he probably slipped the cattle onto the Cee Bar right away."

"Someone at the Slash R is bound to know about it," she said, wondering which ones might be persuaded to talk.

But Quint shook his head in disagreement. "Rutledge would have kept a tight lid on it. I'd be surprised if there were more than one or two people involved. He certainly wouldn't have needed more than that."

"But where could he have gotten the anthrax?" Dallas sighed at the blank wall in her mind.

"It probably wasn't as difficult as we'd like to believe, especially for someone with his money and influence." Stirring at last, Quint sat forward and reached for the phone. "It might be interesting to find out if there is a research laboratory associated with any of the companies he owns."

"Who are you calling?" Dallas asked, her curiosity high.

"An agency the family's used before in investigations." He paused with his hand on the phone. "After that I might try to track down a guy I worked with who was heavily into forensics. An expert can differentiate between manufactured anthrax strains and ones found in nature, but I don't know if the natural strains have any markers that narrow them to a region."

When he picked up the phone and dialed information, Dallas walked over to the kitchen table and sat down to listen.

The phone call to the agency led to a second, informing Jessy of his action. Tracking down his former associate took the most time and the most calls before Quint succeeded in locating him at his new post on the West Coast.

It was nearly midnight when he hung up from the last call. There had been no definitive answers to his questions, but everything was in motion to obtain them, and Quint hadn't expected any more than that.

He stood, flexing shoulder and back muscles that had grown stiff from sitting in one position too long. Turning, he saw Dallas curled up on one of the kitchen chairs, her head cradled on arms resting on the table, sound asleep.

At the sight of her, everything smoothed out inside him, all the knots and twists straightened. There was a moment when he was content to look at her, unaware of the powerfully tender light in his eyes.

Taking pity on her, Quint moved quietly to the chair. She stirred drowsily the instant he slipped an arm under her knees and another behind her back.

"I think you'll be more comfortable in bed," he told her.

Her lashes lifted as she gazed at him through sleep-blurred eyes. "You're going to carry me," she murmured and hooked a limp arm around his neck. "I like that."

Quint discovered that he liked the feeling, too, especially the way she nestled her face near the crook of his neck, her feathery breath all warm and moist against his skin.

"What did you find out?" she asked in an afterthought.

"Nothing yet. But if there's anything to learn, we should know in a few days." Quint paused at the doorway to flip off the kitchen light.

Darkness closed around them, save for a sliver of light peeking from beneath the door to her bedroom. Using it as his beacon, Quint crossed the living room to the short hall, disregarding the creaking floorboards beneath him.

She sighed, a slender hand fitting itself to the ridge of his shoulder. "We probably won't be lucky enough to prove Rutledge is behind it."

"We'll just have to wait and see."

Truthfully Quint thought their chances were slim. He certainly hadn't heard anything tonight that encouraged him to think that they would uncover the equivalent of a smoking gun. But small mistakes could occur in even the most careful plans.

He gave her bedroom door a push with his foot. It swung open soundlessly to reveal a pool of light spreading from a lamp on the nightstand, exposing bedcovers turned back in readiness. He carried her to the bed and lowered her onto it. Her arms immediately tightened their hold on him to keep him there.

"Wait, Quint."

But it was the loose softness of her lips that pulled him down, that and the need to tunnel into them. They were quick to answer the exploring pressure of his kiss. The contact was long and languid, slow to build to an earthy hunger.

Before it did, Quint drew back scant inches. "It's late. You'd better get some sleep."

Regret flickered briefly in her eyes. Then a tiny frown puckered her forehead. "I thought of something. Now I can't remember what it was."

"That's because you're tired. It'll come to you in the morning," he said and braced a hand on the bed to push himself away from it.

"You don't have to go, Quint." It was a statement, issued softly, not an appeal.

More than tempted, Quint studied the heavy lidding of her eyes and smiled. "If I stayed, neither one of us would get much sleep. And you're halfway there right now."

"I know." Her smile was lazy with sleepiness even as she snuggled a little deeper into her bed, settling herself in for the night.

"See you in the morning." He dropped a light kiss on her nose and turned off the lamp as he straightened up from the bed.

"Good night." Her voice floated after him when he crossed to the door.


Only a handful of reporters showed up at the ranch the next morning. They looked with regret at the healthy cattle standing in the pen and halfheartedly recorded the scene when Quint distributed hay to the animals. They lingered for a while until it became apparent no new story would be coming from the ranch. The last one pulled out a little before noon.

During lunch, Jessy called, alerting them to expect a delivery of hay that afternoon. There would be only six of the smaller-sized round bales. Considering that only ten square bales remained in the barn, the news was welcome.

Armed with a grocery list, Dallas headed to the store after lunch. She waved to Quint when she pulled out of the ranch yard. His own trip to the city to switch pickups had been delayed by the arrival of a state inspector.

In less than an hour, Dallas paid for her purchases at the checkout counter and wheeled the cart out of the store into the bright sunlight. The air had a hint of sharpness to it, but the sun blazed a hot counterpoint, the heat of its rays warm on her face.

Dallas rolled the cart to the rear of the white pickup and lowered the tailgate. Turning back to the sacks in the cart, she paid no attention to the tan and white truck that pulled into the empty slot next to hers. She lifted a sack from the cart and pivoted to set it in the pickup just as the driver's door of the other vehicle swung open and Boone Rutledge's muscular frame emerged from it. The bright glitter in his dark eyes and the cocky smile on his face told Dallas that he had known where to find her.

A cold loathing welled up inside her. "Did your spies tell you I was here?" Dallas challenged and reached for another sack, a tightly controlled anger stiffening her movements.

"What do you think?" Boone mocked and strolled over to the tailgate. "I've been waiting to hear from you."

"Why?" She flashed him a chilling look and shoved another sack into the truck.

"Echohawk's bound to be sweating—three cows dead from anthrax, his cattle quarantined, and his hay running low."

Dallas longed to slap that smug look from his face. She settled for taunting. "You seem to know everything already. Obviously there isn't anything I need to tell you."

But it was the phrase "know everything" that clicked in her mind, and Dallas remembered the thought she had wanted to tell Quint last night. With a rare sense of anticipation, she turned to face Boone, tilting her head at a provocative and faintly challenging angle, a small smile curving her mouth. The essentially male side of Boone looked at her with quickening interest.

"You aren't really going to try to convince me that the Rutledges didn't have anything to do with those cows dying of anthrax, are you?" Dallas murmured.

Shock brought a flicker of panic to his eyes, and a telling pause that was heavy with guilt. "What makes you think we did?" He smiled, as if amused by such a ridiculous suggestion, but his gaze was a bit too sharp and searching in its intent study of her.

Dallas had no doubt that Quint's suspicions were true. But she needed more than that. "Because it was so ingenious, of course. And the very last thing anyone would expect."

"You did," Boone stated, unaware that his words were an admission of sorts.

"Experience gives me the advantage of knowing just how dirty and devious the Rutledges can be. There is very little you wouldn't dare, is there?" Venom coated her words, and Dallas made no attempt to disguise it, aware that Boone would instantly be wary if she tried to act friendly or cooperative.

"I knew you were smart. Make sure you stay that way." His eyes had the smug gleam of a man convinced he had the upper hand.

"I intend to." But not in the way he meant it.

"Is Echohawk wondering if we had something to do with the anthrax?"

It was a question Dallas had expected him to ask much earlier. Her nonanswer was all prepared. "Why should he? They were Cee Bar cattle on Cee Bar land. I'm still trying to figure out how you managed that." She looked at him with unfeigned curiosity. "After all, they're range animals, hardly tame enough to be handfed. And if you set out contaminated feed, there was no guarantee it would be eaten right away—and a definite risk that it could be discovered." She paused, not at all sure the ploy would work. "I'm curious. How did you do it?"

Mentally Dallas crossed her fingers, hoping against hope that Boone wouldn't be able to resist the opportunity to boast of his cleverness.

The wideness of his smile signaled her success. "It was a simple matter of throwing up a portable holding pen to confine them and setting out some contaminated feed for them to eat."

"But—you would have had to do that on the Slash R land," Dallas said, feigning surprise.

Boone shrugged. "How can it be our fault if the boundary fence is in such bad shape that a few cows stray onto Slash R range? Naturally we had to push them back on their own side."

"Something that would have looked completely innocent to any chance passerby. But you ran the risk of infecting your own cattle," Dallas said, subtly pressing for more information.

"Hardly," Boone scoffed in amusement. "Not when you have someone with all the training to know the safe way to do it."

"That would be you, I suppose." But she saw at once that her acid flattery wouldn't succeed in getting an answer from him this time.

"That's something you don't need to know," he replied in easy unconcern.

"It never hurts to ask." She turned away and proceeded to calmly transfer the grocery sacks from the cart to the pickup bed.

"So what's Echohawk doing about hay?" Boone prompted.

"Wouldn't you like to know?" Dallas took great satisfaction in throwing the question at his face with cool contempt.

He went from smugness to barely contained fury in a lightning instant, grabbing her arm and viciously digging his fingers into her flesh, finding bone. "Don't get smart with me, you little bitch."

Making no effort to struggle, Dallas gave him an icy stare. "Let go of me or I'll scream loud enough for the whole town to hear."

"Go ahead," he jeered. "Nobody's going to come to your rescue. Now tell me what I want to know."

His grip tightened, the pain intensifying as he twisted her arm higher, but Dallas refused to give him the satisfaction of crying out.

"I guess I forgot to tell you." She fought to keep the pain out of her voice. The effort gave it a constricted sound. "You won't be getting any more information from me."

Dallas tilted her face to him in stubborn defiance, her attention focused on the fiery black glitter of his eyes. There was no awareness of the hand he swung at her until it slammed against her cheek, snapping her head to the side.

There was an explosion of color behind her eyes and a roaring in her ears. She never heard the squeal of skidding tires.

Blinded with his own rage, Boone took no notice of it either as he seized her chin in a viselike grip. "You'd better wise up—"

Quint jerked Boone away from her and shoved him into the tail-gate. "You're the one who'd better wise up, Rutledge." Something savage glittered in his gray eyes. "You touch her again and you're liable to find yourself in a wheelchair like your father."

"You think you could do it?" Boone challenged, smiling with an eagerness that matched the avid and ready gleam in his eyes.

Dallas's voice came between them before a fist could be swung. "The Rutledges infected the cattle with anthrax, Quint. He admitted it."

Stunned, Boone threw her a shocked look, then yanked his gaze back to Quint. "That's a damned lie. I never said anything of the kind."

"Worried, are you?" Quint smiled with a cold kind of pleasure.

"No cattleman would mess around with anthrax." Boone's denial had all the readiness of something rehearsed.

"How true," Dallas said in a voice brittle with control. "But the Rutledges stopped being cattlemen a long time ago." She turned to Quint, her chin lifting fractionally. "Would you like to know why he hit me?"

A puzzled wariness leaped into his expression as if Quint sensed something amiss. "Why?"

"Because I refused to act as his spy and keep him informed about your plans the way I've done in the past." She watched as his gray eyes narrowed on her with an intermixing of disbelief, anger, and pain. The sight was like a fist closing around her heart.

"She's making the whole thing up," Boone rushed in denial. "Everybody knows she's been trying to make trouble for us ever since her grandfather lost his ranch."

Quint unleashed the sharp edge of his temper on Boone. "I don't want to hear another word out of you. Just get in your truck and get the hell out of here."

Boone took a sideways step, hesitated, and pointed an accusing finger at Dallas. "I tell you she's lying. You can't trust anything she says."

"I can't trust you either," Quint fired back. "Now get."

Boone ran a calculating glance over Quint. Satisfied that he had planted all the doubt he could, he sidled clear of the white pickup and backed up a few steps before turning to his own pickup.

Dallas waited in silence, cold all over, but Quint never turned to her until Boone drove off. When he did, his gaze bored into her, demanding and probing.

"Is it true what you said? You've been feeding him information?" Disbelief lingered that she could have betrayed him like that.

The guilt of it weighed on her. "I intended to tell you before now, but . . . the time never seemed right," Dallas admitted.

"But how? Why?" His voice was thick with anger.

"That day I came to the ranch and told you Boone made threats against Empty—that part was true. I knew I could never persuade my grandfather to quit working for you, so I did what I had to do to protect him." It was an explanation. Pride wouldn't let her beg for his understanding. "I hardly knew you then, Quint."

He stared at her, wrapped in a fury and pain that ran deep and hot. Too hot. Not trusting himself to speak, Quint turned and walked back to the idling pickup, slipped behind the wheel, and slammed the door.

Dallas watched him drive off. There were always consequences to be faced with every action taken, but Dallas had never guessed there would be so much pain with this one.

# Chapter Seventeen

The Cee Bar ranch yard was blessedly empty of other vehicles when Dallas drove in. She parked the old white pickup in front of the ranch house and climbed out, hastily scrubbing the dampness from her cheek with her hand.

But it didn't seem to matter how many tears she wiped away; there was always another waiting to slither down her face. It was all part of the big, hollow ache in her chest.

Creaking door hinges came from the porch as Empty emerged from the house. "I'll give you a hand bringing the groceries in." Spindly but spry legs carried him quickly down the steps to the walkway.

Dallas pressed a quick finger to a corner of her eye, blotting away a gathering tear, and took a long galvanizing breath, steeling herself for this meeting with her grandfather. In an attempt at normalcy, she lowered the tailgate and went through the motions of dragging the sacks onto it.

But it was the reddening mark on her face from the hard blow Boone had given her, and not the dampness on her cheeks, that Empty's sharp eyes noticed. His demand for an explanation was instant.

There was no longer anything to be gained by avoiding the truth, and Dallas didn't try. She told him everything, omitting only Boone's admission about the anthrax. The explosion that followed was one she had anticipated.

"You did what!" Empty thundered in outrage. Dallas didn't bother to repeat it. He knew exactly what she'd said. "How could you do that? My own granddaughter siding with the Rutledges! By God, I oughta take a belt to you. What was going through that head of yours?"

"I explained that." Dallas absorbed his wrath with remarkable stoicism, thanks to a pain of a different kind that had left her numb.

"To protect me!" The contempt in his voice told her exactly what he thought of that reasoning. "For your information, little lady, I'm not so old that I can't look after myself. And I sure don't need you stabbing me in the back while I'm trying. I tell you, it flat turns my stomach to think of my own flesh and blood doing the Rutledges's bidding."

"Not anymore," Dallas reminded him. "I told Boone that he'd received the last information from me that he was ever going to get."

"A little late, wasn't it?" Empty snapped.

Her head lifted. "You always told me it was never too late to correct a mistake."

Her words took some of the fire from him, but didn't change the glare in his eyes. "You're through with them. That's something, I guess."

He subsided into silence and Dallas reached for one of the grocery sacks. Empty threw her a sideways glance, measuring and thoughtful.

"What did Quint say when you told him?"

"Nothing." Dallas wrapped both arms around the bag, holding it tightly in front of her as if it might provide protection or comfort. "He just got in his truck and drove off."

Empty dragged in a deep breath and let it gust out. "Guess there wasn't much you could expect him to say after telling him a thing like that. You're probably lucky he didn't tell you to get the hell out of his sight." He grabbed up a sack. "Guess we might as well get these groceries in the house and start packing. It's not likely he's going to want us here anymore. It might be better for us to be gone when he gets back."

"No." Dallas was surprised by the forcefulness of her answer. Yet she felt the rightness of her stand. "Somebody has to be here when the hay's delivered. And if anyone leaves, it will only be me. I'm not going to let him blame you for what I did."

"You aren't going to go anywhere without me," he stated firmly.

Dallas shook her head. "Quint needs you. And if he wants me gone, he'll have to tell me."

Empty offered no argument, but there was a sadness in his eyes. "You love him, don't you?" he guessed.

"Yes." She choked up.

"I just wished you had trusted him a little, Dallas."

His words were a poignant echo of similar advice Quint had given not so many nights ago. And trust was the issue—a broken trust that might never be made whole again.


The upthrust of glass and granite soared four stories into the air. Its sleek, polished sides mirrored the blue of the Texas sky and reflected the image of the black pickup that pulled into an empty slot in the parking lot. Quint piled out of the cab, slamming the door behind him, and headed for the building's entrance, a long-striding walk propelling him toward the door.

There was one thought and one thought only in his mind right now. No matter what rawly emotional road his mind had traveled during the drive to Fort Worth, it had always come full circle back to one thing—the Rutledges. Their black heart had been behind it all.

When he reached the executive suite on the fourth floor, Quint shoved aside the glass doors, mindless of their wild swing. A trim brunette glanced up from her desk and smiled warmly.

"Good afternoon." Her gaze traveled over his face with open interest.

His glance had already darted past her to the closed door just to the left of her desk. "Is Rutledge in?" Quint gestured to the door without ever slackening his pace toward it.

"Mr. Rutledge is in conference right now. If you would care to—" She broke off in alarm when he walked past her desk. Rising from her chair, she protested, "You can't go in there."

Quint spared her a dry, cold look. "Watch me."

A testing turn of the handle revealed the door wasn't locked. He pushed the door open and followed it into the office.

His sweeping gaze ignored the room's sleek, contemporary decor and abstract art, and centered instead on the three men in the room. Max Rutledge sat in his wheelchair behind the steel and wood corner desk. Boone stood facing him. A third man dressed in a western-cut suit and bolo tie hovered next to Max, his manner that of a closely trusted underling.

Boone whirled around, surprise dissolving into a black fury at the sight of Quint. "What the hell are you doing barging in here?"

Unaffected by the angry challenge, Quint continued forward, gripped by the cool dispassion of battle. "I might have known you would race straight here to warn Max that you'd lost your informant."

The frantic look Boone darted at his father and the surprise that flickered so briefly in Max's expression told Quint that Boone hadn't gotten around to relating that piece of news. Something snapped in Boone. Teeth bared, he lunged for Quint.

Sidestepping to avoid the onrush, Quint grabbed Boone's arm, twisted it behind him, and gave him a shove into a nearby chair, all without breaking a sweat. Boone crashed into it and lay there for a dazed second, not at all sure what happened to him or how.

In his side vision, Quint saw the third man pick up the telephone. He pointed a finger at him while keeping a wary watch on Quint.

"I wouldn't make that call to security until you're sure your boss wants them," he warned, and fired a glance at the man in the wheelchair. "Do you, Max?"

After a small pause, Max waved a hand. "Put the phone down, Edwards."

"Smart move," Quint told him as Boone struggled upright in the chair and appeared on the verge of launching himself at Quint again.

With an almost noiseless whirr, Max rolled his wheelchair from behind the desk and glided between them. "Stay where you are," he told Boone, a curl of disgust on his lip, "before he makes a fool of you again." His hand manipulated the control stick, squaring his chair around to face Quint. "What is it you want, Echohawk?" he asked in a perfectly reasonable voice.

Before answering, Quint pointedly divided his glance between the man behind the desk and the brunette poised in the doorway. "You might prefer to have this conversation take place in private."

The touch of his glance seemed to loosen the brunette's tongue. "I'm sorry, Mr. Rutledge. I tried to stop him—"

"That will be all, Miss Bridges," Max told her, then directed a look at the third man. "Close the door on your way out, Edwards."

Silence reigned while the two exited the office. During it, Max Rutledge settled more comfortably in his wheelchair and viewed Quint with a look of great tolerance. Boone displayed no such control, pushing himself out of his chair and pacing over to a floor-to-ceiling window, his body rigid in anger and resentment.

With the click of the door latch, Max assumed charge of the meeting. "Now what is it that's so all-fired important to talk about?" He smiled in amused indulgence.

"It isn't so much what we have to talk about, Max," Quint responded with a cool smile of his own, "as it is what I have to tell you."

"And what might that be?"

"So far you've been dealing all the hands in this game, and I've played them as they came. But not anymore," Quint stated. "I'm taking over the deck. From now on, I'll do the dealing, and you aren't going to like the cards."

Massive shoulders lifted in a vague shrug of indifference. "I'm afraid I don't know what you're talking about."

"In that case we'll start with the most recent one. Anthrax."

The reaction from Boone was instant. He spun from the window, a look of rage on his face. "Damn it, I told you that was a pack of lies. She made up that whole thing as a way to get back at us! Why the hell do you think I hit her?"

Quint never so much as glanced in Boone's direction, choosing instead to observe the sharp, assessing look Max gave him, and the tightening line of displeasure around his mouth.

"You see, Max, I know you infected those cows with anthrax." Quint stated it as a fact. "I didn't need Dallas to tell me that Boone had admitted it to her."

To Max's credit he showed no reaction to that statement, probably anticipating it.

"Yesterday"—Quint stressed the word—"I put a team of investigators on it, all pros. They'll find out where you got the bacteria, who gave it to you, and any middleman you may have used."

"That's ridiculous," Max scoffed. "I had nothing to do with your cattle dying of anthrax."

"Yes, you did. And I'll prove it. Want to know why?" His smile of challenge was full of confidence.

There was an involuntary twitch of a muscle in a gaunt cheek, but Max offered no reply, choosing instead to match Quint stare for stare.

"I'll tell you why." Quint leaned down and braced his hands on the wheelchair's armrests, pushing his face close to Max and destroying any illusion Max might have entertained that his wheelchair was some kind of throne. Fury and loathing warred in the glaring look Max gave him.

"You've been the he-bull around here too long. That breeds overconfidence every time. And that means you've made a mistake somewhere. Anthrax is an ugly word, Max, and your son has already tied you to it. People who would have kept their mouths shut in the past might be inclined to talk now."

"You're talking nonsense," Max insisted, not quite able to pull off a tone of utter indifference.

"Am I?" Quint challenged, with a cold smile of certainty. "Right now your mind is racing, cataloguing everyone who knew or could have known about the anthrax, wondering if any of them let something slip—or might, if questioned, like your son did. You're even wondering if there's someone you can pay to take the fall for this. But you don't dare approach them to make sure there aren't any more leaks, for fear that you would lead my investigators right to them. And you would. But don't think that's your only worry. The team has orders to look into all your dealings. And we both know they'll find something, because your hands are dirty, Max."

"Are you finished?" His temper shortening, Max all but spat the words.

"Not quite," Quint replied, peripherally aware of Boone watching the exchange with a kind of shock. "I'll make you a deal, Max."

"A deal? You stand there and threaten me, then have the nerve to offer me a deal?" His forceful voice trembled with suppressed rage.

"Isn't that the way you work, Max?" Quint countered. "You make all your threats, then offer an alternative. That's all I'm doing. And just like you, I'll carry out my threats if it's necessary—and it'll be the Rutledge name smeared all over the headlines." He paused as Max ripped his gaze away from him. "Are you finding it hard to swallow some of your own medicine?"

"What are the terms?" Max growled.

"The terms are simple: back off." The steel in Quint's voice matched the steel in his eyes. "Back off from the Cee Bar and the Calders."

Max turned back to him, thrusting his chin forward. "If I agree, are you going to call off your dogs?"

This time, Quint straightened himself away from the wheel-chair to tower over the man. "No. Because I can't trust you to keep your word, Max. But I will agree to sit on anything I find."

"That's no deal at all," Max retorted.

"It's the only one you're going to get. Now it's up to you to de-cide whether it's worth the price you might have to pay just to try to get your hands on the Cee Bar—especially now that you know the Calders are going to fight back every way they can."

"You are assuming I had anything more than a passing interest in acquiring the Cee Bar," Max retorted with some of his former poise.

"Is that your answer?" Quint challenged. "Because this is a onetime offer. You take it or leave it right now."

"I don't know why I should agree with your ridiculous pro-posal when I had nothing to do with the trouble you're having at the Cee Bar. But if agreeing will give you some peace of mind, I'll do it," Max declared with dismissive ease.

A smile quirked one corner of Quint's mouth. "I always knew you were an intelligent man, Max. Just remember—I'm going to hold you to this."

He flicked a glance at Boone and walked out of the office. For a moment both men stared at the door. Then Boone finally found his voice.

"He made you back down," he murmured in a dazed and awed tone. "I never thought I'd see the day when someone could do that to you."

Max whipped his chair around, a malevolence in his expres-sion unlike anything Boone had ever seen. "And you never would have if it wasn't for your big mouth! I swear to God you have screwed up for the last time."

"Me? What are you talking about?" But Boone knew exactly what he meant. A kind of panic set in. "I never admitted anything to that Garner woman. She made it all up. You can't blame me just because she managed to convince Echohawk with her lies."

"You don't even have the guts to own up to the truth, do you?"

"I tell you I didn't say anything," Boone protested vehemently. "Are you going to take Echohawk's word over mine?"

"You're damned right I am," Max fired back. "Unlike you, Echohawk is no fool. Regardless of what he might have suspected, he would never have set foot in this office today if you hadn't confirmed his suspicions."

"I tell you she lied to him!"

"And I say you are the only liar around here!" Max bellowed, his gaunt face mottling with rage. "From the time you were able to talk, it's been one lie after another. I've never been able to trust a single thing you say. And I sure as hell have never been able to depend on you to do even the smallest thing right. If you had been anyone other than my son, I would have shown you the door a long time ago. That was my mistake. But it isn't one I'll make again."

"It's always my fault, isn't it? One little thing goes wrong, and I get blamed for it," Boone hurled bitterly, but he was addressing a moving target as the wheelchair zipped Max to the desk. Boone went after him and halted at its side, gripping the edges and leaning forward to vent his pent-up wrath. "Nothing I do ever pleases you! Not the great Max Rutledge."

Deaf to his tirade, Max picked up the telephone and punched the speed number for the main house at the Slash R. The instant it was answered, he ordered curtly, "Pack Boone's things at once. I want every single item of his gone before I arrive home tonight." A question on the other end of the line caused Max to flick a glance at Boone. "No, he won't be by to get them. Send them to the Adolphus for now. He can pick them up there," Max stated and hung up.

"What the hell is this?" Boone demanded, a cold chill creeping in.

"Isn't it obvious?" Max's voice and stare were like iron. "I want you out of my house and my life. As far as I'm concerned, I no longer have a son."

"What the hell are you talking about?" Disbelief was first, then a fear that struck deep. "You can't do that!"

"I can and I am," Max stated. "A check will be deposited in your account on the first of every month, and that is the only contact we will have from now on. You have two seconds to get out of my sight before I call security and have you thrown out."

For Boone, there was an unreality to the moment, a disbelief that this could truly be happening to him. As always, the right words wouldn't come.

When he saw that big hand reach for the phone, he knew Max would carry out his threat and order security to escort him from the premises. Rather than suffer the ignominy of such treatment, Boone straightened up from the desk and walked stiffly from the office, bitter black thoughts whirling in his head.

He didn't remember the elevator ride to the lobby, climbing into his truck, or driving out of the lot. The first thing to register was a beer sign in the window of a bar. The sight of it and his own dry-mouthed feeling had Boone pulling up in front of it and going inside.

The place had the sour reek of beer tinged with stale cigarette smoke, but Boone never noticed as he crossed to the empty stools at the counter and climbed onto one. In a numb kind of haze, he ordered a beer and drank down half of it, then sat there, hot with resentment.

His mind started playing that dreaded and all-too-familiar game of if-only. If only he hadn't let Dallas trick him into admitting they had infected the cattle with anthrax. If only Echohawk hadn't come along when he did. If only she hadn't told Echohawk what he'd said.

His fingers curled into tight fists. If it wasn't for that bitch, none of this would have happened; the certainty of it filled him.

And with it came the first glimmer that maybe there was a way out of this. Maybe there was a way to prove to Max that he wasn't a liar. And Dallas could do that.

It didn't matter to him at all that it would be another lie. Max wouldn't know it, and that was all that counted.

He downed the beer in his glass and ordered another.

# Chapter Eighteen

⌒◞◟⌒

Cloud wisps drifted across the blue of the afternoon sky. The sun was bright, but the air was winter cool, making the sleeves of the sweatshirt that Dallas wore a welcome cover for her arms. She waited next to the tractor, the punctured tire from its nose gear propped against her leg, while Empty backed the white pickup into position.

It braked to a stop a few feet from her. Dallas rolled the tire over to the back of the truck while Empty climbed out of the cab and came around to give her a hand loading it. His assistance wasn't really required, but she didn't object when he helped to hoist it into the truck bed.

Once it was settled into place, Empty lingered, his glance touching on her before skipping to the ranch lane. A believer in dressing for the season, he wore a hat and gloves and an insulated jacket zipped up to his neck.

"I figure Quint'll be back before long." Again his glance bounced back to her, probing with empathy. "If you want, I can take my time getting this tire patched. It might be easier if it's just you and him."

"There's no need." Dallas had already made up her mind that

she would accept whatever decision Quint made, without argument, even if it went against her.

"Quint's a fair man," Empty said in an attempt at reassurances. "After all, no man alive can ever truly understand the crazy way a woman reasons. He might make allowances for that."

Dallas wanted to smile at his slightly sexist statement, but there was too much heaviness within to leave any room for the lightness of amusement.

"Maybe." She was careful not to hope too much. It would only hurt that much more if—but she couldn't finish the thought; even the suggestion of it brought a great hollow ache in her chest that closed off her air.

Empty sighed, a long and forlorn sound. "I'll tell you one thing, I'll be glad when Quint gets back. All this waiting and wondering is working on my nerves."

"True," Dallas agreed, caught somewhere between a blessed numbness and an agonizing tension.

Pushing off, Empty headed back to the front of the truck and opened the door on the driver's side. He paused with one booted foot on the running board and waved a hand in the direction of the opened barn door.

"You might want to close that. No need to advertise to the Rutledges that we got a delivery of hay," he told her.

"I will." But it was his use of the pronoun "we" that made Dallas realize just how much of a home this ranch had become for both of them. It was far from a showplace, but she knew how much she would hate to leave it—and Quint.

With a sharp, quick lift of her head, Dallas turned toward the barn, refusing to anticipate what the eventuality would be, good or bad. While the white pickup rattled out of the ranch yard, heading for town, Dallas crossed to the open barn door and the strong smell of hay that came from within.

Small, round bales stacked two high filled the alleyway. Putting a shoulder to the heavy door, she pushed it, rolling it across the entrance and stopping it within a foot of its jamb, leaving room for the chickens to scamper in and out.

When she stepped away from the barn, the white pickup had already disappeared from sight. Dallas was alone, completely at loose ends. Between putting away the groceries and the arrival of the truck with the hay delivery, she had managed to keep herself occupied. Suddenly she had nothing to do, and too much time on her hands.

Determined to find something that would keep her too busy to think, Dallas headed for the house. The secret was to keep moving, and that was easy with all the inner agitation that pushed her.

But the minute she walked into the house, its silence was almost more than she could stand. Immediately Dallas turned on the radio, leaving it tuned to the country station that always carried the noonday market reports.

With guitar and fiddle music filling the kitchen, she crossed to the sink and put away the lunch dishes drying in the drain rack. After tidying up the counter area, Dallas moved to the living room and straightened it up. It was all busywork—plumping pillows, arranging magazines into neat stacks, and returning the odd glass to the kitchen.

She was on her way to the bathroom to collect the dirty towels from this morning's showers and set out clean ones when a light flashed against the living room, the kind that came from sunlight bouncing off a windshield. Dallas halted in place, her heartbeat skittering like a mad thing.

Suddenly she was all jittery nerves. She pulled in a deep, steadying breath, aware that she would soon find out if knowing would turn out to be worse than the not knowing.

The music on the radio failed to completely drown out the metallic slam of a door and the hard striding footsteps crossing the porch. Bracing herself for that first glimpse of Quint's face and the expression she might see in it, Dallas turned toward the door.

She froze in shock when Boone Rutledge barged into the house, a brutish kind of anger twisting through his features. His raking glance scoured the room and stopped when it reached her.

"I figured you might be here when I didn't see you with the old man in town." The glitter of satisfaction in his eyes had an ugliness to it.

"What are you doing here, Boone?" Every instinct said to run, but Dallas held her ground.

"As if you don't know," he jeered.

"I think you'd better leave. Quint will be back soon," she warned.

"Is that supposed to make me shake in my boots?"

His voice, there was a slight slur to it. He'd been drinking; she was certain of it, and that brought a new sense of fear.

"Let him come," he growled. "We won't be here anyway. You're coming with me."

Boone moved toward her and made a grab for her arm. She pulled it out of reach and took a hasty step back.

"Where are we going? Why?" With a corner of the living room behind her, Dallas had no avenue of escape.

"Max needs to see you. Now. So come on." When Boone reached for her again, Dallas knew she had to act fast.

"Max? Why didn't you say so in the first place?" she said in disgust and pushed his hand away before it could encircle her wrist. She used the movement to brush past him. "My purse is in the kitchen. I'll get it and be right with you."

There was maneuvering room in the kitchen—and a back door. She was almost to the doorway when his hand snared her arm. This time there was no twisting away from it.

"You don't need any damned purse," Boone snarled.

Her reaction was automatic, without any thought of the effect it might have on Boone. "Let me go!" An anger, born out of fear, blazed in her eyes.

"Not a chance." His hands pinned both arms, fingers digging in hard as he yanked her close to him, close enough for the smell of liquor on his breath to wash over her face. "You aren't going anywhere until you set things straight with Max."

"What things? I don't know what you're talking about." Dallas strained away from him and the half-crazed look in his eyes. But her denial only served to further provoke him.

"Like hell you don't! You're going to tell him the truth about what happened today so he'll know I never admitted that we had anything to do with the anthrax. I was just stringing you along to see what I could learn. Do you understand?" The harsh and savage demand was accompanied by a hard shake, so rough it snapped her head back.

Fear licked through her with a cold tongue. Violence—it came from him in waves. Boone wanted her to resist—wanted an excuse to unleash it. Somehow she had to find a way to play along and keep it at bay.

"Didn't you explain it to him?" Dallas asked, uttering the first thing that popped into her mind.

But Boone wouldn't be diverted by it. "It doesn't matter what I did. It's what you're going to do. Your big mouth caused all this trouble. Now you're going to fix it!"

"Tell me again what I'm supposed to say." It was a stalling tactic, an effort to gain more time. Dallas was too rattled to know what she hoped to achieve by it.

It didn't work.

"Don't get smart with me, you little bitch." He grabbed a handful of hair and jerked her head back, pulling viscously on the roots and drawing a short outcry of pain from her. "You know exactly what to say."

"I don't. You're scaring me so much I can't think." There was too much truth in that statement.

"You should be scared—scared of what I'll do to you if you mess this up," Boone warned and gave another twisting jerk of her hair.

"Please." Her voice was thready and tight. "I can't remember."

"All you have to do is tell Max that you made up all that shit about the anthrax—make him understand that everything Echohawk told him was a pack of lies. You got that?"

But only one part of it registered. "Quint saw Max?" The ring of confusion and uncertainty was in her voice and her searching look.

"Hell yes! That's why you've got to set things straight and tell him the truth—that I never admitted anything!"

Dallas could almost see violent forces building up in him, a hair-trigger from exploding. She rushed to defuse them.

"I will. I'll tell him exactly what you said."

Her ready agreement took him aback. "That's better." He let go of her hair, but kept his grip on her arm. "Come on. Let's go."

When he swung toward the front door, Dallas took a chance and stepped into the kitchen doorway, pulling at his grip. "My purse—"

The words were barely out of her mouth before she was forcibly slammed against the framework and a big hand grabbed her by the throat.

"I told you to forget about that damned purse!" Boone thundered, his fingers tightening, choking off her air and silencing her vocal cords.

He hurled more abuse and obscenities at her, but Dallas was beyond hearing them. She opened her mouth for air, but none came in and no sound came out. She pushed frantically at his hand, trying to weaken its stranglehold on her throat with no success.

With her lungs screaming for air, panic set in. Kicking and clawing, she tried to fight him off even as a redness pressed against the edges of her vision. But she could feel her strength ebbing away, fading even as the pain grew to an intense level—her ears, her head, her whole body roaring with it.

Blackness swirled, a relief offered somewhere in its dark void. Even as it closed around her consciousness, the pressure abruptly lifted. But there was no strength in her legs to hold her upright, and Dallas slumped to the floor, sucking in air in great, life-renewing gulps, a hand lifting to her painfully throbbing throat.

A loud crash finally penetrated her dazed senses. With an almost drunken swing of her head, Dallas looked around for Boone, fear surfacing anew.

Then she saw him—there in the kitchen. But he wasn't alone. He was grappling with Quint. She had no idea where Quint had come from—or when or how.

A kind of joyous relief quivered through her, but it didn't last as Quint blocked one blow from Boone, but missed the second. It clipped him on the chin, sending him reeling backward into the kitchen counter. Boone plunged after him, fists swinging.

Her own eyes warned her that Boone was bigger, stronger, and a good forty pounds heavier than Quint. This time Quint managed to duck under an arcing swing and dance out of Boone's trap. But Dallas didn't know how long he could hold him off without help.

Forcing her limbs to work, she struggled to her feet and half staggered to the telephone on the corner desk. Behind her she could hear the gruntings of breath, the shuffle of feet, and the smash of fist against flesh, all of it coming above the radio's tender ballad.

With clumsy fingers, she clutched the receiver to her ear and dialed the emergency number. An operator was quick to answer, the voice coming clearly across the line.

"What's your emergency please?"

But Dallas had trouble making her bruised vocal cords work. "Send the police." It was raspy and weak. She swallowed and tried again. "It's Boone Rutledge. He's gone crazy."

As if in emphasis of her words, a kitchen chair went flying across the floor and crashed into the wall, the racket of it loud enough for the operator to hear.

"Where are you?"

"The Cee Bar Ranch." Dallas threw a worried glance over her

shoulder and saw Quint on the floor, looking dazed and giving his head a shake as if to clear it. But it was the sight of Boone diving for him that made her call a loud and raspy warning. "Look out!"

Quint rolled clear, but Boone grabbed him before he could scramble to his feet. The two men rolled around on the floor, each struggling to gain an advantage.

The voice in Dallas's ear kept demanding answers, but she couldn't seem to focus on anything but the fight.

"Tell them to hurry," she pleaded, fear striking deep when Boone pinned Quint to the floor and closed both hands around his throat, teeth bared, a killing look in his eyes. "My God, Boone's going to kill him."

She dropped the phone and automatically moved to help Quint. Then it all changed in the blink of an eye. One moment Boone's hands were around Quint's throat; in the next his arms were flying outward and Quint bucked him aside.

Gathering himself, Quint lurched to his feet and swayed a little, fists up in readiness, his chest heaving, one side of his face bloodied from a cut above his eye and more blood trickling from a corner of his mouth. Then Boone was up as well, his gaze fastening itself on Quint with a kind of crazed fury and frustration.

The two men circled warily, fists rotating, each searching for an opening in the other's defenses. Boone banged a hip into the corner of the kitchen table. With a sweep of his paw, he hurled the table aside, overturning it.

Quint stepped in and landed two hard blows that temporarily staggered Boone. But he came roaring back with a growl of rage, swinging wildly, more blows missing than landing, but the ones that did inflicted damage.

Unable to stand and watch a second longer, Dallas ran into the living room and fumbled frantically to undo the lock on the gun cabinet's door. At last, she flung it open and grabbed the shotgun from the rack.

She snatched up a box of shells and fed two into the chambers. Heart pounding, she raced back to the kitchen.

Boone was on the floor, a hand pressed to his jaw. Quint stood in front of him, directly between Dallas and Boone. Cursing under his breath, Boone grabbed for the counter edge to haul himself up and missed, catching hold of a drawer handle instead. The drawer came flying out off its track, the utensils tumbling from it and clattering to the floor.

When Boone rolled to his feet, he scooped up something, but not until she saw the glint of a steel blade did Dallas recognize the carving knife.

"Look out, Quint!" Dallas shouted, and this time her voice had some force to it. "He has a knife!"

She lifted the shotgun to her shoulder, but she had no clear shot at the crouching Boone, knife held low. His arm snaked out and Quint jumped back to avoid the arcing slice of the blade point, drawing an ugly laugh from Boone. Again and again the knife slashed through the air in front of Quint.

Dallas wanted to tell him to get out of the way, but she was more afraid of distracting him at the wrong moment. Boone made a sudden stabbing thrust with the knife. Quint sidestepped, but the blade's back-slice caught his arm, cutting through sleeve and flesh, causing an instant spurt of blood onto the material.

Before Dallas could move or cry out, Boone lunged at Quint again. This time Quint grabbed the arm with the knife and tried to wrest it away from him. The two struggled over it, locked together in an ever-changing shift of bodies to counter weight or leverage.

Dallas was never sure what happened next—if it was a deliberate or an accidental tangle of legs that took both men to the floor. She only knew she lost sight of the knife when they fell. Suddenly both men went still.

With her heart in her throat, Dallas waited, the fear of what this could mean stopping her from lowering the shotgun. Then Boone moved, rolling off Quint. She gasped back a little sob and slipped her finger across the trigger. Then she saw the knife buried in Boone's chest and the blood that smeared the front of his shirt.

And there was Quint, grabbing onto the counter and pulling himself upright, the arm with the blood-soaked sleeve hanging limp at his side, his chest heaving in exhaustion as he looked down at Boone.

Relief turned her legs to jelly. Hurriedly Dallas lowered the shotgun, but she was too well schooled in firearm safety to simply lay the weapon aside without first breaking it open and removing the shells.

Only when it was safely unloaded did Dallas thrust it aside and hurry to Quint. He was propped against the counter, a gray dullness to his eyes.

"I'm fine." He made a wan attempt at a reassuring smile.

"No, you're not. You're bleeding to death." Dallas grabbed a dish towel out of the drawer and tied it around his upper arm, pulling it tight across the deep gash.

"Did you call the police?" His voice had the flatness of sapped strength.

"Yes." Until that moment, Dallas had all but forgotten that.

"That must be them coming now," he mumbled.

Belatedly Dallas identified the wail of the sirens in the background, separating their sound from the Hank Jr. classic being played on the radio.

As their scream grew louder, she darted a glance at Boone's motionless form, not really sure if he was alive or dead. Truthfully she didn't care.

"I thought he was going to kill you," Dallas murmured, her voice thick with the freshness of that memory.

"It was close." Quint's glance lifted, touching the red marks on her face and neck. "Are you—"

But he never had a chance to finish the sentence as the door burst open and two uniformed officers charged into the room, one after the other, hands on their holstered weapons. Their lightning scan of the kitchen noted the overturned table and scattered chairs.

"Sweet Jesus, it's Boone Rutledge," the older officer said when he saw the man on the floor. "Get the paramedics in here. Quick!"

While the second officer turned back to the door, the first hurried across the room to Boone's side, sparing only a glance at Quint while obviously deciding he presented no threat. When the paramedics rushed into the house, he straightened up from the body.

"I think I felt a faint pulse," he told them.

Leaving the paramedics to their task, the officer shifted his attention to Quint and Dallas, immediately separating them. And the questions began.

Within minutes the paramedics had Boone loaded onto a stretcher for transport. Dallas watched as they wheeled him out of the house. By then more officers had arrived on the scene. She saw one of them escorting Quint outside.

"Where are they taking him?" she demanded of the two officers interrogating her.

"To the hospital to get that cut stitched."

"You're aren't going to arrest him, are you? I told you it was self-defense. Boone came at him with the knife," Dallas insisted forcefully.

"That's what you said." The older man nodded, but with a touch of skepticism. "Now, can you tell us why Boone was here?"

And the questioning started all over again.

Empty arrived back at the ranch in the middle of it all, his return necessitating another retelling of the events. To Dallas's relief, he didn't demand to know every single detail.


Quint sat atop the bed in the hospital's examination room, a large gauze bandage covering the wound to his arm and a smaller one on the cut above his eye. The nurse went over the doctor's instructions with him, then gave him a copy of them along with a prescription for an antibiotic.

"Remember," she said. "Take it a little easy for a few days. No heavy lifting with that arm. You don't want to tear any of the doc's fine stitching."

"I'll remember." Quint stood up and winced a little as he slipped on his jacket.

The nurse opened the door. Quint wasn't surprised to see an officer standing outside the treatment room. He stepped into the hallway and paused next to the man.

"Do you still need me?" he asked.

"I just got word you're free to go. At least, for now," the officer replied, somewhat grudgingly.

"What about Boone?"

There was a single negative movement of the man's head. "He never made it to the operating room." He paused, his eyes narrowing on Quint with sharpened interest. "A curious thing, though, he had a pattern of small puncture wounds along the back of one shoulder that looked to be recent. You wouldn't happen to know anything about them, would you?"

"Was it the kind of pattern a shotgun might leave?" Quint asked with a thoughtful look.

The officer stared, his eyes widening at the possibility. "It might."

"The night my hay caught fire, I saw someone running away. I fired off a shot. At the time I thought he was too far away. Maybe he wasn't," Quint suggested.

"You don't really think Boone Rutledge set fire to it, do you?" The officer looked at him askance.

"I don't imagine we'll ever know for sure," Quint admitted, although privately he had his own opinion. "Will you be giving me a ride back to the ranch?"

"No. The Garners are out in the lobby waiting for you." He gestured toward the exit sign. "Like I said, you're free to go. Just don't leave the area in case anything comes up that we need to talk to you about again."

"I won't be going anywhere," Quint told him.

"Good," the officer said and moved off, heading in the opposite direction of the emergency room exit.

Quint watched him a moment, then turned to leave just as a

door in a side hall opened and Max Rutledge rolled out in his wheelchair. It stopped abruptly when Max caught sight of Quint.

After an instant's hesitation, Quint approached him. He couldn't help noticing that Max looked older and colder, but the fire hadn't left his dark eyes.

"I'm sorry about your son, Max," Quint told him. "He gave me no choice."

"He was worthless and a liar," Max stated in a hard, flat voice. "But he was my son."

"I know," Quint said calmly. "You paid a high price for your attempt to grab the Cee Bar. Too high."

"I imagine you're wondering now if I intend to avenge his death," Max stated.

"I think you're smarter than that, Max." With a respectful nod, Quint turned and walked back to the main hall and the exit door to the ER's waiting room.

He pushed through the door and was instantly greeted by the cranky cries of a baby refusing to be comforted by his mother. There was a stir of movement on his right as Dallas sprang out of a chair and took a quick step toward him, then checked her headlong rush for something slower. Empty showed no such hesitation, moving quickly to Quint's side.

"I thought you were never coming out of there," he declared. "I never knew it could take so long to sew up a cut. To be honest, I'd just about decided that they'd arrested you and whisked you out some other door."

"I'm free to go, though I imagine there'll be an inquest of some sort." The response was directed to Empty, but it was Dallas who had his attention.

There was a new lividness to the bruise on her cheek and the marks on her neck. Boone had done that to her, and Quint felt some of that old rage. He sensed it must have shown in his expression when he saw that hers took on a look of quick reserve and uncertainty. It reminded him of all the things that had been left unsaid.

"They had a doctor examine you, didn't they?" Quint asked, needing to rid himself of that concern.

"Yes." She managed a short nod. Then a tension crept into her expression. "Quint, this is all my fault—with Boone, I mean. If I hadn't—"

He wouldn't let her finish. "None of us can be sure of that. One way or another it took a lot of courage to do what you did. I'm sorry I didn't see it right away. In the long run, it doesn't really matter why you went along with Boone; it only matters why you stopped."

Her lips parted in an unsteady smile as Dallas let out the breath she'd been holding and took a step closer. "Do you really mean that?"

"You damned well better believe I do," Quint declared with fervor.

The quick shining light that leaped into her eyes drew a low, exultant laugh from him as he reached with his good arm and pulled her against him. There were no words to describe the powerful emotion that filled him, and Quint much preferred to show her.

# Epilogue

The sun was at its zenith, stripping the ranch buildings of their shadow and giving a summer warmth to the December day. Dallas hummed to herself as she crossed the ranch yard, bound for the house.

There was a radiant look to her face that rivaled the Texas sun. Not even the purpling bruises on her cheek and neck were visible, concealed by an adept application of makeup.

As she reached the porch steps, she caught the distinctive sound of a vehicle traveling up the ranch lane. Pausing, Dallas turned and cast a curious glance its way, but the blue sedan that rolled into view wasn't one that she recalled seeing before. At first she assumed it was a health inspector coming to check on the quarantined herd, but the car carried no government identification, either on its tags or its doors.

When it came toward the house, Dallas walked out to meet it. The sun's glare on the windshield blocked her view of the driver, but she had a clear look at a large box in the rear seat, filled with wrapped gifts.

The door on the driver's-side swung open and a smartly dressed woman stepped out, slender and petite with raven-dark hair. A smile spread across her face when she saw Dallas. Without hesitation, she came to meet her, quick to extend a hand in greeting.

"You must be Dallas. We spoke a couple times on the phone. I'm Cat Echohawk, Quint's mother."

Dallas stared at the woman's startlingly green eyes for a stunned moment. Other than the black color of their hair, there was little resemblance between mother and son.

Recovering from her initial surprise, she grasped the woman's outstretched hand. "Mrs. Echohawk," she murmured. "I didn't know you were coming. Quint must have forgotten to mention it."

"That's because he didn't know. I decided to surprise him. And please call me Cat."

"Welcome to the Cee Bar, Cat." Dallas struggled to sound natural, but she felt oddly flustered and nervous.

"The old place hasn't changed much," Cat remarked, her glance making an idle sweep of her surroundings.

"Of course, you've been here before," Dallas remembered. "I'd forgotten. Would you like to come in? I was just going to fix some lunch."

"Is Quint inside?"

"He's in the barn, repairing a bridle strap. Would you like me to—" Dallas broke off the offer when she saw Quint emerging from the building. "There he is now."

Clearly recognizing his mother at once, Quint broke into a jogging trot, a laughing smile of welcome on his face. He greeted her with a hug that was mostly one-armed.

"What are you doing here?" he declared, drawing back to look at her.

"It was obvious you weren't coming home for Christmas. So I didn't have any choice but to fly down here." A hand reached up to cup the side of his face. "I've missed you, you know."

"I know." His simple reply conveyed a depth of understanding that reminded Dallas that it hadn't been that many months since he'd lost his father. Then the smile was back, and he was turning to include her. "Have you met Dallas yet?"

His mother nodded. "We introduced ourselves."

"I hope you're going to be able to stay for a few days," Quint told her.

"That's the plan," she admitted.

"Good. That'll give you a chance to get acquainted with your future daughter-in-law." Smiling with a kind of pride, he curved an arm around Dallas's shoulder and drew her to his side, uniting them before his mother. He didn't seem the least bit concerned that his announcement was a total surprise to his mother.

"My—you—" Cat stammered briefly, then laughed, the happy sound dispelling all the tension that gripped Dallas. "What a Christmas present this is! Have you set the date yet?"

"There hasn't been time, but it will be soon," Quint assured her.

"Quint," she began on a note of excitement, "our old house at the Circle Six is sitting there empty. It will be the perfect place for the two of you to live."

"Don't get your heart set on that, Mom," Quint cautioned.

"Why not?" Cat frowned in bewilderment. "It would be ideal. Where else would you live?"

"Maybe right here," he told her. "I plan on talking to Jessy about taking over the operation of the Cee Bar on a permanent basis."

"Are you serious?" she murmured in disbelief.

"I am." He lifted his gaze to the Texas hills, drawn by the wide sweep of them. "This is Calder land, Mom. It's time a Calder lived on it again."

*A single star,*
*A Texas brand,*
*There is no doubt*
*He's on Calder land.*